BURNING TRUTH

A DCI BOYD THRILLER

ALEX SCARROW

D1321568

GrrBooks

A BURNING TRUTH

Published by GrrBooks

To my mother, Audrey – an oasis of calm, compassion and wisdom

To my mother, Audrey – an oasis of calm, compassion and wisdom

PROLOGUE

'Shit! Jesus! What the hell? T.P. – what the fuck did you do to her?'

T.P. shook his head as he crouched to examine the body. She was clearly dead. She'd been dead for some time, in fact. Her skin had started to turn blotchy as the immobile blood in her body began to settle and become livor mortis stains. Vomit filled her mouth and had spilled down the side of one cheek onto the chaise longue.

'The drugs did it.' T.P. turned round to look at the others – all of them looking worse for wear after the blow-out into the early hours.

'We *all* played a part in this,' he said.

'This... is... going to...' started one of them. 'Oh, God, we're so fucked!'

'Shut up!' T.P. stood up. 'This can be fixed. This *CAN* be fixed.' He stared at the others. 'This *WILL* be fixed... or it's over for everybody.'

The guest room was silent, but from down the hallway the faint sound of 'Jump in the Fire' by Metallica could be heard, still playing on the sound system.

'We're all *Spartans* here,' he said. 'Right? Fucking Spartans!'

T.P. took in the blanched faces in the room.

'*Right?!*'

The others nodded mutely.

'Remember the pact,' he said. 'This is between us. No one talks.'

1

Firefighter Alison Tucker was hopeful that the house was now empty. The fire had taken a firm hold of the old stone-walled building. They were going to have to pull back and fight it from the outside.

If anyone was left inside, especially upstairs, there was nothing more that could be done – smoke inhalation would have finished them off by this point. She could hear frantic comms chatter coming in from the lads outside about the stability of the roof. Eagle House was a grand old Regency-era building with stone walls, but there was a hell of a lot of sturdy oak at the top holding up a heavy lead slate roof.

'*Ali, it's looking dodgy. Clear your team out right NOW.*'

'All right,' she replied. Then louder, so that her voice dominated the comms channel. 'Everyone out,' she called to her two colleagues in the building. 'NOW!'

A moment later, the bulky outlines of Ed and Graham emerged from the swirling smoke, both moving as quickly as they could, burdened like packhorses in their bulky flame retardant jackets, with oxygen bottles on their backs.

ALEX SCARROW

'Anyone?' she asked as they squeezed past her to get to the exit point – the conservatory.

'Nothing,' said Ed, shouting over the roar and crackle of the flames.

They disappeared through the smoke, barging past still-undamaged furniture that looked exquisite and expensive, and all destined to become charcoal and ashes very shortly.

Eagle House was one she knew well. For Alison, a denizen of Hastings all her life – a *Hastonian* – it had been a lifelong landmark for her: one of life's perennial things, always there, but hidden away by trees and bushes and a moss-encrusted stone wall that ran alongside London Road. Now the historical building was ablaze. Another piece of Hastings' grand past would be a smouldering blackened shell by the morning.

Over the comms, one of the team outside hosing the roof shouted a warning that part of it looked about ready to cave in.

Enough lingering. She turned to follow Ed and Graham when she heard a faint gurgling scream above the roar of flames and the whistle of air being drawn through the building.

She paused.

She had two daughters, Mia and Penny, and a lovely guy called Brian waiting for her at home.

But the scream cut through the noise of the fire – a pitiful yet very *human* moan.

Shit.

'I think I heard someone else inside!' she yelled into the radio.

'Too late, Ali. Roof's beginning to sag. Get the fuck out now!' It was Grant, leading firefighter – and the grumpy old sweat who'd begrudgingly, finally, permitted a woman to join his team.

'*Get out now!*' he barked.

The scream came once more. It sounded feminine, almost childlike.

Fuck it.

'There's definitely someone!' she relayed to Grant. 'I'm going to take a quick look!'

Without waiting for his response, she made her way through the thickening smoke, stumbling as her thigh banged painfully into the corner of a side table.

'Ali! That's enough!' barked Grant. 'Out now!'

The next cry was close. Very close. The problem was that the smoke was now so fucking thick she could be within a yard of the person and walk straight past them.

'Ali, the roof is going!' shouted Grant. 'GET OUT!'

Through the whorls and mini tornados of swirling black smoke, Ali glimpsed something. An outline, a silhouette.

She took a step closer and bumped straight into it.

It was a snooker table. One of those expensive full-sized ones. The surface baize was mostly burned away; it was the corner pockets that actually gave it away. Lying on the table was a man. The poor, screaming, blackened wretch was flailing around like a bluebottle stuck to flypaper.

In the last few seconds – because that's what she was down to now – she could make out the struggling form. He was tied down, wrists and ankles, like a starfish. A face, blackened and burst, split cheeks running with liquidised human fat, itself fuel for the fire. And... among that blackened flesh, the startling whiteness of two rounded eyes and a gaping mouth full of gold fillings.

A horror mask that would have haunted her sleep for the rest of her life.

But she was spared that.

The roof collapsed.

She never had a chance.

2

DAY 1

Boyd's own little piece of grisly hell occupied his current dream. Not the car wreck, thank God, but the Heinz mayonnaise jar, filled with formaldehyde, that was sitting at the back of his safe in the study.

A parting gift from the Russians, it contained what he strongly suspected was Gerald Nix's severed ear. As in reality, beside the jar was a wad of cash bound with an elastic band and smudged with dried blood – also, presumably Nix's. About ten thousand pounds in twenties, but Boyd hadn't counted it. Hadn't touched it, in fact. There'd been a clear message there: Carrot and Stick. Threat and Reward.

Be good and we'll be nice... And remember: we know where you live.

Boyd could have – indeed, definitely should have – taken them straight in to be forensically examined. But there was that other thing: his chief superintendent. He had no way of knowing for sure whether Her Madge was in some way directly linked to the Russians or (taking a more charitable view) following orders handed down from someone who *was* taking their dirty money.

In his view, what he had sitting in the safe was evidence that he'd been both threatened and bribed. Evidence that he might one day need – and he didn't trust that even if he handed it in, it wouldn't simply disappear. He'd told the only other copper he could completely trust: DC Okeke – and she had shared his concerns.

So there they were, ticking like a time bomb in his safe that could either blow up in his face or exonerate him if an anti-corruption investigation: two pieces of toxic waste that were percolating into his dreams along with the play-repeat, play-repeat image from his second Hastings murder case, of Kristy Clarke's snarling face as he'd jumped to his death.

The gasp of Clark's breath being expelled as the rope pulled taut had morphed over the recent weeks to form its own distinct word – *haaa-rck*. The 'ck' at the end was his neck snapping.

Tonight, though, in Boyd's dream, Kristy Clarke was still alive, swinging, grinning and saying that word over and over...

'Dad! Dad!! Wake up!'

Boyd opened his eyes to see his room soaked with the bluish-grey light of pre-dawn. He'd yet to put curtains up in here and having tall windows on two walls made it something of a goldfish bowl. Lovely for those sunny mornings of which there had been less than a dozen in the six months they'd been living down here.

'What's the...? What's going on, Ems?'

'Dad, it's Ozzie. He's not well.'

He palmed the sleep out of his eyes as he sat up. Ozzie normally slept beside him on the double bed, entitled bloody sod, his head on the pillow like a human.

'Where is he? What's the matter with him?'

'It looks pretty bad. He's sick.'

Boyd swung his legs out from under the quilt and onto the cold wooden floor. 'You sure?'

'He needs a vet, Dad.'

He looked at his bedside clock. It was quarter to five in the morning. 'Okay, we can take him in after breakf–'

'No. Dad... *now*,' Emma said firmly. 'He keeps throwing up and he's not moving.'

She led him to her bedroom. Ozzie was lying on his side on her bed, panting rapidly with his head beside a pool of dark and drying vomit.

'Bollocks' was the only useful thing Boyd could think to say.

Five minutes later, they had him spread out on a towel in the back seat of the car and were driving uphill to the vets in Ore.

'Has he been poisoned do you think?' asked Boyd as he eased to a stop at a red light.

'It's right at the next lights,' said Emma, checking her phone. 'I don't know. I've been googling it. It could either be a toxin, a reaction or a blockage.'

'Reaction?'

'Allergy.' She looked at him. 'Dogs have them, Dad. Just like humans do.'

'To what?' He couldn't think of anything out of the ordinary that Ozzie had had in the last twelve hours. Dried Kibble – the usual brand. A corner or two of toast with Marmite and butter on. A broken-off bit of a chocolate digestive, nothing exactly exotic or lethal.

'Have you given him anything different?' she asked.

'I was just running through that. I don't think so.'

The light turned green and he gunned the car forward across the all-but-deserted crossroads. Ozzie whimpered in the back seat.

'He shouldn't have most of the things you give him anyway. It's not good for him,' scolded Emma.

'Oh, come on,' he said with a heavy sigh. 'When I was a kid, Grandma gave her dog all sorts of crap. She didn't often buy them dog food. They lived mostly on our scraps.'

'Jesus,' muttered Emma. 'And they lived to how old?'

Boyd shrugged. 'Old-ish. Nine. Ten, I think?'

'And they were fat, I'm guessing.'

He shrugged again. They were, to be fair, both chunky, lolloping chocolate Labs. He turned right at the next light.

'That was *then*,' she said. She made '*then*' sound like it was pre-war Britain. 'This is now. The additives we get in our food are pretty horrific. Especially for dogs.'

It was too early in the morning to get a lecture from her on the recent flood of US imports. Anyway, Ozzie might have picked up something in the garden, or on the beach last night. The rubbish that out-of-towners left behind on the shingle at the end of a bank holiday weekend was pretty depressing to witness.

'It's up ahead, there,' said Emma. 'See?'

Boyd saw the sign: BODINE GROUP VETERINARY SURGERY. The car park was empty except for one car, but there was a light on in the building. 'You're sure they're open this early?'

'I called. They're expecting us.'

He parked his Captur and, between them, Boyd and Emma, carried Ozzie, limp and lifeless, to the front door of the vets. The door automatically swung inwards and they carried him into the waiting room.

'This is Ozzie?' said a woman in green scrubs. To Boyd, she looked only a couple of years older than his daughter.

Emma nodded. 'You the one I spoke to?'

'Uh-huh.' The vet pushed over a low trolley on castor wheels. 'On here,' she said.

Boyd gently rested Ozzie on the blue plastic mattress. 'He's been vomiting repeatedly,' he said. The vet squatted down and lifted Ozzie's jowls. She tutted.

'What is it?' asked Emma, stroking his side.

'His gums are a bit pale. Has he had any blood in his stool?'

Emma looked at Boyd. 'You walked him last night. Can you remember?'

Boyd shook his head. 'I... I don't really tend to study them that closely, Em. Thinking about it – I'm not sure he actually went.'

The vet exchanged a quick glance with Emma and then turned to Boyd. 'I'm going to admit him. He could have eaten something that's got stuck. Do you have pet insurance?'

'Uh, no. Not really. Should I?'

She raised her eyebrows. A face that Boyd interpreted as meaning *'This isn't going to be cheap'*. 'Let's worry about that later,' she said.

'Right.'

'Okay.' She stood up straight. 'I'm going to take him through now. I've got *your* phone number?' she said to Emma.

She nodded.

'It's Emma? Isn't it?'

'Emma Boyd, yes.'

'Right. When our receptionist comes in, I'll get her to call you back and we can set up Ozzie's treatment record.'

'Thank you,' said Emma. 'Thank you so much for coming in so early.' Then, one hand stroking his ear: 'Ozzie Bear, please be okay.'

Boyd watched Ozzie being wheeled through the double doors and out of sight, wondering whether the queasy flopping sensation in his own gut was his concern over the size of the bill or concern for the survival chances of his dog.

Annoyingly he suspected it was the latter.

3

'Morning, sir,' said DC Warren without breaking his gaze from the microwave's window.

'What've you got in there?' replied Boyd, bending down to see what was so fascinating.

'Chocolate Oats-So-Simple. I overfilled it, I think. Don't want it all bubbling out.'

Warren glanced across at him. 'Blimey, you look rough, sir.'

'I was up at stupid-o-clock this morning with a sick dog.'

'Oh, right. I'm a cat person. They're less work.'

'I'm beginning to wish I was too,' said Boyd, waiting in line to warm up his sausage roll. The leaking grease had rendered the paper bag almost transparent.

'What's wrong with the dog?' Warren asked.

'Dunno, he's at the vet's now – he's probably eaten something.'

The microwave pinged and Warren opened the door. He pulled out the steaming plastic pot of brown sludge. 'All yours, sir. Hope he's okay.'

Boyd placed his paper bag in and pushed start. Just then DS

Minter entered the kitchenette, carrying a freezer bag of boiled eggs and a protein shake, his dark hair slick from a shower.

He wrinkled his nose at the smell coming from the microwave. 'Oh, Christ. Is that another of your rancid snack pots in there, Warren?'

'Boss's breakfast,' Warren replied, thumbing over his shoulder.

'Ah, morning, Boss. Didn't see you there.'

'Morning.'

'Late night?'

'Early morning,' replied Boyd. 'My daughter woke me up because our dog was vomiting everywhere.'

Minter pulled a face. 'Nice. You take it off to the vet's?'

'At five in the morning, yes.'

He winced. 'Oh, crikey. That's going to cost you a pretty penny.'

'Yup,' said Boyd. 'That's what I'm expecting.'

'But you've got pet insurance, right?'

Boyd shook his head. 'He didn't poop last night. They think it might be a blockage.'

Warren pulled a face and let his spoon drop into his pot.

'Goodness, surgery too?' said Minter. He made a whistling noise, which sounded to Boyd very much like money escaping from a punctured balloon.

DCI Flack poked his head into the small room. He had a jacket over one shoulder and his face had the puffy look of one that had endured a long night shift. 'Oh, Boyd, there you are.'

After six months of being stationed here, Flack was one of the few detectives Boyd had yet to properly interact with. They'd probably exchanged fewer than a hundred words since Boyd had relocated from the Met at the beginning of the year. He'd had to turf Flack and his team out of the Incident Room twice in the six months he'd been here, so it was no wonder

Boyd felt like he was one angry exchange away from being headbutted by the man.

'What's up?' he asked.

'The fire last night in St Leonards. The East Sussex FIO's just finished his preliminary inspection and he's on the phone to Sutherland. There are signs of an accelerant.'

'What fire?'

'London Road. Up Silverhill way. Couldn't you smell it coming in this morning?' asked Flack.

Boyd had cycled in this morning since it was nice-ish. And actually, yes, he'd picked up the faintest – to be honest, rather pleasing – tang of wood smoke as he'd come up Bohemia Road towards the station.

'The fire inspection officer suspects arson.' Flack looked at his watch. 'Since I'm off now and you're on...' He nodded. 'It's all yours, Boyd.'

He flicked a taut and insincere smile at Boyd and the others, then tapped the kitchen counter with a finger. 'Have fun.'

4

'Ah, DCI Flack managed to find you then?' said DSI Sutherland.

'Yes, to toss the fire over to me,' replied Boyd.

'As it well should be,' said Sutherland. 'He's busy, you're not. Come in. Take a seat.'

The detective superintendent had been sticking to his ten thousand steps a day, and had recently announced that he'd begun a Couch to 5K regime as well as Sunday cycling. Sutherland gestured to his visitor's chair but remained standing behind his desk.

Boyd sat down, his coffee in one hand, his still-steaming paper bag of fat, salt and carbs in the other. Since Sutherland had begun his health kick in March, he'd become a food Nazi. Even worse than Emma, if that was possible.

At this moment, Sutherland was staring at the greasy bag in Boyd's fist.

'Breakfast,' said Boyd. 'I haven't actually had mine yet.'

'Well, whatever horror's in there, it's staying put until we're done.'

'You can have a bit if you like, sir?'

'Bugger off. Not interested. Plus, I don't want your pastry flakes all over my floor.'

Boyd removed the offending paper bag from view. 'So Flack mentioned something about a fire last night in St Leonards?'

'Just up the road,' said Sutherland. 'You could probably have seen the flames from the top floor of this building.'

'I could smell it coming in.'

Sutherland reached down for his mug of tea and cupped it in both hands.

He's really not going to sit down, is he? At least this way, Boyd mused, their heads were almost on the same level.

'There were three fire engines trying to save the building, but –' he took in a deep breath – 'it's just a shell now. Crying shame that, another piece of Hastings' history gone.'

'Like the old pier,' said Boyd.

Sutherland scowled. The pier had gone up in flames back in 2010, leaving a row of blackened stumps like rotten teeth. 'The pier's still there, Boyd,' he replied defensively. 'It didn't go anywhere. It's had a make-over, that's all.'

'One hell of a makeover,' Boyd muttered.

'Eagle House. You know who lives there?'

'Uh, no.'

'Sir Arthur Sutton.'

The name rang a bell for Boyd. It took him a moment to place the name. 'The ex-politician?'

'That's right.' Sutherland paused, then said, 'Look, I've just had the East Sussex FIO on the phone.'

'Flack said "traces of accelerant"?'

Sutherland nodded. 'Yes. The FIO's convinced it was arson, so we're looking at the house as a potential crime scene. His name's Mark Wells; he's still over there if you want to meet 'n' greet.'

'I'll head over there now,' said Boyd, lifting himself up out of the chair; he needn't have bothered sitting down in the first place.

'There's something you should know, Boyd.'

'Sir?'

'They lost one of their own fighting the fire last night.'

'Shit.'

Sutherland nodded again. 'The building collapsed. I don't think they've managed to recover the body yet.'

'Right, thanks for the heads-up.'

'According to Wells, she was a very popular member of the station and much loved. So be mindful that emotions will be running high over there.'

5

Boyd found their forensics co-ordinator, Kevin Sully, and their crime scene manager, Leslie Poole, sitting at the same table in the canteen.

'Ah, got you both. Good. There's a job,' he said by way of a greeting.

'No "*Good morning, lovely day, isn't it?*" Just straight in with the work talk,' said Sully to Leslie.

Boyd ignored him. 'I'm heading over to the arson incident on London Road.'

'Arson?' repeated Leslie. She'd recently cut her silver hair into a practically spherical bob. Being stout and short, in her dark trouser suit with her – now – perfectly round head, Boyd thought she vaguely resembled DSI Sutherland. His evil twin sister, perhaps.

'The FIO's detected accelerant, so we're looking at a crime scene. Sutherland wants us over there to tape it up as soon as the fire engines have gone,' said Boyd.

'I hear it was Eagle House?' said Sully.

'*Eagle House?*' Leslie looked horrified. 'Oh, no!'

Boyd nodded. 'A local landmark, I'm led to believe. Or it was.'

Leslie sighed and pushed her nearly finished breakfast plate away. 'That's awful. So sad. It was a lovely building.'

'I'm heading over on foot,' Boyd said. 'Apparently it's just up the road?'

'It is,' said Leslie.

'No point driving?'

'It really is only five minutes,' she said. 'And there'll be nowhere to park if the driveway's still clogged with fire engines. The house – well, its driveway anyway – opens straight onto London Road. It's going to be busy now.'

'Right. On foot it is, then,' said Boyd. 'See you two out front in five minutes?'

BOYD ASKED DC OKEKE ALONG. She was starting to look like wilted rhubarb behind her desk and he reckoned she could do with some fresh air and daylight. She lit up a cigarette as soon as they stepped outside.

'You know I used to smoke?' said Boyd.

She nodded. 'You said.'

'I worked out I spent about thirty thousand pounds on fags in my lifetime. Crazy, eh?'

'Working it out or spending it?' she asked.

'Fair point,' he replied.

'I should quit,' she offered, 'but I'm worried I'd replace smoking with eating.' She nodded at his modest pot belly.

'One battle at a time, Okeke, one battle at a time.'

He could smell the smoke in the air from the fire as they headed up Bohemia Road. 'I've been told the place was a local landmark.'

She nodded. 'Everyone calls it Eagle House because of the two eagles. I don't think it's actually called that.'

'What two eagles?' Boyd asked.

Ahead, Poole and Sully were deep in conversation about something that involved a lot of air-drawing with their fingers. They stopped at a pedestrian crossing and Sully hit the button.

'They're old stone eagles. Either side of the driveway,' Okeke explained. 'They're right on London Road. They loom out of the bushes like scary gargoyles. You can't miss them.'

The walking man flashed green and they followed Sully and Poole across the busy road. To his right, further up the hill, Boyd could see faint twisting skeins of smoke rising into the blue sky and the rear butt of a fire vehicle poking out from greenery, partially blocking one lane of the northbound road.

'Sutherland told me Arthur Sutton lives up there,' said Boyd.

'Who?'

'Sir Arthur Sutton?'

She frowned as if the name was vaguely familiar but she couldn't quite attach a face or a reputation to it. Boyd had had a bit more time to recall what little he knew about the man. 'He's that pompous sod who writes those crappy airport thrillers. Used to be in the government for a few months, I think,' said Boyd.

'Oh.' Okeke nodded. 'The one with the bushy eyebrows?'

Sutton had silver-grey hair that was always cropped army-short, but thick, dark eyebrows that curled up at the end, giving him a distinctive Alistair Darling/Norman Lamont contrast.

Arthur Sutton's name had become woven into the scruffy patchwork quilt of British culture. Like Eddie the Eagle or Nicholas Parsons, he was somebody everyone thought they knew but didn't really.

Sutton's bushy brows and coarse buzz-cut hair were as much a part of his public image as his caustic wit and political incorrectness. He'd been an Oxford scholar, a government advisor, an MP, and briefly a cabinet member, before he'd been tossed into the political wilderness to become an author of shiny paperbacks, with large, embossed foil fonts and vaguely Shakespearean titles. With, of course, an obligatory guest spot from time to time on *Have I Got News For You* and a rumoured upcoming appearance on *Strictly Come Dancing*.

They arrived at the driveway. A fire engine was overhanging the road and flanked by the eagles that Okeke had told him about. They were matching weather-worn stone monstrosities standing astride sandstone columns; each of them a yard tall and leering out from untamed bushes that rendered the narrow pavement outside the low wall unusable to pedestrians. The stone birds marked the entrance to a sloping gravel driveway that ran almost parallel to London Road like a slip-road. Boyd imagined it had to be a bloody nightmare coming out of there at rush hour.

Poole turned round beside the rear of the fire engine and gestured for Boyd to lead the way in. 'Eagle House,' she announced like a tour guide.

The fire engine virtually filled the driveway. They had to squeeze past it, ducking beneath low-hanging branches and wrestling with the many brambles and nettles that were spiking out, testing their boundaries.

The drive angled up steeply, which put the old house on a tree-shrouded prominence from which, Boyd imagined, Sir Arthur Sutton gazed down over his kippers every morning upon the hoi polloi of Hastings.

They passed two more fire engines, every equipment hatch wide open and their contents spilled out onto the ground. A procession of weary, soot-faced firefighters were getting ready to pack all their stuff away.

The smell of wood smoke, a charming ambient bouquet from a distance, was now unpleasantly overwhelming. Boyd could feel the back of his throat tickle with the acidity of it. It wasn't just the smell of charcoaled wood but all the other odours that came with a house fire – the stench of burned rubber and melted plastic, the unsettling sting of unidentifiable toxic chemicals and the nasty suspicion that in a building this old there'd be particles of asbestos hovering in the air.

Boyd squeezed past the final fire service vehicle and had his first unobstructed view of the remains of Eagle House.

The building had been tall; in fact, technically speaking, it still was – if the blackened stone cadaver could be counted as a building. Three storeys high, it was topped with a folly of a Gothic tower on one side and the steep ribcage of a tall attic on the other. The stone walls were pretty much all that remained of it. He could see through empty eye-socket windows shards of daylight that shouldn't be there. It looked as if the entire middle of the building – rooms, furniture, roof beams, every-thing – had collapsed in on itself, producing a mound of smoul-dering debris that reached to the first-floor windows. A thick pall of smoke and steam still rose from it, even though the firemen were packing up to leave.

Boyd spotted a man with a tightly clenched mouth, wearing white hard hat that was pushed back, revealing silver hair. He was carrying a clipboard and making notes as Boyd approached.

'Are you Mark Wells? The FIO?'

The man looked up at him. 'Yes. And you are?' He spotted Sully standing behind and seemed to recognise him. 'Ahh, took your time this morning.'

'Didn't want to get in your way,' replied Boyd. He offered his hand. 'DCI Boyd.'

Wells shook it. 'You're the new DFL, aren't you?'

DFL – Down From London. He'd got used to hearing that acronym over the last six months. 'Not so new now. I've been here since the start of the year.'

'I saw you on the local news a few months back...'

'Yeah,' Boyd said. 'It seems everyone has. I had to be bleeped. Apparently it was hilarious.'

'It was.' Wells smiled faintly. He nodded at Sully. 'You keeping well, Kev?'

Sully nodded. 'Not too bad, thanks for asking.'

Boyd introduced Okeke. 'This is DC Samantha Okeke, and...' He stepped aside to introduce Leslie Poole. 'Our CSM, Lesl–'

'I know Leslie,' butted in Wells. 'We've worked together enough times.'

They exchanged a quick smile. Introductions done, there was a momentary conversation vacuum and Boyd suddenly remembered Sutherland's mind-how-you-go warning.

'I'm very sorry to hear that you lost one of your firefighters last night,' he said.

'Yes. Ali Tucker. She was...' Wells took in a deep breath and let it out slowly. 'She was a lovely girl. Everybody loved her.'

'I'm really very sorry,' Boyd said again.

Wells accepted this with the slightest tip of his head. 'We recovered her body about an hour ago.' He clamped his lips together hard. 'She nearly made it out.'

Leslie placed her hand on his arm. 'My God. I'm so sorry, Mark.'

It looked as though Wells wanted to say more, but his mouth closed, then clenched. He patted Leslie's hand.

'My DSI says you're calling this arson?' Boyd said, keen to bring things back to a less emotional footing.

Wells looked relieved to have something else to focus on. 'We've had strong hydrocarbon readings on the electronic sniffers already,' he said. He inhaled loudly through his nose. 'But you can smell it yourself anyway.'

Boyd copied him, detecting a faint but distinctive tang of benzene – that *petrol station smell.*

'Yeah, I'm getting it.'

'So, it's arson, absolutely. And because we lost Ali... manslaughter. Right?'

Boyd nodded. 'What about the owner? Arthur Sutton?'

'We rescued a woman who'd been badly burned,' Wells said. 'She's at Conquest Hospital now. I'm told she's stable but unconscious...'

'Ali was investigating what she thought were sounds of screaming when... well, then it all came crashing down around her.' Wells took another deep breath.

'Did she find anyone? Could it have been Sutton?'

'She didn't have a chance to say. She just said she thought she heard someone screaming for help.' The FIO shook his head. 'It could have been wind devils.'

'Wind devils?' Boyd asked.

'When the fire starts drawing in oxygen to feed, it creates a strong draught. That can create sounds that can be mistaken for cries for help. They can be particularly high-pitched, like a child's voice,' Mark explained.

Boyd nodded and looked down at his pad. 'I'm told Arthur Sutton lives alone? Mostly.'

'He has a housekeeper,' Wells said, 'which is probably the woman we rescued.'

Boyd glanced at the smouldering pile of debris within the stone husk of Eagle House. 'So there's a chance Sutton's body is still in there?'

'If he was at home last night, then that's where it'll be. I can't get a sniffer dog in there until it cools down. We'll be able to pick through that debris tomorrow hopefully.'

'In the meantime, we could try and track Sutton down, guv,' said Okeke. 'See if he's away on a trip or something?'

Boyd nodded. 'Get on to any next of kin. Family, friends. Find out if they know where he was supposed to be last night.' He turned back to the FIO. 'So... you're saying you're going to need another day with this before we can tape it up as a crime scene?'

Wells nodded. 'There'll be vehicles in and out for another twenty-four hours.'

'Fire scenes,' Sully huffed. 'I hate them. They're already horribly compromised by the time I get my hands on them.' He rummaged in the bag he'd slung over his shoulder, pulling out a pair of blue nitrile gloves. 'Mark? Mind if I go walk the perimeter?'

'Be my guest,' Wells said.

Poole also dug into her own bag and took out a notebook. 'Mark, can I grab you for a moment and get a list of everyone on your team who was working on this last night?'

'Yes, of course,' he replied. 'Come with me; we've got a roster in my van.'

As Poole and Wells headed across the wet and grimy gravel driveway, Boyd spotted Sully, already sniffing around the thick foliage of the house's small garden like a dog looking for the right spot to go. The trees in this garden were all mature ones, the nearest of them to the building had scorched branches, but none looked as though they'd been burned enough to die. They formed a thick and impenetrable wall of privacy around the property and its little secret garden. The small lawn – and it was small, about the size of a badminton court – was covered with fire hoses and damp equipment, stretched out across it to dry off in the daylight.

The trees kept most of the garden and the bottom half of the building in permanent shade. 'The house that time forgot,' muttered Boyd.

Okeke didn't answer. He turned to see that she'd walked a little way away from him; she was on the phone to someone. From her hectoring tone, it sounded to Boyd as though she was talking to Warren.

He decided to get a closer look at the smouldering building.

He could see why the place had been something of a Hastings landmark. As he craned his neck to look up the stone walls, at the castle-like crenellations along the top of them, and the faux watchtower with a three-sixty view of Hastings, he got a distinctly Gothic vibe from the place.

Though knowing little of Arthur Sutton, Boyd thought the building seemed to reflect his eccentric, Edwardian-Englishman public image. He could imagine the interiors had been stuffed with overly expensive, tasteless furnishings, colonial-era statues and the like, and above some grand mantelpiece the mounted head of some poor bloody mammal on an endangered species list.

Boyd approached the empty frame of a large ground-floor bay window and peered through the shattered teeth of blackened glass at the mound of debris inside. He glanced upwards and saw that a few stoic joists of wood had withstood the avalanche of the slate roof coming down. They held up what remained of the first floor and, further up, the jagged bones of what remained of the second. Beyond that, it was pretty much twists of smoke and July blue sky beyond.

What a bloody shame.

He could understand why Leslie Poole's shoulders had sagged at the news Eagle House had gone up in flames. It was another part of Hastings' Grand Past, permanently erased. It looked to Boyd that the building was well beyond restoring. Undoubtedly this prime real estate would be snapped up by some hungry developer and turned into a block of studio flats.

6

Boyd had seen enough for now. He rounded up Okeke, who was so engrossed in what she was doing on her phone that he had to lead her down the sloping driveway by the arm. He left Sully probing the treeline and Poole discussing with Mark Wells when precisely she could take possession of the keys to the crime site.

They walked back to the station, Okeke busy thumbing her screen while Boyd steered her around both people and lamp posts. By the time they returned to the CID floor she had found what she was looking for and was immediately on another call.

'So when was the last time?.... Okay, so that would be normal for Sir Arthur?...'

Boyd threw his jacket on the back of the chair. He'd actually worked up a sweat on the walk down. After half a year of solid grey skies and pissing rain, it seemed that summer had finally arrived. At the weekends, Hastings was usually busy with a steady trickle of out-of-towners buying bags of doughnuts and plastic tat from the gift shops come rain or sleet, but now the warm weather was here, and the schools had broken up, the town was mobbed all week long.

Boyd glanced at his desk and noticed his forgotten sausage roll, still sitting in its paper bag and cold as a corpse.

Sod it. Stone cold would do. But he needed a coffee to go with it. He signalled to Okeke, who was still busy talking. She mouthed back a *yes please.* He raised his eyebrows; he hadn't actually been offering – just letting her know where he was going. She grinned back at him.

Boyd returned from the canteen ten minutes later with a black for her and a frothy cappuccino for himself. She was finally off her phone.

'Thanks, guv.'

He sat down at his desk, took a sip of his coffee and began to hungrily devour his long-overdue sausage roll. He checked the clock. It was ten to twelve. No wonder his stomach was grumbling noisily.

Okeke wandered over to his desk. 'I can't get hold of Sutton. His phone keeps clicking over to answerphone.'

'That doesn't bode well.'

'Well, not necessarily. I spoke to his publishing editor. Apparently he has a habit of going off to write his books in remote windswept rental cottages, phone off, internet off, that kind of thing.'

Boyd vaguely recalled an exchange on *Have I Got News* between Sutton and Hislop about writing regimes and Sutton grandly announcing that he wrote when the muse hit him and took himself off to some dark and moody corner of the country to do so. Hislop had eye-rolled at the pomposity of the man.

'What about his family?' Boyd asked.

'He has two grown-up children. Neither see him. Or even like him, it seems. An ex-wife who *really* doesn't like him, and that's it for immediate family. I'm going to carry on, guv. See if I can get through to any of them.'

Boyd nodded. 'Fine. I'll bone up on his background details. If this was arson, then perhaps Sutton's pissed off one to many people in his life. If he was home last night,' he continued, 'then I guess he'll be buried in that debris somewhere, poor bastard.'

He turned to his computer and pulled up the LEDS interface in one window and opened Explorer in another, took another greasy bite of his cold sausage roll and began to dig.

A COUPLE of hours later and Boyd had a much clearer picture of Sir Arthur. The man was something of a maverick. A chancer. A Dodger-like character who'd climbed from working-class obscurity and found himself hobnobbing with the good and the great.

Boyd had cut and pasted snippets from Wikipedia, the BBC and various papers into a Word document and now reviewed the messy montage of extracts on the page.

Sutton had started out as a grammar-school boy from Broxbourne, Hertfordshire. He'd managed to get good enough grades to go to Imperial College, London, to study economics and then, partway through that, he'd parlayed his degree course into one at Oxford.

At Oxford in the early 1980s, it seemed he'd struggled at first with his humble background and give-away accent, but he eventually adjusted to his new environs, in a vaguely Walter Mitty way. There were tall stories about his family's wealth and origins, which his university friends all seemed to have taken with a pinch of salt. But Sutton had managed, through sheer bullishness and charm, to inveigle himself into the elitist social circles of the Eton School Old Boys.

After Oxford, he'd worked for a while as a Fleet Street journalist, finally editing a tabloid for six months before stepping across into the world of Thatcher-era politics.

He'd worked in the office of the Business Secretary in some

nebulous advisory role for a few years, then in 1997 he was 'parachuted in' to become an MP for Mid Staffordshire and served in a junior position in the cabinet for a few months.

Boyd speed-read the parliamentary career part of Sutton's life; politics wasn't really the man's thing. Sutton spoke far too bluntly – like Norman Tebbit with his famous 'Get on your bikes and find a job' quote. And 'Hardship is there to filter out the wasters and weaklings' had been one of the soundbites that had hastened the end of his political career. Sutton had given up on politics after the second Labour win in 2001. He'd leveraged his name and connections to get a generous book deal writing political thrillers, which he'd been doing ever since, churning them out once every two or three years.

Those were the broad brushstrokes of Sir Arthur Sutton. As for his personal life – in 1989 he married Kate Munton-Jones, the daughter of some businessman doing exceedingly well out of the international arms business. It might have been a marriage that had evolved from a genuine love, but marrying into money and influence would have been, Boyd thought, almost certainly the icing on the cake for Sutton. Arthur and Kate Sutton had two children: one son – Henry; one daughter – Hermione.

Sutton had found himself on the receiving end of a little tabloid attention in 2002 when he'd had an affair with a much younger woman who worked in publishing. The Suttons separated the same year and finally divorced in 2012.

Since then, Arthur Sutton had been a confirmed bachelor. None of that second-wife nonsense for him. He'd written in a *Telegraph* op-ed four years ago: '... *having sawn off an arm and a leg (financially) to get rid of the ball and chain, it would be the very definition of madness to chain a brand-new ball to my remaining leg.*'

Of course he'd drawn some fire for the 'ball and chain' comment. Boyd tried not to smile at the five hundred and something comments beneath the online article. Opinions were firmly polarised and in some cases the comments were hilarious.

As for his kids, Arthur Sutton and his offspring were not particularly close, to say the least. His son, Henry, ran a business that had something to do with corporate events; his daughter, Hermione, owned a cake shop in Brighton.

Okeke managed to get hold of his ex-wife's contact details, and a little more rummaging around on the internet yielded the contact details of Sutton's literary agent.

'How're you getting on with his kids?' Boyd asked, but Okeke had headphones stuck on her head and was busy watching something on her monitor. Boyd tore a sheet of paper from an A4 pad, screwed it up into a ball and tossed it across the seven or eight feet between their desks to get her attention. His aim was unintentionally accurate and the paper ball bopped off the side of her head.

Okeke pulled her headphones off and turned to glare at Warren. 'Oh, grow up!' she snapped.

'Huh?' Warren looked up from his screen and pulled *his* headphones out. Music hissed from them as he held them away from his ears. 'What's up?'

'I said...'

'Sorry,' Boyd said. 'That was me!'

Okeke turned to glare at him, though a little less ferociously than she had at Warren. 'Well then, *you* grow up... guv.'

He waved an apology at Warren. 'My bad. As you were.' He turned back to Okeke. 'I was just trying to get your attention. What's got you so sucked in anyway?'

'YouTube,' she said. 'It's Arthur Sutton on *Have I Got News For You.*'

'Oh? What's he like?' He vaguely recalled Arthur Sutton resembling virtually every other politician exposed to the cut and thrust of the show's regular characters: awkward and embarrassingly unfunny.

'I'll send you the link,' she said. A moment later, the chat window of LEDS pinged open with Okeke's name, a thumbnail of her ID photo and a link.

Boyd clicked on it and LEDS' proprietary internet browser offered him the standard warning box about viewing illegal or inappropriate content. He clicked 'OK' and then hunted for his own pair of headphones before he started playing the video clip.

His phone buzzed in his pocket, and he pulled it out. It was Emma. He felt his stomach drop.

'Hey, Ems. How's Ozzie?'

'He'll live.'

'What's wrong with him?'

She sighed. 'A sock.'

'What?'

'He ate a sock. It was stuck in his gut. They operated on him and took it out, and he'll be ready to pick up from about three this afternoon.'

Boyd looked at his watch; it was nearly lunchtime. 'Can you pick him up? I won't be able to get away early today.'

'We'll need the two of us,' she replied. 'One to drive, one to sit with him. I'll drive down to the police station for five and then you can drive us both to the vet's. Sound good?'

'Sounds good,' he confirmed. 'Stupid bloody dog,' he muttered, surprised at the relief that flooded through him.

7

'How. Bloody. Much?!'

'Seven hundred and ninety-three pounds, ninety-nine pence.'

'You've got to be fu–'

'Dad!' Emma snapped. She was raising one of her dark eyebrows – and shooting him a look just like her mother would have done.

'All that for a bloody sock!' Boyd exclaimed.

'You're lucky it wasn't a toxic substance,' said the receptionist. 'He'd have been in observation for another forty-eight hours. Look... do you want me to double check it's been tallied up correctly?'

'No, no. It's fine,' he managed, as Emma continued to glare in his direction.

'Sorry,' the receptionist said sheepishly. 'I forgot to add the course of antibiotics onto the bill.'

On the way back, Boyd found himself gripping the steering wheel so tightly he was getting what felt like shin splints in his wrists. 'Eight hundred and fifty quid, because that moron in the back ate one of my bloody socks!'

'It's quite common, Dad. Lots of spaniels do it. It's not just Ozzie.'

'What? Eat random things that nearly *kill* them?'

'You can't blame Ozzie,' said Emma calmly. 'You should try being a little less messy and sorting out your floor-drobe.'

'So, what? It's *my* bloody fault?'

'And mine, Dad. We've both got to be a bit tidier in our rooms, that's all.'

It would have taken some of the sting out of things if the slimy, mucous-soaked sock they had pulled out of Ozzie's gut had been one of hers, or even Danny's, now that he slept over some nights. But no... it had to be one of Boyd's big, black, for-work Primark socks.

'Bollocks!' he grumbled to himself. 'Fucking unbelievable amount of bloody money.'

'Maybe we *should* have medical insurance for him?' said Emma. 'Like I suggested?'

He shook his head. 'Either way you get gouged for money, Ems. It's ridiculous. The whole thing's a money-making racket!'

Boyd looked in the rear-view mirror to see Ozzie on the back seat, looking sorry for himself with the 'cone of shame' surrounding his head. His eyes blinked blearily, as he sat upright, bobbing and swaying like a Friday-night pisshead waiting for a night bus. For a fleeting moment, Boyd felt something like affection towards the stupid animal that had cost him the best part of a grand.

'Oz, you big muppet,' he huffed. 'I'm glad you're all right, boy.'

8

DAY 2

Boyd placed his cup on the draining board and dried his hands.

He was about to leave the kitchenette when he realised Okeke was hovering outside, waiting for him. 'What's up?' he asked.

'I finally managed to speak to Arthur Sutton's daughter, Hermione,' Okeke said.

'Ah... and?'

'She said she can't meet us until next Tuesday as she's on holiday in Turkey.'

'Is she aware of what's happened?' Boyd asked.

'She's aware that her dad's house burned down, yeah.'

'Does she have any idea where her father might be at the moment?'

Okeke shook her head. 'She said she hasn't spoken to him in a few weeks.'

'A few weeks? I thought they were estranged?' Boyd said.

She shrugged. 'Don't believe everything you read. That's what she said. That she'd spoken to him a few weeks ago. She said her dad has a flat in London; he sometimes goes up there to write. She said it's not unlikely that he's holed up there, phone off, internet off and busy knocking out his latest masterpiece.'

'What about the son? Did you manage to get through to him?' Boyd asked, picking his phone up and heading out onto the office floor.

'No. Not yet. I've got his number, but he's not answering his phone,' Okeke said, following Boyd back to his desk.

'Well, keep trying,' he said. 'Look, after lunch I think I'll drive up to London to try this writing getaway of his. I could do with an extra pair of eyes.'

Her eyes widened as she realised he was offering a trip outside the station. 'God, yeah. I'd love to come along. Thanks, guv. Is there any more news from the fire investigation officer?'

'Wells said they're going to begin picking through the debris this afternoon. So perhaps either *we'll* find him later on or they will.'

OKEKE TURNED the pool car right and headed onto Bohemia Road and up towards London Road. She caught a glimpse of the twin pillars, the eagles marking the entrance to Eagle House as she drove past.

'Can you see any smoke still?' she asked.

Boyd twisted in his seat to look back as they went over the crossroads and carried on north. 'I'm not sure. A tiny bit maybe.'

He turned back round and settled back in the passenger's seat. It was nice to have Okeke for company. She was the one person at work he was beginning to feel comfortable enough to *not* have to make small talk with.

Plus, it meant she could drive and he could relax.

'How're you doing, guv?' she asked.

Strike that about no small talk.

'I'm fine, thanks, Okeke, and how are you?' he said in an overly bright voice.

She glanced across at him. 'Have you spoken with HR about some PTSD counselling yet?'

Boyd rolled his eyes. 'Nope. And I'm not planning to, either.' In error he'd told her about his recurring dream of Kristy Clarke dropping from the rafters above him and snapping taut with that sound – *haaar-ck* – and she'd suggested he talk to someone about it. It seemed she wasn't giving up.

'That is an idiotic attitude, guv, if you don't mind me saying. You really should take it seriously. Mental trauma is as real an injury as –'

'I'm not injured and I'm not traumatised, for crying out loud!' he cut in. 'I've just had a couple of bad dreams. But noted,' he said, sighing, 'and added to my to-do list.'

'Good,' Okeke said. 'It really is best to deal with these things.'

He rolled his eyes again. 'Right. Great. Thanks, Oprah.'

9

oyd looked at the sign beside the buzzer. The building appeared to be home to two businesses as well as Sutton's writerly bolthole: a firm of accountants and a 'holistic therapist'. He presumed another way of wording that was an 'everything doctor', the kind of expensive consultant you'd go to see if nothing was actually wrong.

He pressed the buzzer for the top floor, Sutton's place.

'It looks pokey,' said Okeke, peering up at the narrow façade.

Boyd nodded. Number 176 Chancery Lane in Holborn was so narrow it looked like it had been built between two older buildings simply to fill an unsightly gap. The bricks were stained dark with the soot and grime of London past, and the ledges had been pebble-dashed with pigeon crap.

He rang the bell again.

Chancery Lane opened onto Fleet Street at the far end, busy with suicidal Deliveroo cyclists, inept wobbling Boris-bikers and ponderous bendy buses. This off-shoot was a quiet haven by comparison. Okeke miraculously had managed to find a parking space right in front of the building.

ALEX SCARROW

Tired of waiting, Boyd knocked heavily on the door. To the left of it was a small window filled with the charmless vertical slats of an office blind. He saw them part slightly, then a moment later the front door clacked and opened.

An old woman in a smart white blouse and a dark cardigan peered out. 'Can I help you?' she asked.

'We're after Sir Arthur Sutton,' Boyd said. 'On the top floor.'

'And you are?'

'Police. CID. Do you know if Mr Sutton has been using his flat recently?'

The woman shook her head. 'I have no idea about the comings and goings of other tenants here,' she replied.

Beyond her, in the narrow hallway, Boyd could see a small side table on which post had been dumped. 'Do you mind if we come into the hallway?'

She frowned suspiciously. 'Don't you need some kind of warrant to come barging in?'

'Well, we're not exactly *barging*, are we?' he replied. 'Just asking. Politely.'

The woman huffed. 'Can I have your names then?' she asked.

'DCI Boyd and DC Okeke,' Boyd said patiently.

'And your first names?'

'Bill and Samantha,' he replied, this time not so patiently.

'Which is which?'

He raised a brow. 'Well, I'm hardly going to be a Samantha, am I?'

The woman narrowed her eyes at them both. 'How do I know you're not reporters?'

Boyd and Okeke produced their warrant cards.

With that, she seemed happy with the information she'd collected and she stepped back to one side to let them in. Boyd led the way and Okeke closed the door gently behind them.

'So do you work down on this floor?' asked Okeke. 'At the accountant's?'

'Yes,' the woman replied. 'At Watson and Dorridge.'

Boyd went over to the side table to pick through the pile of unopened post.

'That's mostly addressed to Mr Sutton,' said the woman. 'I've been tripping over his post every morning for some time.'

'So he's not been here for a while?' Okeke asked.

'He's not bothered picking up his junk mail if he has been.'

'We should try knocking, since we're inside,' said Boyd.

'Don't you need a warrant or something to do *that*?' asked the woman.

'We're concerned for his well-being,' Okeke explained. 'This isn't a police raid.'

'Oh.' Now the woman just looked disappointed. 'Well... yes, if you want to. But make sure you shut this front door properly when you leave.'

'We will,' said Okeke. 'Thank you.'

They made their way up two flights of old and worn mahogany stairs to the second-floor landing. At the end, a solitary stained-glass window cast a crimson and lemon glow across the tired, scuffed linoleum floor. The lead lining projected web-like lines of shadow across the hall and up the walls.

'Okay, so not at all creepy,' said Okeke.

'Okay then, let's knock,' said Boyd. He stepped past her and rapped his knuckles on the door. 'Mr Sutt–'

The apartment door swung gently inwards with a creak.

10

'D o you smell gas?' asked Boyd.

'What?' Okeke sniffed.

'*Do you smell gas?*' He looked meaningfully from the door, which was ajar, to the trespassing threshold of the door jamb, and back again.

'Oh,' she said, the penny dropping. 'Maybe. Yes.'

'Good. Reasonable grounds to enter.' He held a finger up. 'Stay back,' he said quietly.

Okeke raised her eyebrows at him, then she took a step forward, over the threshold of the apartment and onto the tired door mat just inside. 'POLICE!' she shouted into the small hallway of the flat.

'Anyone in here?' Boyd added, as he stepped in beside her.

Their voices bounced off the wood panelling and tiled floor of the hallway, reverberating into what appeared to be a large room at the end. He could see sunlight streaming diagonally across the room's floor from above. Skylight windows, he guessed. The cast-down beams of light cut through clouds of lazily swirling dust motes.

They advanced cautiously until they stood in the opening

to the room. Sutton was clearly a fan of the creepy, crusty antique look; the floor was set with black and white tiles, the walls lined with either more wood panelling or shelves of faded book spines. Above them, he could see the bones of the building, oak beams running across to support the slate roof. He suspected that if he shone a torch up into the rafters he'd see the eyes of a few dozen spiders shining back.

'Mr Sutton! Are you in here?' Okeke called out.

There was no reply.

Boyd ventured into the large open room. 'This is the police? Anyone in?'

There was still no answer.

He pulled out a pair of forensics gloves and snapped them on. 'Right, given the door was unlocked, either Sutton forgot to lock it or...'

'Someone else has got a key.'

'Or picked it.' He made a mental note to check the door frame beside the lock for signs of scraped paint or wood indentation that would indicate a little jimmying to coax the lock's tongue aside.

Beneath a dormer window that looked out onto Chancery Lane and the buildings opposite was a mahogany writing desk and ink blotter. Both in keeping with Sutton's apparent obsession for all things dark, polished and antiquarian. Boyd expected to see an old Singer typewriter, but when it came to his work Sutton, it seemed, embraced more modern methods. Beside a photograph of a much younger version of himself in a rowing crew was his Wi-Fi router, on and merrily blinking away.

There was no sign of a laptop, though.

'No family pics,' said Okeke, pointing. 'Just lots of himself.'

'I noticed. He's obviously not that close with his kids.' Boyd wandered across the floor towards a galley door with a stained-glass design. He pushed it inwards to find a modest kitchen, the kind that a single man with little interest in cooking would have: a small fridge, a hob and oven and a dishwasher. There were three pans in descending size, hanging from hooks that Boyd suspected were a design statement more than anything else.

He opened the fridge. It was on and contained a few essentials: milk, butter, pate, a pot of stoned olives and feta cheese. Nothing smelled offensive. He uncapped the milk and sniffed. It was on the cusp. He'd have braved it for a builder's tea if there'd been nothing else to use – but that was it.

'So he was here relatively recently,' Boyd called out.

'Guv?'

'Yeah?'

'There's something you should see.'

Boyd stepped out of the kitchen back into the main room. 'Where are you?'

'Bedroom.'

He saw another open doorway punctuating the relentless wooden panelling. He went over and poked his head inside to see an elaborately carved four-poster.

Of course... he's got a four-bloody-poster.

Okeke was in front of a painting on the wall beside it, something Turner-esque in a thick and swirly gilt frame.

She grabbed one corner of the frame and casually flipped her wrist. The frame swung out on hinges to reveal a wall safe.

Boyd joined Okeke and peered inside.

'It's open,' she said, 'and empty. Someone's been looking for something.'

Just then Boyd's work phone buzzed. He pulled it out of his jacket. It was Sully.

11

'I think we may have located Sutton,' said Sully. He took a few steps away from the small crowd of fire crew who'd been pulling the debris mound carefully apart, piece by piece, and who were now gathered around the body laid out on a board.

'Just a moment, Boyd,' said Sully. He turned back to the four firemen who were peering a little too closely at their discovery and put his hand over the phone. 'Gents! Gentlemen! If you wouldn't mind...'

Sully hated shouting. Shouting reminded him of mothers in playgrounds, or monobrow apes squaring off at each other outside pubs. It was vulgar. But these idiots were looming over his cadaver and probably spattering drops of sweat and goodness knows what else on it.

'Can you please get the fuck away from the body!' he snapped loudly. Then: 'If you don't mind... *gents*.'

'Sorry, Boyd,' Sully continued. 'Just shooing away the rubberneckers.' The firemen returned to their task of pulling away carbonised wood beams and floor boards, leaving Sully alone to squat beside the corpse.

'What have you got for me, Sully?' Boyd asked.

'We have a male body attached to a rectangular section of slate,' Sully explained. The body looked as though it had been merged with the slate.

'Attached? What... like nailed?'

'No, he's stuck to it... Do you remember that Superglue advert from the eighties? The one where that poor chap in a cheap white boiler suit was glued to a plank of wood and then dangled over a shark pool?'

He heard Okeke let out a snort of laughter.

'But, of course it's not that.' He peered a little closer and with one gloved hand pressed at the resin-like seam between the blackened body and the flat board. It dented easily, like butter left out of a fridge.

'Yes, it's body fat. The body's stuck to it – welded. Like a fried egg or a sausage if you left them in a frying pan for too long.'

'Jesus, Sully...' Boyd exclaimed. 'Why does it always have to be a food metaphor?'

'It's a simile, actually,' Sully corrected him. He leaned in to examine an extended arm and hand. The top side of the corpse was blackened and cracked, almost completely carbonised, but the underside, protected by the seal of fat, looked less well done. He probed the fat with his gloved hand and managed to coax the wrist and hand free of its adhesive. 'The top is completely blackened but underneath... Hang on, I'm just looking...'

He crouched down further and looked beneath the arm, not wanting to lift it too high in case he caused further damage. Remarkably, the skin was intact, reddened from the heat, and marbled with livor mortis stains, but essentially still raw meat.

'I think I can see a ligature mark around the wrist.'

'A ligature mark?' Boyd repeated. 'Are you sure?'

'Uh-huh. Looks like our man was tied out on a slate

surface.' He stood up and took a few steps back to look at the blackened slate board itself. 'Which, I'm almost certain, was a snooker table.'

Sully smiled as he listened to Boyd suck in a deep breath on the other end of the line. It was vaguely satisfying to hear the DCI's normally gruff and steady tone tempered by an all-too-human inflection.

'Want me to send you a picture?' Sully asked mischievously.

'Christ, I can wait for that,' Boyd said, and hung up.

'Oh, and thanks very much for the prompt update, Kevin,' Sully muttered to himself as he tucked the phone inside his forensic suit and turned back to the body in front of him.

'Well, it looks like we have a definite murder,' Boyd said to Okeke.

'Sutton?'

'It's male. Sully can't possibly know if it's Sutton yet. But, given what's been going on here, I think that's a reasonable assumption.' He glanced at his watch. It was getting on.

He made a call to the nearest station and an hour later a locksmith was on site with a toolbox to secure Sutton's flat. He handed Boyd a set of keys and a job slip to sign. Okeke stuck some crime-scene tape across the doorway and they were done.

'I've left a message with –' Boyd checked his notebook – 'DI Ashtiani to log the crime and to contact me if they're planning on looking in on it before Monday,' he told her.

'Are we knocking on downstairs before we go, guv?' Okeke asked.

'I think we can let the Met do the legwork on Monday,' Boyd said. 'We may as well make the most of their manpower. They're a senior force, but we've got the murder. Unfortunately it stays ours. Anyway, I expect the local CID will be glad that someone else has taken the load.'

'In that case, while they're at it, can we get them checking the cameras down this road?' said Okeke. 'We might get lucky.'

'Good shout,' Boyd said, tucking one of the keys into his pocket and putting the rest in an envelope addressed to DI Ashtiani.

They finally exited the building, pausing for Boyd to take a snapshot of the business names on the brass plate beside the door. He preferred to give them both a call himself rather than rely on the third-hand messages from a Met officer going through the motions.

They were both quiet as Okeke drove them out of central London; she was busy with the typical stop-start traffic and Boyd sat beside her, gazing out of the window and gathering old memories like a milkman collecting empties. The route took them south across Blackfriars Bridge, and as he looked out at the South Bank, bathed in sunshine and crowded with tourists, he wondered how many times he and Julia had walked along there on a Sunday afternoon, Emma and Noah in tow.

The car picked up just enough speed south of Brixton to get out of third gear and they kept up a steady pace down to Croydon and the M25.

'Whoever broke into Sutton's place was either after Sutton or something Sutton had,' Boyd said, finally breaking the silence.

'You don't say, guv,' said Okeke.

'All right,' Boyd said with good humour. 'But it never hurts to state what you think is the obvious, does it?'

'That's true, guv,' she replied. 'And, if I may say so, you're bloody good at it.'

'Up yours,' Boyd said, laughing. 'Seriously, though. Maybe they found Sutton there?'

'What? Kidnapped him?' said Okeke. 'Then what? They dragged him down to Hastings to his own house?'

'Yeah, okay. It's pretty unlikely,' Boyd said. 'More likely they were looking for something. There were no signs of a struggle, and the flat was pretty tidy – so whoever it was knew it was empty and knew exactly where to look. Obviously, the timing's too coincidental for this *not* to be linked. So, until something says otherwise, we're looking at a sequence of events that ties in his London flat and his Hastings house. And whatever happened it ended with the fire two nights ago.'

'So that's your weekend, is it? Puzzling this out?' Okeke asked.

Boyd sighed. 'I was planning to tame my wilderness of a back garden this weekend. I'm thinking I might have to take a chainsaw to the whole bloody lot.'

The 'garden' – sixty feet of brambles and nettles – had been neglected and allowed to run wild by the previous owners. For a couple of decades, by the look of it. Now that summer had come to Sussex, Boyd had decided it was time to get out there with a zero-tolerance weeding policy and level everything. Emma and Daniel had promised to help him this weekend, but he was pretty sure that wasn't going to happen now that Ozzie needed looking after.

'Not gonna lie – it is a bit of a jungle out there,' said Okeke, then she added, 'You should have a gardening party.'

'Well, maybe I will one day when I finally have a garden to have one in,' Boyd replied.

'No... not a garden party. A garden-*ing* party. Get some friends to come over and help you flatten the place, then you could have a bonfire, barbecue and beers after.'

'When you say friends...?' Boyd said, shooting her a side-ways glance.

'Yes,' she replied. 'Me and Jay would come. Minter might too. And Warren, if his mum lets him out at weekends.'

Boyd laughed. 'Yeah, maybe. That actually sounds like a pretty good idea.'

She looked at him. 'You should, guv. You really should. Get to see us outside work for once. In our *civvies*.'

'Christ. That's what worries me. I'd be expecting Minter to turn up in a mankini and flip-flops.'

She laughed.

'Or Sully in some bizarre cosplay costume.' He pulled a face. 'Whatever weird and worrying things you lot get up to in your spare time is of no interest to me!'

'Relax. We'll all come in sensible casual-ware and make short work of your jungle. Seriously, guv, you should do it. It'll be a good team-building thing.'

'Right. So not just a piss-up then?'

'Well,' Okeke said. 'That's a distinct possibility.'

13

DAY 3

Boyd finished his toast and stood up. 'Right, I do believe the plan today is to make a dent in the garden.'

Emma and Daniel were still eating their breakfast. Neither looked particularly keen.

Boyd turned to look at the TV. Andrew Marr was on and interviewing some sprightly and well-groomed junior minister who'd recently been promoted to the cabinet.

'*So, Tim Portman, finally off the substitutes' bench and onto the pitch. How does it feel to be promoted by the prime minister? To join his team?*'

'*Exciting, Andrew, of course. I've given the party a long period of loyal service and I think the PM sees me as a mature pair of hands in a relatively young cabinet. A seasoned veteran in this politics game –*'

Boyd picked up the remote and switched the TV off. 'Come on, you idle buggers.'

THEY SURVEYED THE GARDEN, armed to the teeth with a formidable array of tools that Boyd had picked up in a B&Q trolley dash on his return from London. He felt like some conquistador staring uncertainly at an impenetrable wall of an Amazonian jungle.

Daniel and Emma stood either side of him, Ozzie at Emma's feet, his head encased in his cone of shame.

'So, what's the plan, Dad?'

'There isn't one, really. Just hack and slash everything to the ground.' Boyd looked at Daniel. 'No prisoners.'

'No mercy,' Daniel added.

'You got it.'

Emma went and sat down on the low brick wall that had kept the jungle from engulfing the house. She looked warily at the extension cable coming out through the dining room's sash window, the orange flex snaking up from the plug block to Boyd's electric chainsaw and Daniel's hedge trimmer.

'Well, me and Ozzie are going to retire to a safe distance if you're going to be swinging those things around,' she said.

Boyd turned to Daniel. 'Locked and loaded?'

Daniel raised his strimmer like it was a heavy machine gun. 'Remember, Egon: never, under any circumstances, let the plasma beams cross.'

Boyd laughed at the *Ghostbusters* reference. That was why he liked the lad. 'All right, let's proceed with Operation Slash 'n' Burn.'

They both fired up their power tools and began to tear into the tangle of undergrowth.

An hour later, they stopped for a break. Emma brought them out a bottle of beer each and they surveyed the ground they'd cleared. Depressingly it really wasn't very much; both of them had carved uneven semicircles around themselves a couple of yards in diameter, leaving a shin-deep bed of severed bramble stems and nettle heads at their feet.

'Um, Boyd? This trimmer's a bit rubbish,' said Daniel. 'It keeps clogging.'

Boyd's chainsaw was the same. He'd bought at the budget end, assuming that even the cheapest power tools would be more than a match for tender green stalks.

'Maybe Okeke's right,' he muttered to himself.

'*Scre-w-w-w... you.*'

Boyd looked at Daniel sharply.

'I didn't say –'

'*Screw you.*'

Boyd turned back to look at Emma. 'What?' she asked innocently.

'Did you just –'

'*Screw you. And you.*' It sounded like a female voice. '*... And you. And you.*'

It was coming from beyond the fence to his right. He turned to see a head peering over the top. It belonged to a woman with long frizzy grey hair, held back on her head by an Alice band. She was wearing glasses that made her eyes look relentlessly owlish.

'Ah! Finally taming that fucking wilderness!' she hooted over the fence.

She stepped up onto something and the rest of her face, and the culprit who'd been telling them all to go screw themselves, came into view.

'This is Fergie,' she said, introducing the parrot. 'The little bastard's got a bit of a potty mouth.' She shoved a hand over the top of the fence. 'I'm Angela,' she said. 'And you're Mr Boyd?'

'Just Boyd,' he replied, holding her hand lightly. 'This is my daughter, Emma, and her boyfriend, Daniel.'

Angela waved at Emma. 'Hello again.' Then nodded at

Daniel. 'I can't believe it's taken this long to say hello,' she said to Boyd.

Boyd glanced up at the blue sky. 'It's the weather, I guess. Brings us all out of our little caves, doesn't it?'

'Your parrot,' said Emma. 'Won't he fly away?'

'He's tethered,' Angela replied. 'But I doubt he would anyway. He knows he's on to a good thing here. He's got free run of the house.'

Boyd looked up at her side of the building, which was a mirror image of theirs. At one time the entire building had been a small Victorian girl's school and their backyards a generous and well-kept walled garden.

'The whole place?' he asked.

'Oh, yes. He's the man of the house, you know. He can be a bit of a rude bugger at times, though.'

'I noticed.'

She turned to look at Fergie, tickling him just beneath his beak. 'He finds other males a little threatening, don't you, little man?'

The parrot's beady eyes remained resolutely on Boyd. 'Arse,' he said.

It was at that moment that Ozzie's cone of shame angled towards the bird and he finally figured out what had been tossing hostilities over the fence. He jumped to his feet and unleashed a barrage of his own.

Fergie squawked and flapped his wings frantically, dislodging a couple of feathers as he took to the air.

Emma reached down and caught Ozzie's collar. 'NO! Ozzie!'

Angela withdrew from the fence, reeling in Fergie by his tether, green feathers raining down on her as he flapped his wings in a frantic bid to escape to safety.

'Sorry about that!' Boyd called.

'It's all right!' Angela replied. 'I'd better take him in!'

Ozzie let rip with another rapid sequence of loud window-rattling barks that merged into one long woo-woo-woo.

'Enough!' Emma scolded him. '*Enough!* No barking!'

Ozzie did as he was told and finished off with a series of indignant huffs that made his jowls flap.

LATER THAT NIGHT, as Boyd lay in bed with one of the bedroom sash windows open to let in a little breeze, he heard a volley of woo-woo-woo barking coming from next door and realised Fergie the foul-mouthed parrot had learned a new put-down.

14

DAY 4

Boyd rapped his knuckles on Chief Superintendent Hatcher's door and *almost* waited for her to call him in. It was a small but childishly satisfying act of rebellion.

'Ahh, there you are,' she said. 'Come on in and take a seat.'

Her office felt somewhat crowded this morning with Sutherland sitting in one of her visitor seats and another man in the other. Despite Her Madge's invitation for Boyd to sit down, there was little opportunity for him to do so. The only available chair was backed into a far corner, and her handbag and a pair of comfy walking shoes were on the seat. He decided to remain standing.

The other man turned to look Boyd's way and nodded a greeting. He had the tidy look of an ex-services man, with his auburn hair clipped short and side-parted. He could have been in his early forties, but was doing a good job at looking trim and ten years younger.

'Boyd, this is DI Douglas Lane,' Hatcher informed him.

Lane stood up and offered Boyd a hand.

'And this is our SIO on the case, DCI Bill Boyd,' Hatcher continued.

They shook hands. Lane smiled. 'So, *you're* the detective who found the Ken Doll Killer after all this time?' He had a very soft Scots Border accent.

Boyd nodded. 'Well, blindly stumbled across him, more like.'

'DI Lane is from the PaDP,' added Hatcher.

The Parliamentary and Diplomatic Protection unit was one of the more publicity-shy and lesser-known departments of the Met – or it had been until Keeley Hawes' character in a TV show a few years back had decided to have a tumble with one of its young officers.

Boyd raised a brow. 'Arthur Sutton had a security assignment?'

'Aye, but not an *active* one,' replied Lane. 'You're aware he used to be a cabinet member?'

'For all of five minutes, wasn't it?'

'That's long enough that he's on our Christmas card list,' said Lane, smiling .

'DI Lane's going to tag along with you Boyd, until....' Chief Superintendent Hatcher cocked her head as she looked at Lane for an answer.

'Until?' prompted Boyd.

'The truth is... I'm here as a sacrificial lamb, a gesture of contrition,' said Lane. 'My department dropped the ball and we failed to protect Sir Arthur Sutton, so... I'm here as a spare pair of hands for you to make use of.'

Boyd smiled. 'I wasn't aware the Met sent apology-o-grams.'

Lane laughed. 'It's actually more about arse-covering. We messed up; we need to be seen as taking part in clearing up the mess.'

That was refreshingly honest. Boyd had a feeling he was going to like him. 'Okay. Well, are you any good at making tea?'

Lane grinned. 'Whatever you need me to do, Boyd.'

A free detective. He suspected Sutherland was doing mental cartwheels.

'Also...' continued Lane, 'because of *who* the victim was...'

Ah, here we go. The caveat.

'I'm here as an intelligence firewall. There may be confidential documents that pop up during this inquiry.'

'And you're here to redact them?'

'To review what can go team-wide, and what can't,' said Lane. 'I'm sorry, but anything to do with Sutton's short period in cabinet needs to have an eye run over it.' He softened that with a genuinely contrite smile. 'There's an agenda behind the gesture, I'm afraid.'

'Has the body been officially ID'd yet,' asked Hatcher.

'Not yet officially, but it's looking more than likely that it's Sutton. The first thing on my list this morning is to chase up Ellessey Forensics.'

'Ah, about that,' said Hatcher. 'The Met said they'd have their own pathologist look him over.'

'Why?' Boyd asked. She dipped her face slightly to look over her glasses. 'Ma'am,' he added.

Lane answered. 'Again. It's about damage limitation. To spare any blushes,' he said with a hint of disdain. 'Signs of substance abuse, or any... unsavoury behaviours.'

Right. Boyd nodded. *Can't have the Good and the Great looking bad now, can we?*

'And the Met's paying,' said Sutherland, trying not to sound too pleased about that.

'I presume we can attend, though?' said Boyd. Not that he particularly wanted to.

Hatcher nodded. 'It's our investigation, so I insisted that our

SIO should have access to the examination and the report.' She glanced at Lane. 'But you'll be accompanied.'

Lane offered him another apologetic smile. 'I'm sorry... I'm afraid I'm going to be hovering around you like a mosquito.'

'Has Sutton's next of kin been told about the body?' asked Sutherland.

'Second job this morning,' replied Boyd. 'Once we know for sure.'

'Well then, I'll let you press on with that.' Hatcher stood up to indicate that the meeting was done. 'DI Lane, is there anything else you need?'

He stood up. 'No, ma'am.'

She nodded and turned to Boyd. 'Right, Boyd you've got another murder inquiry team to set up. Do try to pick some different people; we need to spread the experience around our CID.'

'I'll try, ma'am,' he lied. 'But there aren't that many spares. DCI Flack has most of the rest.'

'Well, see what you can do. And tread very carefully with this one. Sir Arthur was something of a national treasure. He guest-hosted *Countdown* once.' She went to her door and opened it. 'Show Lane the essentials: the canteen, toilets. Find him a desk and a spare mug.'

Boyd led the way out of her office and Sutherland squeezed past the two men as they lingered outside in the hallway.

'Incident Room's free,' said Sutherland. 'No need to evict Flack this time. It's all yours.'

'Dammit. That's my favourite bit,' Boyd muttered.

15

Five minutes later, Boyd and Lane were up in the canteen with a coffee each and sitting at a table away from the noisy counter.

'I didn't know ex-members of cabinet got special attention too,' said Boyd. 'I thought it was just ex-PMs.'

Lane shrugged. 'Ex-PMs and chancellors get the *deluxe* service; the rest get someone like me to check in on them every now and then.'

'None of the glamour and excitement of a close protection unit then?'

Lane laughed. 'No standard-issue Glock and shoulder holster, no hidden earpiece or dark glasses, I'm afraid. Not for poor Sutton.'

Boyd tore the corner off a sachet of sweetener. 'So how long will you be attached to our operation? Until…'

'Until the investigation has an outcome. I need to find somewhere to lay my doss bag.'

'Doss bag?' Boyd laughed. 'So you *are* ex-military!'

Lane gave him a resigned shrug. 'Does it show?'

He nodded. 'Army?'

'Paras.'

He didn't offer any more than that and Boyd had spoken to enough ex-military in his life to understand when not to probe.

'You know, Lane, this may take months. Where are you based?'

'London,' he replied. 'But I've got an accommodation allowance.'

'Nice. Well, there's a decent seafront hotel not too far from the station. The Lansdowne Hotel.'

Lane sighed. 'I'm on a budget. It'll be a B&B for me. Close enough to walk to work and the train station would be handy.'

'You could borrow one of our pool cars,' said Boyd. 'I'm sure Sutherland wouldn't mind springing for –'

'I can't drive. Medical reasons,' Lane added. 'I have tonic-clonic muscular seizures. Used to be known as Grand Mal seizures.'

'Shit,' said Boyd. 'Sorry to hear that.'

'Ah, it's not a big deal. They're rare and avoidable, but enough of a risk that I don't get to drive any more. That's why I'm doing this instead of guarding a minister or an ambassador, but it works for me. I've got a little boy. A desk job and nine-to-five hours are a much better fit.'

'How old is he?'

'Four.'

Boyd smiled. 'Well, we'll try our best to get you back home as soon as we can.'

16

'Morning, everyone, said Boyd.

He looked at the tin of Celebrations in the middle of the conference table. Sutherland's moving-in gift for the team.

Boyd had ignored Hatcher's request to pull in new faces. Those that hadn't been sucked in by Flack's ongoing resource-drain investigation were the very bottom of the barrel: a mixture of old sweats serving time until they could take their pensions, and a few younger ones who just weren't cutting it and would inevitably be bumped horizontally into another role. Boyd had picked the same core team he'd had with the Ken Doll Killer case. *His* team, as he liked to think of them.

Sitting round the table were DS Minter and DCs Okeke, Warren and O'Neal. Sully was riding shotgun at one end, ready to handle any crime scene queries. Leslie Poole was beside him with her notes on the state of the crime scene and the personnel who'd entered it in the initial thirty-six hours.

'First of all, I'd like to introduce DI Douglas Lane – he's from the PaPD. Everyone say, "Good morning, Mr Lane."'

The room filled with their chorused voices sounding like an unruly class welcoming a new supply teacher.

'All right, let's keep this looking professional for as long as we can.' He caught Minter's eye and nodded at him to slide the chocolates up the table. Minter gave the tin a hearty shove and it came to rest like a curling stone right in front of Boyd. 'Lane's here as a spare pair of hands and a knowledge resource on the levels of protection Sutton had, which were...' Boyd looked over to Lane to fill in the rest.

'Not a great deal,' Lane said. 'Ex-cabinet members get a panic button, CCTV fitted and an annual security review, but that's about it. It's the ex-PMs and ex-chancellors who get a close protection assignment for life.'

'Right. So, since Sutton served as a junior minister for about six months, he got the very basic security plan?' asked Boyd.

Lane nodded. 'Indeed.'

Boyd prised the lid off the Celebrations. 'I got confirmation this morning that the body pulled out of Eagle House *is* Sutton's body. They identified him through his dental records. There is clear evidence that he was tied down and, as of right now, this is officially a murder inquiry. Her Madge will be hosting a press briefing later today. Given that Sir Arthur Sutton is... *was* a very recognisable name, we're going to have press descending on this station and they're almost certainly going to try and catch us coming in and out on our own. If that happens... the answer is "no comment" every time. Clear?'

The room filled with muttered affirmatives.

'Good. Right then, I suppose the best way to get you all up to speed is to give you a bio on Sutton.' He looked at Lane. 'Care to do the honours?' He picked out a Bounty from the tub, unwrapped it and tossed the chocolate into his mouth.

Lane nodded and stood up in front of the whiteboard. 'Okay.' He looked around awkwardly for a moment; it was obvious he hadn't been expecting to deliver a presentation of any kind this morning.

'Sir Arthur Sutton was a writer of trashy political thrillers, a cabinet member under Cameron back in 2015, an occasional TV guest on panel shows, as well as a commentator on some of those it-was-okay-in-the-eighties clip shows. He was significantly wealthy –'

'From the books?' asked Minter.

'Some of it was,' Lane replied, 'but there was also the settlement with his ex-wife. He did very well out of that – and the after-dinner speaking. He dabbled in a bit of lobbying on the side and got a yearly consultancy fee with a number of finance and construction companies. So his wealth was fed by a variety of connections made during his time in public service.'

'There's a surprise,' said Okeke.

Boyd gave her both eyebrows. 'Politics at the door, please, Okeke.'

His comment was met with an eye-roll from her.

'She's right, though,' Lane conceded with a shrug. 'For people like Sutton, a political service is pretty much an audition for the lucrative career that comes afterwards. And he used his few months in cabinet to make some helpful connections.'

Lane went on to cover Sutton's path to Westminster, his time at Oxford and his time as a Wapping-based red-top sub-editor. He also mentioned his private life, the kids, the affair and the divorce.

Boyd stood up and took over once he'd finished. 'So, then the first go-to is usually money if there's a stash of it lying around... We have an ex-wife and two grown children to take a close look at.'

He turned to Okeke. 'I want you and Warren to have a chat with Sutton's daughter, Hermione. She said she was back from her holiday after the weekend, right?'

Okeke nodded.

'Hermione first,' confirmed Boyd, 'and keep trying to get hold of the son, Henry.' Next, his gaze settled on O'Neal. 'I want you working on CCTV along London Road and Bohemia Road, and ANPR hits for Sutton's car.'

Sutton's Mercedes had been transported to the division's vehicle compound. Parked right outside the front door of the burning Eagle House, it had suffered surprisingly little damage, only some paint blistering on the side nearest the building.

'I want you to look at Sutton's movements, call history, whatever digital forensics we can get. Warren, you can help O'Neal with that. Minter, you're my action log gatekeeper. O'Neal, evidence coordinator. Oh, and we're working with a Met forensics contractor, not our usual folks at the Ellessey labs.' He turned to Lane. 'Do you know who they're using?'

Lane shook his head.

'Mace and Mackintosh,' said Sully from the other end of the table. 'And, if I recall correctly, they're based in Putney. They emailed me this morning for a copy of my SOC report.'

'You got a contact name for me?' Boyd asked.

Sully consulted his iPad. 'Dr Raddon. I copied you into my reply. Check your inbox.'

'Thanks, Sully. Will do,' Boyd said. 'Which reminds me... DC Okeke and I visited Sutton's London apartment on Friday. It had been broken into – nothing obvious had been taken, but the safe was open and empty. The Met forensics team have been processing it over the weekend. Sully – can you make sure you're up to date on their findings? If you need to pop up and take a look yourself, then let me know.' He looked around the table. 'Everyone else, this is something to take into considera-tion as our investigation progresses. I'll share any forensic find-ings on this as they come in. Right, any questions so far?'

'Do we have any witnesses to the fire, boss?' asked Minter.

'One possible... if she survives, that is. Sutton's live-in housekeeper was the woman pulled out of the fire.' Boyd flipped through his notebook. 'Her name's Margot Bajek. She was pulled from a room on the ground floor, a pantry or larder of some kind.'

'And you said there was evidence that Sutton had been tied up, boss?' Minter said.

'Tied *out*, actually,' Boyd replied. 'To a snooker table. One limb to each corner pocket.' Boyd glanced at his team. 'Any of you lot seen that Da Vinci movie with Tom Hanks?'

Most of them nodded.

'So like that... like Da Vinci's Vitruvian Man.'

'Is that, you know, symbolic?' asked Warren. 'I mean, is the pose meant to mean something?'

Boyd shrugged. 'Could be. Equally it could be that the corner pockets were the easiest way to anchor his wrists and ankles. Let's not jump down that rabbit hole just yet.'Are Sutton's books linked in anyway?' asked Okeke. 'You know, any weird stuff? Occult stuff?'

Lane answered. 'He writes routine political thrillers. The usual Ian Fleming tropes: terrorist plots, gadgets and sex-object female characters.'

'So a bunch of cringy misogyny, casual racism and lots of guns, explosions and car chases,' Okeke clarified.

Lane nodded. 'All very Boys' Own.'

'I might give one a read,' said Minter.

Lane grimaced. 'It's not really a recommendation, Sergeant.'

Boyd decided enough was enough. 'All right. Back on topic, please, boys and girls. We're investigating a murder, not running a book club... Sutton has people in his life who may benefit financially from his death, and we'll be taking a look at those first before we cast the net wider.'

'What does "casting the net wider" mean?' asked Okeke. 'Are we looking at his political and lobbying links?'

Lane caught Boyd's eye. 'May I, Boyd?'

'Go on.'

'Part of the reason I'm here is to keep an eye out for official secrets leakages. So, yes, I'm afraid if the investigation swerves in that direction, I'll have to –'

'Cover it all up with one of those big black marker pens?' offered Sully.

Lane shrugged apologetically. 'Confidentiality is the way the business of government works. Ministers need to be able to talk freely... and privately.'

'That's convenient,' muttered Okeke.

Boyd stood up. 'Okay. That's enough. Lane's got his job to do, and we've got ours. If I had his job, I'd be pulling out that black pen if it was necessary. Right. You've all got jobs folks... so let's get busy.'

As the room filled with the sound of chairs being pushed back, Boyd remembered one last thing he'd wanted to announce while he had them gathered.

'One sec! Everyone!'

They paused.

'I'm having... a sort of barbeque-stroke-garden-clearing party this Sunday. In the spirit of many hands make light work, just bulldozing the lot. You're all welcome, well... I mean, I'd be grateful, if you'd drop by and help.' He was dimly aware that he wasn't exactly selling the idea. 'There'll be beers and food and... stuff,' he added.

There were a few muted half nods, some muttered 'yessirs', but not a great deal of direct eye contact from around the room.

'Anyway, Sunday from midday. Let me know if you're up for it.'

He suspected next Sunday was going to be a complete no-show.

17

'All right, I'll take a few questions,' said Chief Superintendent Hatcher. Boyd begrudgingly had to admit that Her Madge handled the press better than Sutherland (who droned), Minter (who got stage fright) or himself, now notorious for being bleeped. *Once.*

Hatcher seemed to have cajoled the press pack into behaving itself, silently raising their hands and waiting patiently to be picked rather than all shouting out at the same time.

'Yes,' she said, pointing to a journalist in the front row. 'You.'

'Amanda Brooks, the *Guardian*. You said the body pulled out of Sutton's house has been identified as Sir Arthur Sutton. Has his family been informed?'

'They have.'

'How are they? Have they commented?'

'They're understandably distraught and have made no public comment – they've asked for their privacy to be respected at this moment.'

Hatcher picked another.

'Heather Crombie, the *Mail*. There's been a suggestion that the fire was deliberate. Arson. Can you confirm that?'

'No, I cannot. Nor will I. The fire investigation officer has yet to submit his final report and we're keeping an open mind until then.'

'But we've heard rumours that you've assembled a murder investigation tea–'

Hatcher silenced her with a stern look over the top of her glasses. Boyd wondered how the hell a slight gesture like that could have such an impact. Some people were obviously born to be school teachers... or press-pack wranglers.

'*Of course* we've got a team looking at it. If there turns out to be an indication of foul play, I would like us to have that evidence to hand.' Hatcher smiled wryly. 'It's called policing.'

Calm as anything.

Boyd caught DI Lane's eye. Lane smirked. He was obviously thinking the same thing.

'Matthew Donegal, the *Canary*. If evidence surfaces that this is arson, will you be looking at motives linked to Sutton's political career?'

'*If* evidence surfaces, we will look at all possible inquiry leads –'

'It's worth noting that he was in cabinet during the fundraising for the Brexit campaign and had links to Cambridge Analytica and that –'

Hatcher interrupted him tersely: 'We will examine all angles, Matthew, rest assured.' She pointed to another journalist. 'Yes?'

'Sue Pascal, the *Argyle*. You mentioned that there is a witness in hospital.'

'Yes, Sir Arthur's housekeeper. She's currently in an induced coma because of the severity of her burns. Her condition, unfortunately, is critical at the moment, but, if and when she makes enough of a recovery, we will of course want to talk to her.'

BOYD WATCHED the journalists rise from their seats and vacate the press-briefing room. It was muggy and hot inside from the number of bodies and the lack of a window to open. Boyd noted there was an AC unit but it was off. He wondered if it was off deliberately to hasten the journos' departure from police premises or whether it was something else in the building that had fallen victim to budget cuts.

'She's good.'

He turned to see Lane at his side. 'Rather her than me,' he replied. 'Half the time I want to groan and eye-roll at the questions they ask.'

They made their way back to the Incident Room and found Okeke.

'I'm going over to Conquest Hospital to have a chat with Margot Bajek's mother and daughter,' he told her. 'Want to come along?'

'Well, I *was* just about to take Warren out for a trip to Brighton,' Okeke replied. 'Sutton's daughter, Hermione, lives there,' she added at the slightly puzzled look on Boyd's face.

'I thought she could only do tomorrow?' he said.

'She called to say she's okay to talk this afternoon, guv.'

'Ah, right. Then let's get this visit done first. I'd like you to come along. You're good in these situations. It's a courtesy call foremost... maybe a little gentle fact-digging. After that, you can take Warren and go to see Hermione.'

'Mind if I tag along to the hospital?' asked Lane.

Boyd nodded. 'Be my guest.'

18

'Where is she?' asked Boyd.

'She's down there in room eleven, but you, Detective ...' The nurse had been entirely unimpressed by Boyd's warrant card and had already forgotten his name. 'May I ask you and your colleagues to wait in the family room.'

She led them to the room, opened the door and gestured for them to step inside. 'I'll let her family know you've come to visit.'

The door closed and Boyd took a seat. He looked up at the clock on the wall. It was three already. He had no idea how long they'd be here talking to Margot Bajek's family. 'Okeke, I'm sorry. Can you bump Hermione Sutton back to tomorrow?'

Okeke nodded, picked up her phone and started tapping out a text.

'So how long have you been in the force?' asked Lane.

'About twenty years,' Boyd replied. 'Five of them in uniform. What about you?'

'Twelve.'

'Before that, the paras?'

'Aye.'

Okeke looked up from her phone. 'I thought so.' She nodded at his shoes. And, for the first time, Boyd noticed that Lane was wearing a pair of Oxfords, polished and buffed immaculately.

'I have tried to kick that habit, but not giving them a once-over feels like not brushing your teeth.' Lane laughed. 'I know. Sounds ridiculous. Nobody but ex-forces types understand that one.'

Boyd looked down at his own scruffy brown loafers. There was a dusting of dried mud on both and, if he wasn't mistaken, some tooth indentations on the left toes, courtesy of Ozzie.

'The army does that,' said Lane. 'It messes with your head. Gives you unhealthy obsessive compulsions like shoe-shining, bed-making...'

The door opened and the nurse ushered in a young woman. 'These are the police who wanted to talk with you.' The nurse looked at her. 'But if you don't want to...?'

'No, I'm fine. Thank you,' the young woman said.

The nurse pulled the door shut. Boyd stood up and offered the young woman his hand. 'I'm DCI Boyd. This is DI Lane and DC Okeke.'

'Lena Bajek. I am her daughter.'

'Can we get you anything?' asked Boyd.

'No, I am fine.'

'Take a seat, Lena, please.'

They all sat down. Boyd began. 'Before we start... how is your mum doing?'

Lena Bajek had the look of someone battered and worn out by the cross currents of life. She seemed to be about the same age as Emma, give or take a few years, but prematurely aged.

'Mama... she has third-degree burns over eighty per cent of her body,' Lena said quietly. 'Babcia, my grandmother, and I are not sure she is going to survive.'

'I'm so sorry, Lena,' said Okeke. 'How are you and your grandma coping?'

'Not good,' she replied. 'Babcia is not well. I am her full-time carer. Mama helps.'

'With your grandma?' asked Boyd.

'With bills mostly,' Lena replied. 'She pays for the medicine, the rent, the utilities.'

'The medicine?' asked Lane.

Lena nodded. 'We are not... what is....?' She flapped her hands as she searched for the right words in English. 'We cannot have free healthcare. We did not get the settled status. So....'

'So you have to pay for it all?' asked Boyd.

She nodded. 'And now also this too...'

Christ. Boyd presumed there had to be some emergency fund that covered this kind of situation. He made a note in his pad to get their FLO, Sergeant Gayle Brown, to have a chat with her about that.

'Margot worked for Sir Arthur Sutton?' Boyd was still unclear about her role. 'As his housekeeper?'

Lena shook her head. 'First. Yes. Now she was his *carer*.'

'Carer? Was he sick?'

Lena nodded. 'Yes. He was dying. He had motor neurone disease. Mama has been looking after him for last year now.'

That explained why Sutton's public profile had decreased in recent years, Boyd thought. There'd been fewer appearances on *Question Time*, not so many guest op-ed pieces in the broadsheets. Maybe Sutton hadn't wanted the world to witness his gradual decline.

'Lena... when was the last time you spoke with your mother?' Okeke asked.

'Four days. The afternoon, before the fire.'

'Was there anything she said that concerned you? Did she sound worried?'

Lena shook her head. 'Normal.' She laced and unlaced her fingers absently. 'She told me about taking him to London. He stayed there sometimes. He has very nice place there.'

Boyd nodded. He certainly did. 'And would she stay there with him?' he asked.

'Of course,' replied Lena. 'More recently, yes. He needed help with stairs.'

'And had they just come back when you spoke to her?'

She nodded.

That matched up with the relatively fresh contents in Sutton's London fridge.

'And was she concerned about anything to do with Sir Arthur?'

'No. Opposite. She was very happy.'

'Happy? What about?'

'Sutton give her a pay rise and also asked her to go abroad with him... soon.'

'Where?' Boyd glanced at Okeke.

Lena shook her head. 'I don't know.'

'On holiday?' asked Okeke.

'I think so,' said Lena.

'As his carer?' Okeke prompted.

Lena nodded. 'And his good friend too.'

'They were close?' said Boyd.

She nodded again. 'Sutton like her very much. She felt very sorry for him. No family helping him. He lived all alone, you know?'

'Your mum sounds very kind,' said Okeke.

'But she may die for that,' Lena said sadly.

Okeke reached out and clasped Lena's hand. 'Your mum's got a fighting chance, Lena. She's strong, right? And she's in the best place.'

Lena nodded. 'Stronger than me.' Her voice was beginning to falter now.

'Then she *must* be strong,' Okeke said, smiling gently. 'We're going to help you, okay?' She glanced at Boyd. 'We're going to see if there's some financial assistance that can be organised.'

Boyd nodded and dug out a card from his jacket. 'This is my number. If you or your grandma need help, or if either of you can think of anything that might help us find out who did this, then you call me, okay?'

Lena took the card.

'We're going to find out what happened,' said Boyd. 'And who did this, and then we're going to put them away for a very long time.'

Lena nodded absently, her eyes down on the floor, hearing but not really listening.

Boyd leant forward to meet her eye line. 'Lena, thank you. We'll talk again soon, okay?'

She looked up at him, then at Lane and Okeke. 'Would you be here if this was just about my mother?'

Boyd nodded. 'Yes.'

She shook her head. 'Mama has been a carer for many years, since we came to this country. She caught the Covid and we caught it too... and we lived. She cared for so many people but there is no help for her...' She narrowed her eyes. 'Britain just clap, then say, '*Thank you very much – now go*. Maybe you can help. Maybe you cannot.'

With that, she got up out of her chair and headed out into the corridor, leaving the door creaking closed behind her.

Lane nodded slowly. 'She's quite right.'

19

They drove back to the station, and Boyd left Okeke to catch up with Warren about the re-arranged interview with Sutton's daughter.

It was getting towards five and Boyd was aware that Lane had placed an overnight bag beside his desk earlier today.

'Right. We need to get you some accommodation sorted.'

'Aye,' Lane said, nodding. 'That or I'll sling my doss bag under your desk.'

Boyd turned to look for Minter and found him digging in a stationery cupboard for something. 'Minter!'

'Boss?'

Boyd waved him over, and Minter joined them holding a printer cartridge. 'We're out of ink, boss. Flack and his cockwombles left it completely bloody empty, didn't they?'

'Minter, we need to get Lane into a B&B. Somewhere that's walkable to the police station. Could you suggest anywhere?'

'Ah. Right. There's a whole row of them, just beyond the pier, heading towards Bexhill. They've got "vacant" signs up in the front windows if they got any rooms going. You only need to drive along the seafront till you spot one.'

Boyd offered Lane a lift and they drove slowly up the seafront road, looking for vacancy signs and quickly found one – Linton House B&B. The whitewash paint was flaking slightly on the outside and a lone weed was reaching skyward from the guttering, but apart from that it seemed okay.

The little reception nook was staffed by a withered old man who spoke like a frustrated thespian, rolling his Rs and projecting his voice further than was necessary. He seemed excited to be providing a roof for a police detective and offered Lane a discount.

'I'm not sure how long I'll be staying, but is it possible to have a rolling weekly booking?'

'Of course, sir. Of course!'

'Well then...' Boyd said, offering Lane his hand. 'Welcome aboard, and see you tomorrow.'

Lane nodded. 'Aye. Before you go, can you point me in the direction of a good place to eat?'

Boyd shrugged. 'I've not really dined out in Hastings much yet. Down my end, the old part of town, there are some nice pubs that do decent pub grub. I'm not too sure about this end of town, though.'

'Ah well,' Lane said. 'I can have a little mooch around, see what's what. See you tomorrow, Boyd.'

Lane picked up his bag and Boyd headed to the door.

Oh, for fuck's sake, he thought. He felt shit leaving the poor bugger stuck here. He turned back round. 'Lane... how are you with dogs?'

20

'Are you sure you don't want a glass of wine, Mr Lane?' asked Emma.

'No, thank you. I don't really drink. Or try not to. Water's fine.' Lane reached across the table and helped himself to one of the spring rolls.

'Ems, I can't believe you allowed me to order in a Chinese,' said Boyd, spooning sweet and sour sauce out of the foil carton.

'Well, since you've been such a good boy dodging the chips at work, it doesn't hurt to have the occasional bad day,' Emma replied. She turned to Lane, 'So Dad said you're down from London until this Sir Arthur case is all sorted?'

'Aye, in a spare-pair-of-hands kind of way,' Lane said with a shrug, 'and in an advisory capacity.'

'Sutton was a cabinet minister for a short while,' explained Boyd.

'Ah, okay.' Like most people, Emma recognised Sutton's name, his fiery eyebrows and that he was some stuffy middle-aged man who'd had something to do with politics.

'Which means,' Lane added, 'there are potential official secrets to catch and bag.'

'Like a sneeze?' said Emma.

He nodded. 'Not that we're expecting any. Sutton's been mostly busy writing cheesy pot-boiler thrillers for the last ten years.'

'You read any?' asked Emma.

He pulled a face. '*Enough* of one. I'm not a fan of protagonists who can *conveniently* speak Northern Vietnamese, or quote Nietzsche, or who suddenly know how to fly a helicopter when it suits the story.'

Boyd nodded to that. 'Brilliant at bloody everything.'

'I think it was Stephen Fry who called Sutton's hero, Max Trent, an obnoxious Bond knock-off with blond hair, blue eyes and back-dated values.'

Emma laughed... but then, remembering Trent's creator had recently died, cut it short.

'Do you think it was deliberate, Dad?' she asked.

'Yes, I do.' He gave Lane a look. 'Anyway, enough work talk, Ems,' Boyd cut in. 'We've been at it all day.'

Lane nodded. 'Aye. It's probably best we don't say any more.' He glanced at Emma. 'Sorry, this is potentially a sensitive case. Sutton wasn't well and –'

'What was wrong with him?' Emma couldn't help asking.

'Motor neurone disease. It's that condition a lot of footballers and rugby players have begun to succumb to, some people think, because of the repeated head trauma involved in contact sports.'

'Had Sutton been a sporty type then?'

Lane shook his head. 'It can also be hereditary.'

'It's a horrible disease, Ems,' said Boyd. 'Your brain shuts down, bit by bit, gradually disabling functions until something critical finally goes kaput... and then –'

Ozzie's coned head and paws suddenly appeared at the table.

'Oh, you crafty bugger,' said Boyd. Ozzie had jumped up

onto the spare chair and was now surveying the buffet of open cartons like a late dinner guest.

'Ozzie! Watch your stitches!' said Emma, moving the cartons back. 'He doesn't normally do this,' she said to Lane.

'It's all the incredible smells. It must be torture for the poor sod,' said Boyd. 'Let him have a prawn cracker at least, Ems.'

'Do you even know how unhealthy this crap is?'

'You're letting *me and Lane* eat it,' Boyd pointed out as he posted a cracker into the cone of the eagerly awaiting Ozzie.

BOYD HELPED Emma to clear the plates after dinner, then went outside to find Lane, who was having a cigarette in the partially cleared back garden. It was pleasantly warm still and Ozzie was snuffling around, in spite of his cone, thwacking it on practically every branch and stem he encountered.

'I can see why you've invited everyone over this weekend,' Lane said, surveying the tangled spread of undergrowth.

'I suppose I could take a bloody flamethrower to it. Or napalm the lot. That'd be easier, but –' Boyd hunched his shoulders – 'it's going to be nice this weekend according to the BBC – a chance for a barbeque and a few beers. You're welcome to come and help out if you want.'

Lane smiled. 'I'd love to, but I'm back home for the weekend.'

'Oh, right.' Boyd remembered what Lane had said. 'You've got a little 'un.'

'Uh-huh. A little rascal called Josh.'

'And he's four?'

Lane nodded. 'He's just at that stage where he keeps eyeing up my phone. So I've had to load some kiddie apps onto it. It amazes me how quickly he picks up all this technology stuff.'

This was another thing Boyd knew he'd never have to do. '*Candy Crush*?' he asked.

'*Zombie Gardener*.' Lane shrugged. 'You play a zombie, tapping the screen to look after your plants. I'm not entirely sure what Joshy gets out of it.'

'And Mum approves of this, does she?'

'*My* mum doesn't,' said Lane. He looked at Boyd. 'We lost Josh's mum when he was a baby.'

'Oh,' Boyd said. 'I'm sorry to hear that.'

'It is what it is,' said Lane quietly. 'I've still got some of Sarah in my little boy. The expressions on his face, little tics that remind you of....' He stopped and took another pull on his cigarette. 'How about you?'

'Emma's mum?' Boyd sniffed the smoke and it triggered a fleeting memory – his old band days, touring in the back of a van. 'Same boat as you. Julia died a few years back.'

'Shit. My turn to say sorry,' said Lane, blowing out a cloud.

'As you said... it is what it is. You just bumble forward. Not much else you can do, right?'

'Right.'

They listened to Emma as she stacked the plates in the kitchen. She was humming along to something by Taylor Swift playing on her phone.

'So you're teetotal, then?' said Boyd. 'Is that because of the seizures?'

'Yes. Alcohol *can* trigger it. It's best to play it safe, I find.' Lane chuckled softly. 'It also triggers my dormant Scottish accent... which is far worse.'

'When did the seizures kick in for you?'

'A long time ago.' Lane looked at Boyd. 'Right after I came out of the army.'

Boyd nodded. That was a whole other conversation for another day. He reminded himself that some PTSD sufferers were talkers and some weren't.

'Right,' said Boyd. 'I suppose I'd better drive you back to your luxury five-star hotel.'

Lane laughed and stubbed out his cigarette. 'Where do I...?'

Boyd looked at the stub. 'Just chuck it on the floor. It's fine.'

Lane let it drop to his feet. 'So what's the plan tomorrow, Boyd?'

'Sutton's wife and son are our top priority. Neither have answered their phones. Okeke's off to see the daughter. And I'm heading up to Putney for the autopsy. You're welcome to tag along if you want.'

'Yes, I suppose I probably should.'

Boyd stretched. 'Okay, let's get you back to your budget prison cell.'

21

_A_nd here it is – the home of Sir Arthur Sutton. So close to this busy road, yet tucked away. You'd never know he lived here: the man, the myth, the legend... in his own mind, at least.

A figure pauses beneath the sickly sodium-orange glow of a street light, beside the first of two old worn stone eagles, and pulls a spray can from a rucksack.

This is usually a busy junction. The lights are red right now, but it's late and there's no one around, impatiently waiting for green. No one to idly watch the lone visitor.

The figure quickly ducks down and sprays something on the low flint wall.

It's a simple design. Several strokes of air-sprayed paint and, there, it's done.

It will go mostly unnoticed, totally without meaning to the world at large, but, to a select few, it will serve as a very stark reminder.

You made a vow of silence. Keep it.

The figure returns the spray can to the rucksack and, looking around to be sure there are no witnesses, hops up over the low wall and ducks down under the heavy bough of a mature oak tree – now completely invisible to the outside world, just like Eagle House.

The figure crawls through the undergrowth and peers out at Sutton's small lawn. There is a decorative fountain in the middle of the grass. A stone cherub urinating into a shallow dish – an indicator of the man's idea of humour.

On the other side of the small lawn sits Sutton's Mercedes parked on the gravel and, beyond that, lights from inside the house cast tall ghostly window projections across the tidily clipped lawn.

Through a bay window can be seen movement inside the house. A woman brings a cup of something into a grand drawing room. The trespasser can see burgundy walls and a low-hanging chandelier, portraits in gilded frames that are certainly not prints, but – in keeping with Sutton's social climbing ways – aren't his distant relations either.

The figure gets his first glimpse of Sutton – receiving his drink. A mug of something hot. A mouthed 'thank you' to the woman, then she's gone again, leaving Sir Arthur alone, cupping his drink in both hands and staring out of one of his tall windows into the night.

Are you scared yet, Sir Arthur? You should be.

Oh, I'm going to have fun with that pompous bastard tonight.

22

DAY 5

Boyd pulled up outside the B&B and found Lane waiting, finishing off a cigarette, his jacket over one arm. He stubbed his cigarette out, placed his jacket neatly on the back seat of Boyd's car and climbed into the front.

'Good morning.'

'Morning,' replied Boyd. 'How was the room?'

'Small and stuffy.'

'You look tired.'

Lane did. He looked like he hadn't slept a wink. But he was still immaculately turned out. 'It was a bit noisy,' he said.

'Pub goers?' Boyd asked.

'No, next door,' Lane said, laughing. 'I learned their names, though: Ron and DeeDee.'

Boyd signalled and pulled out. 'Like that was it?'

'Most of the night, noisy buggers.' Lane reached into his pocket and pulled out a packet of mints. 'Want one?' he offered.

Boyd shook his head. 'No thanks. So, Mace and Mackintosh have Sutton on the slab at eleven,' he said, glancing at the time on the dash. It was a few minutes after eight; he'd allowed an extra hour since they were driving into London. The last time he'd driven through Putney, he could have crawled on his hands and knees faster.

Eight wasn't great for getting out of Hastings either and Boyd found himself crawling slowly past the layby on the A21 where they'd found 'Nike Boy' two months ago. They still had no ID for him. The layby looked different. Somebody from the Highways Agency had tidied up the picnic area, mown the grass, fixed the wooden tables and even cleaned up the picnic signpost – presumably shamed into sprucing it up after having seen the state of it on the national news.

'Thanks for dinner last night, by the way,' said Lane.

'No problem. It was a win for me. I'd have been force-fed rabbit food by Emma if you hadn't come over.'

'She's a character, isn't she? Definitely not the shy type.'

'Nope. She's just like her mother. She was a people person too. Friendly and extravert... and always asking questions.'

'And you?'

'Me? I'm the polar opposite – arsy and private. Which is why Julia was perfect for me. She maintained our friendships and family links, and I got to dip in and out at will.'

'Ha! Same here,' said Lane. 'I'm not brilliant at small talk. What's the term...? Schmoozing. Sarah was like Julia; she kept all the friendships going. Maybe it's a male thing?'

'Or a grumpy bastard thing,' said Boyd.

THEY ARRIVED OUTSIDE KILN HOUSE, just north of Putney Bridge at half ten. It was tucked away on the right-hand side of Fulham Palace Road, a six-storey kidney-bean-shaped building of bright vanilla brick and dark tinted windows. Luckily there was a guest parking space beside the old disused pottery kiln that sat in front of the building.

Mace and Mackintosh Forensics' corporate plaque proudly announced in smaller lettering that they were 'partnered with' the Met.

Lane pulled his jacket on, shrugged out the rumples and straightened his tie. Boyd's only concession was to grab his jacket from the back seat and fling it over one arm. It was far too hot to wear the damned thing.

He led the way inside, flashed his warrant card and gave his name to the receptionist who instructed them to take the lift to the first floor. The lift doors opened to reveal a clinically lit lobby and a slim young man wearing a dark polo neck and a lanyard.

He reached out a hand to Lane. 'You're the SIO, DCI Lane?'

'No, I'm DI Lane,' he said, then gestured to Boyd. 'This is the SIO, DCI Boyd.'

The man looked at the dishevelled detective. 'Oops, sorry. I got that all wrong.'

Boyd shook his hand briskly. 'I believe it's Dr Dayne handling our session?'

'Correct, you're in the Johnson theatre this morning.'

'Johnson?'

'They're named after prime ministers.'

Boyd and Lane were led into a theatre that contrasted with the muted Gothic ambience of Dr Palmer's at Ellessey Forensics. It was brightly lit and starkly clinical. Sir Arthur Sutton's blackened cadaver was stretched out on a brushed steel table that was set beneath several diffused but bright ceiling spotlights.

Dr Dayne looked up from the notes he was reading as they entered. 'Ah, you're the guys up from Sussex police?'

Boyd nodded. 'I'm DCI Boyd and this is DI Lane on secondment from the Met.'

Dayne checked a wall clock. 'Bang on time, thank you, gentlemen.' Dayne had an accent that sounded gently East Coast American. His tanned skin looked a sickly grey beneath the bluish tint of the spotlights.

'Because this body has been so badly carbonised, we had it sent across to Hammersmith Hospital yesterday for a scan. That's why we had to delay this until today. The PMCT slides...'

Christ, here we go. Boyd realised, belatedly, that he should have dragged Okeke along with him.

'Post-mortem computed tomography,' Dayne explained, seeing the blank expression on Boyd's face. 'Multi-slice density scans. When a body is this badly burned, it's virtually impossible to carry out a conventional autopsy. You're looking at a load of charred meat in essence. So I'm looking for parts of the body, usually right in the middle that might still retain fluids, which we can sample for toxicology, and undamaged bone segments that we can take stem cell samples from.'

'You think there's uncooked fluid in there?'

Dayne looked at Boyd. 'Correct. We'll get something almost certainly; it takes a helluva lot of heat and time to cook everything right out of a body. The spinal column is usually the last place to hold out, so I'm going to go probing in there for a viable sample.'

'What about the fatty deposits that were around the body?' asked Boyd.

'To have boiled out as grease eruptions, the body would have been heated to oven temperature, like a Thanksgiving turkey. The fatty deposits are where it's cooled back down to what is essentially lard. There will be nothing useful there.' Dayne pulled out some slides from the scan and showed them to Boyd and Lane. 'We're looking for liquid density, and I can see what looks like some in the spinal cord here.' He pointed at an area on one of the scans. 'And also here, the dura mater. We might get lucky with one of these, but the rest of the body is probably unviable.'

Boyd nodded. This was going to be a little easier than the last autopsy he'd attended. He was looking at charcoal in the shape of a splayed man. One arm had been broken off and was lying on the table like a spare, but the other three limbs were doing their best rendition of a star.

'The SOC report says he was found in this pose?' said Dayne.

Boyd nodded again. 'He was tied down to a snooker table.'

Dayne grinned. 'Love how you Brits call it that.'

'Was the arm broken off before the body reached you?' asked Lane.

Dayne nodded. 'It may have thermally amputated during the fire; that happens. Boiling pressure at the joints can create an explosive force. Like when sausages burst.'

Lane pointed at a glistening texture around the wrist of the separate arm. 'What's that?'

Dayne came round the table and bent down to look more closely at it. 'It looks like melted plastic. Perhaps a watch strap?'

'Or a cable tie?' offered Lane. 'Plastic, though. If it was that hot, surely it would have melted enough for him to snap himself free?'

'Unless he was dead before the fire?' Boyd looked at Dayne. 'Is there any way you're going to be able to determine that?'

Dayne winced. 'Probably not. If he was less burned, yes... there's be signs of scorching of the trachea, signs of smoke inhalation. I'm not going to get that sort of information out of this body. Toxicology samples might... I repeat, *might* give us chemical traces that could have been inhaled from the smoke or the accelerant used. But, honestly, it would be guesswork, a suggestion only.'

'And there are no indicators of cause of death other than –'
Boyd stopped himself saying *death by cooking.*

Dayne looked again through his slides. 'Nothing that indicates a deep penetration or laceration or blunt trauma.'

'What about a bullet wound?'

Lane looked at Boyd. 'You're thinking – a professional hit?'

He nodded. 'Then disguised as something more emotive.'

'If there was a bullet or bullet hole in there, the passage would have showed up, crystal clear,' replied Dayne. 'And a bullet inside? Metal presents *wonderfully* clearly in a scan.'

'Right,' said Boyd.

'I'm going to start the examination by digging for any remaining soft tissue. We'll get viable DNA, I'm sure. If we're very lucky, we'll get a few more details from the toxicology report, but the scans I'm afraid aren't telling me much more than where I need to begin excavating.' Dayne picked up a serrated blade. 'By the way, where do I send the report? The Metropolitan force is our client.'

'Although the Met's paying,' said Lane, 'the report needs to be directed to me in Sussex.'

'Okay.' Dayne nodded. 'I've got your email address... I think.'

Lane pulled out one of his cards and left it on the corner of a kit trolley. He tapped it. 'Just in case.'

As they stepped outside into the sunlight, Boyd savoured the warmth on his face and the glow of light on his closed eyelids. He took several deep breaths to dispel the growing nausea he'd been feeling. It wasn't the body; it was the odours that did it – the faint tang of formaldehyde, the residual whiff of fuel, the grotesque scent of cooked meat.

He was suddenly relieved to detect the smell of cigarette

smoke as Lane sparked up. Boyd fought the urge to ask Lane if he could spare one. But the return of that old habit was just one bad choice away. He wouldn't go there again.

'It would be useful to know for sure,' said Boyd.

'What?'

'Whether Sutton was alive or dead before the fire got going.'

'He was tied out,' said Lane. 'You don't need to tie a dead body.'

'Which suggests more than a professional hit. Doesn't it?'

Lane nodded.

'So he was probably tortured first,' said Boyd. 'But why? To get information? To exact revenge?'

'Aye... you're thinking it's less likely the ex-wife or one of the kids had a hand in it?'

'Maybe, yeah. But... it's possible they hired someone and things got out of hand. These things do happen.'

'Or maybe it was an attempt to disguise the motive?' offered Lane.

'Right – make it look weird and ritualistic.' Boyd pondered that in silence while Lane finished his cigarette. He'd seen that tactic a few times before. It worked pretty well as a smoke screen, especially if the press got hold of it. It wasn't popular with the higher-ups, though. Pressure to investigate satanic groups or weird cults – stoked up by the papers, of course – meant spending critical resources chasing down blind alleys.

He looked at Lane. 'You said there could be official secrets that came out during the investigation?'

Lane puffed out a cloud, then bit his lip. 'Not that I'm expecting any. Sutton wasn't a big cog in the government.'

'But he would have attended cabinet briefings?' Boyd said.

'Aye.' Lane nodded. 'Mind you, he was a junior minister, so probably only attended full cabinet meetings, and those tend to be little more than photo opportunities.'

Boyd looked out past the car park, across to Fulham Palace

Road and the park that ran alongside this side of the glistening Thames. He'd had a picnic there not so many years ago. With his family. A memory of a £5 Tesco disposable BBQ and burgers, and Noah waddling across the grass, barefoot, in a nappy and dinosaur T-shirt.

He closed his eyes again and concentrated on the last of the cigarette smoke, in a bid to dispel the association of that precious moment with that blackened corpse on the slab.

23

'I think this must be it,' said Okeke. She'd spoken to Hermione Sutton first thing this morning to get the address of her cake shop that it was in Brighton's Dukes Lane arcade .

The shop looked out onto a cute little square with space for half a dozen small round tables and parasols. Next door was a café, and opposite a Ted Baker's. Since it was sunny, warm and lunchtime, the tables were full with ladies lunching and, Okeke noted, seagulls that seemed to show a little more respect than the louts back in Hastings.

Warren stepped forward to open the door to Hermione's Treats, but Okeke gently stopped him. 'A word before we go in.'

'What?'

'I'm leading this interview.'

He frowned. 'What? Hey.' His voice hardened slightly and he stuck his chin out, challenging her. 'I don't remember the boss putting you in charge.'

'I spoke to her on the phone. I talked her into seeing us.' Okeke shrugged. 'I've built a little trust with her. It makes sense for me to lead. You just sit tight and look cute.'

She pushed the door inwards before Warren could respond, and a bell tinkled inside the shop.

It was busy. There was a queue at the glass counter for cakes, pastries and coffee – everything on display was one hundred per cent vegan. There were stools in the front window, neatly lined up along an eat-in counter, and a few tables at the back, all of which were occupied.

A woman with long blonde hair tied back in a ponytail, and wearing a green apron, approached them. 'Are you Samantha?'

Okeke nodded. 'And this is DC Warren.'

Warren nodded politely.

'I'm Hermione,' said the woman. She was carrying two plates stacked in one hand and a cloth in the other.

'This seems like a bit of an awkward time,' said Okeke.

'It's busy, yes, but it'll clear in ten minutes,' Hermione assured them.

'Do you want us to go and come back in a bit?' asked Okeke.

Hermione shook her head. 'There's a back door beside the toilet, with "Staff" on it. It's a quiet outdoors space where the girls can take a break. Grab a seat. Can I bring you a coffee?'

Okeke smiled. 'Thanks, that would be nice.'

She looked at Warren.

'You got anything cold?' he replied. 'Like a Coke or something?'

She shook her head. 'Sorry, we don't stock any of the branded fizzies. I can get you an iced coffee or an ice tea?'

'I'll just have an orange juice, thanks,' he said.

Hermione nodded at the staff door. 'Go through – I'll be with you in a little bit.'

Okeke weaved around the queue to the door and pushed it open, stepping into a tiny courtyard that was a pleasant little suntrap. If it wasn't for the waste containers, it would've been a perfect space for a couple more customer tables.

They sat down, Warren whipping off his jacket and loosening his tie. 'It's fucking warm today.'

He pulled out a packet of cigarettes.

'Hold on,' said Okeke. She looked around and saw an ashtray sitting on top of a blue plastic drum. 'All right, I guess it's okay.'

He pulled one out for himself and offered her one.

'Go on, then,' she said. 'But we'll have to make it quick.'

He lit them both, handed her one and sat back. 'So *did* the guvnor say you were to take the lead?'

'No,' she replied. 'But this is going to be a sensitive conversation. Her dad's dead.'

'I did all the family visits for the Ken Doll case,' Warren pointed out. 'I'm not going to go blundering in.'

'All the same,' Okeke said, 'let me lead. If you think I'm missing something, you can give me a hint.'

They finished their cigarettes and stubbed them out just as Hermione came out with a tray. She set their drinks down and pulled up a chair.

'Okay then, so how can I help you?' she asked.

'There's a few questions we want to ask you about your father... and about the fire,' Okeke said.

'The first one being... why are you back at work and not sobbing your heart out?' Hermione said.

Okeke watched her closely. There were complicated flickers of emotion fleeting across her face – not at all easy to read.

'No.' Okeke shook her head. 'We deal with things like this in our own way, right?'

'Well, for your information, I despised the man,' Hermione said. 'He was a bully. He mentally abused Mummy for thirty years, until she couldn't take it any more. I think the term to use now is "gaslighting", isn't it?'

Okeke pulled out her notebook. 'In what way did he abuse her?'

'Oh, he told her she was stupid, constantly. She was useless, an air-head. He shouted at her all the bloody time.'

'Was he ever physical?'

Hermione shook her head. 'I never saw him hit her, but... I mean, he didn't need to. It was all non-stop put-downs and sarcasm and saying cruel things to her. He undermined her self-confidence, her self-worth, and of course he cheated on her... probably several times.'

'But she did divorce him eventually?'

'With my help. I had to convince her. I told her I could see he was killing her slowly. Killing her with meanness. Even then, he screwed her over in the divorce. He bullied her into giving over half her money.'

'*Her* money?'

'Money from Grandma and Grandpa – from her side of the family. It was obvious he married Mummy for the money, the connections, the social standing. Daddy was a grubby oppor-tunist. I hated him.'

Warren caught Okeke's eye and raised his brows.

'Did you have much of a relationship with your father's family?'

'Not really. Daddy was ashamed of Nanna and Grandad Sutton. His working-class roots always bothered him. He was their only child and pretty much blocked them out.' Hermione looked at her. 'It takes a cold-hearted arsehole to be able to do that, right?'

Okeke nodded. 'Did he not want you and Henry to have a relationship with them?'

'Oh, God, no! He frequently told us they were a waste of space. Non-achievers.'

'Wow, that's hard,' said Okeke.

'I know! He was all about climbing up the social ladder. That's literally ALL he cared about. A little man with very little time for anyone but himself.' She laughed harshly. 'Did you ever watch that old comedy show *Dad's Army*?'

Okeke frowned; she vaguely recalled the show from her childhood. Something about stuffy old men in army uniforms.

'My dad was a bit like Captain Mainwaring. Not in appearance, just in his manner. It was all about making an impression. All about show. He was a pompous little social climber.'

There's not an ounce of love there, Okeke mused. *Or grief.*

'He was complete bullshit,' said Hermione. 'Parlaying himself upwards from one useful connection to the next. That's how he ended up in the government. All talk.'

'Did he ever abuse you?' asked Warren.

Hermione's mouth clapped shut.

Shit, thought Okeke. *Far too blunt.* She glared at him.

'What do you mean... physically?' Hermione asked.

Realising he'd been leaden-footed, Warren glanced at Okeke, unsure as to how to proceed.

'Or mentally,' Okeke said, kicking Warren under the table.

'Well, not sexually, if that's what you're suggesting. No, not really. He had no time for me. For either of us.'

'And does your brother feel the same?' asked Okeke.

'Henry?' She laughed sharply again. 'He's cut from the same cloth as Dad. A complete self-serving prick. They weren't any closer, if that's what you mean. Henry's out for Henry, no one else.'

'Do you know where he is?' Warren cut in. 'We've been trying to contact him for several days now.'

Hermione shrugged. 'No idea. Dubai, maybe? Probably trying to con someone out of their money.'

'What does he do?' Okeke asked.

'Something to do with raising investment funds. But, if you strip away the fancy business title and trappings, he's basically a salesman who wants your long card number and sort code.'

'Right,' said Okeke. 'A used car salesman in very smart clothes?'

'Exactly. But with some very rich old school friends to vouch for him. You wouldn't believe the number of doors *that* opens.'

'So you're not close with him, then?' Warren asked.

Hermione pulled a sarcastic face. 'Can you tell?'

Okeke took a deep breath. 'Now I know this is an uncomfortable question to be asked...' she began, 'but in the event of your father's death...'

'You're asking whether Henry or I would benefit?' Hermione guessed.

Okeke nodded.

'As in, "Did either of you do it?"' Hermione added bluntly.

'No, I'm not asking that. I'm only trying to get a complete picture of your father's situation, the people –'

'Who'd want him dead?' she finished for her. 'Well, much as I hate the narcissistic, self-serving bastard, I wouldn't want to kill him.' She leant forward. 'Is that what's happened? Was he... *murdered*?'

'We believe the fire was started deliberately,' said Warren. 'With the intention of catching him inside, yes.'

'God,' said Hermione, wide-eyed.

'Had he made any enemies you can think of?' Okeke asked. 'Anyone who'd want to exact revenge on him? Or want something from him?'

'Well, I'm sure he has lots of enemies, but what do you mean by "want something from him"?' Hermione said.

Okeke shot Warren a warning look. She didn't want the London break-in mentioned. Not yet. Not until Boyd said it could be used in interview.

Hermione shrugged. 'I don't know. It wouldn't surprise me if his relentless social-climbing made use of some dirty little secrets along the way.'

'Okay,' Okeke said, nodding. 'Thank you, Hermione. I think we've got enough for the moment.'

'Were you aware he was dying?' Warren blurted out.

Okeke nearly choked on the last mouthful of her coffee.

'Dying?' Hermione stared at Warren, genuinely shocked at that news. 'Dying? How? Of what?'

'Motor neurone syndrome.'

'*Disease*,' corrected Okeke. She was strongly tempted to kick him again, but managed to restrain herself. 'We only learned he was suffering from that yesterday,' she explained to Hermione.

'Dad had MND?'

Okeke's instinct was telling her again that Hermione's reaction to the news was authentic. She hadn't known anything about this.

'When?' she asked. 'I mean how long ago was it diagnosed?'

Okeke shook her head. 'I don't know, but we're aware that he had a carer for the past year. Do you think your brother would have been aware of this?'

'I... I don't know. Probably not. He barely speaks to him unless he wants something from him. You said dying.... How long did he have left?'

'I'm afraid we don't know that either.'

'God,' Hermione whispered, her head dipped.

'I'm sorry, we thought you would have known,' said Warren.

'Are you okay?' asked Okeke.

'What? No, I'm not grieving. God, I despise the man, but... He would have hated going that way. He's completely vain. Do you understand? He thought he was Nigel Havers, James Mason.... He'd have hated shrivelling up into a wheelchair and wasting away.' Hermione glanced at Okeke, then at Warren. 'Was it suicide, do you think? Because that *would* be like him. A screw-you-all, melodramatic way to make an exit. Oh, that sounds exactly like, Daddy.'

Okeke shook her head. 'We're keeping our investigation

open-ended, but we're confident it wasn't suicide.' She spread her hands. 'Which is why we're very keen to get hold of Henry and your mother to have a chat with them.'

'Oh, Mummy's been in Spain all summer and has a new number. Let me get you that...' said Hermione, getting up and making her way back inside.

Warren looked at Okeke. 'Well,' he said, 'if Mummy's in Spain, then that's one down.'

24

'Ma'am?'

The door to Hatcher's office was open. She looked up from her laptop and smiled. 'In you come, Boyd.'

He entered, closed the door, and she gestured for him to take a seat. He was expecting to see Sutherland in there too, for the afternoon progress meeting.

'Where's –'

'Broken ankle.'

'What?'

Hatcher sighed. 'Iain, the silly idiot, fell off his bicycle and broke his ankle last night. He told me yesterday he'd ordered a racing bike, helmet, Lycra suit... the works.'

Boyd smiled. 'All the gear, no idea?'

She nodded. 'Exactly. The first time he gets on it, the wally goes and fractures his ankle.'

'Ma'am, I just want to let you know I've got a team update meeting in about twenty minutes,' said Boyd, glancing at his watch. He'd arranged it for four to allow Okeke and Warren time to get back from Brighton.

'That's okay. I only wanted you to bring me up to speed on the Sutton case.' She closed her laptop. 'Well?'

'It's looking like a deliberate murder rather than arson-slash-manslaughter.'

'Deliberate, as in...'

'Pre-meditated. Our killer came looking for Sutton, tied him down and may have tortured him before killing him and setting the building on fire.'

'I see.'

'We may have a witness, if she lives, that is. His housekeeper and carer.'

'He had a carer?'

Boyd explained about Sutton's condition and then how his body was found. Hatcher's grimaced. 'Poor bugger,' she said.

'The thing is, the body's so badly burned that the pathologist in Putney said there's little chance of determining what exactly was done to Sutton on that snooker table. But I think that it's important to find out as much as we can.'

Her Madge looked interested.

Boyd cleared his throat. 'I mean, if he was... tortured, then that could imply the killer was after something.' He shrugged. 'A password, a code... I don't know... the whereabouts of something. That would tie in with the London break-in.'

She nodded slowly, thoughtfully. 'Sir Arthur Sutton was a bit of a maverick... I think some *Guardian* journalist called him a Walter Mitty character. I mean, I personally don't know much about him, apart from what I've caught on TV... but I do know he made some powerful and influential friends.'

She reached for a tube of hand cream on her desk, dabbed a little into her palm and began to rub her hands together. 'Would it be possible that he maybe...'

'Had some compromising material on someone?'

She nodded. Her brows raised for a microsecond. 'He used to be a journalist, didn't he?'

'He was a sub-editor. I don't think he was ever out on the streets with a notebook and pen.'

Her Madge frowned and changed the subject. 'Do you think his illness might have a bearing on this?'

'How do you mean?'

'It's a degenerative condition, isn't it? Well, if he knew he only had a limited time left... maybe he decided to unburden himself of something before the condition rendered him incapable of doing so?' She finished rubbing the cream into her hands. 'A mea culpa? An attempt at redemption?'

'Or revenge,' said Boyd. 'Maybe somebody had something on him, or he'd been threatened to keep quiet about something?' He paused. 'Knowing you're going to die tends to make a person a little less worried about repercussions.'

'Quite.' Then she spoke with an unusual sense of urgency: 'Boyd, a word of caution. Sutton has – *had* – powerful friends. Be careful where you step.'

Those last words gave him an unpleasant chill, as if some ghostly spectre had gently teased a fingernail up the nape of his neck.

'Be careful... ma'am?'

There was something unsettling about her sudden directness. If Sutherland had been present, he suspected she wouldn't have been this straight with him.

'With Sir Arthur and... his associates, you're wading into some very deep water.'

What the fuck is that supposed to mean?

'Very treacherous water,' she added.

'I'm not really that clear on what you're telling me, ma'am,' Boyd said, wondering if he was being unbelievably thick – or if Hatcher had finally lost the plot.

She leant forward. 'What I'm saying, Boyd, is that you're stepping into a private members' lounge area, an Old-School world of connections and favours. What they do *for* each other, or even *to* each other... in their quiet clubs over gin and tonic, well, it's expected to stay there. Behind closed doors. It's *their* business and woe betide anyone who thinks otherwise. If Sutton had some old scores to settle, just remember this: you and I are little people to *them* and a quiet word in an empty Westminster corridor is all it takes to decide the fate of little people.'

The conversation was beginning to make Boyd feel decidedly uncomfortable. The last time he'd had one of these eye-to-eye, carefully nuanced conversations with her, it had been about the Nix case.

This was definitely less nuanced, but just as disturbing. *Is she telling me to do my job, but be careful – or to look the other way? Fuck it...*

'Is that what happened during the Nix case?' he asked. 'Favours for favours?'

She stiffened slightly. 'You're not here to discuss the Nix case.' She held his gaze for a moment, daring him to say another word about it. Then she shook her head. 'You're a good detective, Boyd. One of the better ones. If you go digging into Sir Arthur's past, I have no doubt whatsoever you're going to find dirt on someone.'

He still couldn't work out how whether that was a *threat* or concern.

'I'm trying to tell you to watch your back,' she said. 'Just be careful, Boyd.'

25

B oyd decided to hold the meeting standing up and take charge of the whiteboard. He figured he was far less likely to dip his fingers into the Celebrations tin if he had a pen in his hand and was a step back from the table.

'Okay, it's a late-in-the-day meeting, I know, folks, but there's some stuff to share before we all clock off.'

'Where's Sutherland?' asked Minter. 'He's not been in all day.'

'Ah, I think he had aspirations to join you on the Iron Man challenge,' said Boyd. 'He bought himself a racing bicycle, fell off and fractured his ankle.'

Minter groaned and face-palmed. O'Neal and Warren chuckled, while Okeke tutted and said, 'Oh, for God's sake.'

The room was hardly awash with sympathy.

'Anyway,' said Boyd, 'back to the briefing. First off, my chat with –' he checked his notes – 'Lena Bajek yesterday. She's the daughter of Sutton's carer and keeper, Margot Bajek.'

Boyd wrote *Sir Arthur Sutton* in the middle of the white-board and drew a circle around the words. He added a short line and drew another circle with *Margot Bajek* inside it.

'Margot had been, until recently, Sutton's housekeeper. But, according to her daughter, Sutton confided his illness to her nine months ago and basically her role has been that of carer as his condition has steadily worsened. Lena suggested a bond had been growing between the two, so –' he thickened the line on the board with an extra couple of strokes – 'do we have a relationship there? A motive?'

'She's the only one earning money for her family,' Okeke offered. 'She has a mother who needs expensive meds and therapy. So money is a possible motive. Perhaps Sutton had written her into a will?'

O'Neal sniggered. 'Well, that's got to be the world's crappiest murder plan if she ended up nearly burning to death with him.'

'Things can go wrong,' said Boyd, 'especially if you're arsing about with petrol. She might have backed herself into a corner somehow. Anyway, it's something we have to look into.'

'Warren, Okeke? How did it go with Sutton's daughter?'

'Yeah, we had a revealing chat with her.' Okeke flipped open her pad. 'There are several bullet points for you, guv. One – she hated him; I mean, *really* hated him. She called him a bully; he abused her mother, a complete shit. Two – she had no idea about Sutton's MND. No idea at all.'

'Seriously?' said Boyd. 'I thought she'd been in recent contact with him?'

She shrugged. 'By telephone, yes. But she definitely had no idea. I suspect the son doesn't know either. She was shocked, but then she also seemed to think that was in character. He didn't have time for weakness or pity. She wasn't surprised he'd kept it quiet. She thought that sounded very much like him: too vain, or proud, to admit being terminally ill. Which leads me to my next point. Three – she floated the idea he might even have done this to himself.'

'Suicide?' Boyd tried not to sound too dismissive.

'That he didn't want anyone to know he had this condition. Didn't want anyone to inherit his house; he was the kind of person who'd choose to go out in a blaze of glory –'

'Literally,' said Sully, snorting with laughter.

'Clearly he didn't do it to himself,' said Lane. 'He was tied.'

'And come on,' said Minter, 'that's a horrible, grotesque way to die. No one would choose that.'

'Warren,' Boyd said, looking over at him, 'you're quiet. Do you have anything to add?'

'Just letting the boss lady speak first,' he said, smiling sweetly at Okeke. 'Well, what if he was dead already? Took an overdose? Then paid someone to make his death look like a murder?'

Okeke rolled her eyes.

'Why?' asked Boyd. 'Give me a workable motive for that.'

Warren paused for a moment. 'He's dying. He doesn't want to be remembered as weak, taking the coward's ways out with some pills. And he wants to frame someone... take someone down with him.'

Boyd shook his head. 'I don't buy that. What about the break-in to his apartment?'

'Well, if he staged the rest, he could have staged that. He was there last week,' Warren pointed out.

It still felt too far-fetched to Boyd. 'Okeke says Hermione hated him. That's a more plausible motive.'

Okeke cut in. 'He was abusive to her mother,' she said. 'Mentally. And Hermione did mention that he screwed her over with their divorce. He helped himself to half her family's wealth.'

Boyd nodded. 'Now that sounds more credible.'

Boyd wrote Hermione's name on the whiteboard with a thin line linking her to Sutton. *Abuse/revenge/inheritance* he wrote beside it. 'What about his son, Henry?'

'I'm still trying to contact him,' said Okeke. 'I've got a

mobile number that keeps going to a recorded message. Which means it's probably switched off.'

Boyd wrote *Henry* on the board. 'So, he's not looking particularly innocent right now is he? Is there a similar motive there?'

'Inheritance?' said Warren. 'Knock off the old man for his big stash?'

'And then what about the ex-wife, Kate Munton-Jones?' said Boyd.

Okeke replied. 'Hermione said she's been in Spain for the summer; I've spoken to her. Her flights and travel records confirm that, so she didn't do it herself, but could still have been involved in a plan to do it.'

Boyd nodded. He drew a linking line and the word *inheritance* beneath it. He turned round and picked out Sully. 'Anything on the digital forensics?'

'My resident digital expert informs me that the hard-drive discs have warped massively from the heat. We won't be getting anything from them.'

'Bollocks.'

'Worry ye not. All is not lost,' said Sully. 'There's obviously iCloud storage.'

'And?'

'I've submitted a data-access request to Apple, which I'm still waiting on. Also a request to Facebook. Again, waiting to hear back.'

'What about phone tracking from his network provider?' asked Boyd. 'Can we build a map and timeline of his movements leading up to the fire?'

Sully nodded and smiled. 'Yes... you can.'

Boyd nodded at Okeke. 'Yours.'

'On it,' she said.

'Someone entered his London flat,' Boyd continued, 'before or after the fire. If it was before, maybe that someone was looking for him; if it was after... then presumably they were looking for something he had.' Boyd drew another squiggled loop on the whiteboard and a question mark in the middle. He drew a connecting line and scribbled *information?* beside it.

'If Sutton had something, perhaps compromising material on someone, that would be a very powerful motive. Particularly,' Boyd added, 'if that person was a public figure.' He turned to look at the whiteboard. 'So, we have several lines of enquiry to consider. Minter...'

'Boss?'

'Do a deep dig back into Sutton's past. He used to be a sub-editor. Did he write a poison-pen piece on someone? Did he damage someone's reputation? Their career?'

'On it, boss.'

'Warren and O'Neal. Door to door along London Road, please. I recall there are some shops opposite Eagle House. Were any open in the evening? A takeaway or something? Find out what you can.' He tossed the pen onto the table. 'Right. It's been a long day. Prep what you can and be ready to go first thing in the morning.'

The room filled with the sound of scraping chair legs as everyone got up to leave. Boyd's gaze settled on the middle of the conference table where someone had plonked a number of today's papers. Three of them had put Sutton's death on their second page, one of them as a secondary item on the front page. The picture they'd all gone with was one of the two stone eagles, the rear-end of a fire engine and the overgrown front wall. He'd flipped through the articles over lunch in the canteen.

Boyd picked up the *Mirror* and studied the photograph on the front for a few moments, his attention drawn to the low flint wall and the out-of-place graffiti sprayed on it.

'O'Neal?'

O'Neal was halfway back to his desk, chatting with Warren. He stopped. 'Sir?'

'Warren, you too... Get a tally of the CCTV cameras going up along London Road.' His eyes narrowed as he studied the flint wall. 'That wall at the front of the property is really low. If I recall correctly, it's only chest high – very easy to scale. Is it that height all the way around?' He lowered the paper. 'Does anyone know?'

There was a chorus of murmured 'no's.

'Okay, you two,' he said to Warren and O'Neal. 'If Sutton's property is as easily accessible from another side, can you see if there's any CCTV footage from any of the other roads bordering it? Check all sides of the property.'

Warren and O'Neal chorused a 'yessir'.

'Once you've rounded that up, we can get in some popcorn and all have a CCTV-watching party.'

There was a collective groan across the Incident Room.

26

'Can I buy you a beer?' said Lane as they emerged from the station's clinical lighting into an invitingly warm and sunny evening. Boyd took in a deep breath and weighed up the offer.

Quite honestly, he was done in. He fancied hastening back home, taking Ozzie down onto the beach at the Rock-n-ore end and stopping for a pint and a packet of crisps at the Pump House, where Emma would be working, before heading back up the hill. But Ozzie was grounded for the foreseeable – or at least until his wound healed. Boyd would more than likely end up slobbed out on the sofa with a large glass of red and teatime TV for company.

'Go on, then,' he said to Lane, 'if you're buying. But I can't stay long – I'm on poorly dog duty tonight.'

Fifteen minutes later, he had a pint of Caffrey's in his hand and was leaning against the safety rail of the pier, looking out across the Pelham portion of Hastings beach. It was six o'clock and still warm, and, even though the sea must have been brass-monkeys cold, there were still plenty of kids splashing around in it.

'I could quite happily up sticks from London and move down here,' said Lane.

'What's stopping you?'

He opened his mouth to answer, then hesitated. 'I was going to say family reasons, but... I suppose they're all solvable.'

Boyd nodded. 'It's thinking about the hassles involved that stops you doing anything.'

Lane blew out a cloud of smoke that spun and swirled in the breeze. 'Responsibility's like superglue,' he said.

'Ain't that the truth,' Boyd said, raising his glass.

'Anyway, close protection work tends to be London based.'

Boyd looked at him. 'You're not too old to change department.'

Lane waved that idea away. 'I've got my hands full with my mum and my lad. I don't want to be worrying about a career change as well.'

'Fair enough.' Boyd sipped his Caffrey's and wiped the suds from his top lip. His mind kept circling back to Her Madge's supposedly friendly words of warning.

Just be careful, Boyd.

'Lane?'

'Yeah?'

'Did you ever do close protection for Sutton?'

Lane shook his head. 'I haven't done anything like that for the last few years – the seizures...'

'But you would have – what – reviewed his security measures?'

'Along with everybody else on our constantly expanding list, yeah.'

'How much do you know about his connections. His associations?'

Lane took a swig of his Coke. 'He was like the rest of them – there's a constantly swinging door between top boarding schools, Oxford, Westminster and Downing Street. Followed by a comfy seat in a corporate board room. It's handshakes and nods all along the way.' He looked at Boyd. 'What the Lefties like to call the "chumocracy".'

'The old boy network. Alive and well, as always,' said Boyd.

'The way it always has been... *yea, even unto the Middle Ages.*' Lane took a long pull on his cigarette. 'We're no more democratic or accountable than the usual villain nations out there; we're just much better at disguising it with a bit of charm and British eccentricity.'

'If Sir Arthur was tortured then murdered... do you think those kind could have anything to do with it?'

'Those kind?' Lane smiled. 'You getting all masonic on me?'

'Just a thought,' Boyd said with a shrug. 'Sutton schmoozed with the establishment. And the picture I'm getting is that he was a bit of a chancer. A bit of a loose cannon? Could he have pissed off someone in that world enough to do something like this to him?'

Lane gave that some thought, then nodded. 'I could imagine that. But... that's too brutal for a bunch of old boys. That's more your Columbian cartel way of dealing with things. In Britain we're a tad more civilised, I think. We just destroy reputations.' He smiled. 'That's usually all it takes, right?'

'With most people, yes. But Sutton... I'm getting the impression he was a belligerent bastard. And I suppose, if you're dying, perhaps you wouldn't give so much of toss about your name being dragged through mud?' Boyd sipped his beer again. 'What if he was about to spill something and the threat of being publicly shamed into silence wasn't enough?'

'So *they*... whoever they are, paid him a visit in the dark of night?'

Boyd nodded. 'I hate sounding like I'm wearing a bloody tinfoil hat, but you have to go where the thinking takes you.' He watched a gull hovering almost motionless on the breeze a dozen yards out from the pier. 'Even if it's unthinkable.'

'Sheesh,' said Lane. 'That's not a thing I'd like to think happens here.'

'Well, *somebody* tied him down and burned him. And I don't see Sutton going all Walter White and getting involved with a bunch of Columbian drug barons.'

Lane chuckled at the thought. 'No, me neither.' He stubbed out his cigarette and flung the dimp over the side.

They finished their drinks watching the last of the ghostly blue-skinned kids being herded out of the freezing water by parents keen to pack up and get going.

'Just be careful,' said Lane finally. 'If this investigation starts taking you into creaking Westminster corridors filled with creepy old Sir Humphreys... watch your back.'

27

DAY 6

'What's the crazy rush?' Boyd looked at his watch. It was eight fifteen. He'd come in early to get a quiet start, with a hot coffee and a bacon butty, ahead of everyone else coming in and had found Okeke waiting for him at the front door, car keys in hand.

'Henry Sutton says he has a plane to catch at Heathrow at midday,' Okeke explained minutes later, as she signalled right to turn out of the station and headed up towards London Road.

'So what? We're barrelling up there to suit him?'

'It looks like we are, yeah.'

They could have interviewed him over the phone, but she was right – in person was better and if he did blurt out anything incriminating they'd be there to stop him boarding his flight.

'Where did he say he was going?' Boyd asked.

'I didn't speak to him. It was his PA. She just told me that Mr Sutton was aware the police wished to talk to him and would be in the British Airways Concorde Room, terminal five, at eleven o'clock. She said he might be able to donate half an hour of his time, but then he'd have to fly.'

'Donate?' Boyd queried, incredulous.

She looked at him. 'Her words, guv.'

'He sounds like an entitled bloody bellend. Oh, I'm looking forward to this one.'

She smiled. 'My thoughts exactly.'

'AND YOU'RE HERE TO SEE?'

'Henry Sutton,' said Boyd again. The concierge checked her guestbook and finally nodded. The fact that he and Okeke had flashed their warrant cards didn't seem to have impressed her one bit.

'Ah yes, I do believe he's checked in,' she said, smiling.

'Right, well, can we see him, please?' He looked at his watch again. It was five past eleven and their valuable *donated* time with Henry was ticking away.

'Let me call someone to find him and check whether he's –'

'Mr Sutton knows we're coming,' Okeke said with an edge to her voice.

The concierge – platinum blonde, fine-featured and with a Russian accent straight out of a Bond movie – recoiled slightly. She directed her reply to Boyd. 'We will check if he's ready to see you.'

She stopped a young man in a gold-trimmed waistcoat. 'Antoine?' She spoke a sentence in Russian that ended with the English words 'cabana three'.

Boyd nodded. 'Cabana three, is it? Thanks.' And he strode off after Antoine.

Okeke gave the concierge a tight smile, then followed the two men, who were striding side by side in a polite speed-walking race past leather couches and Ibiza-style loungers to see who could reach Sutton first. She let them dash ahead, as she dawdled behind, taking in this rare glimpse of the luxury that the One-Percenters enjoyed when in transit.

To her right was a breakfast/brunch buffet set out on a row of beautifully dressed tables, staff in waistcoats and BA livery, waiting patiently to assist. To her left was a tall apron of windows with an uncluttered and panoramic view of the runway and planes both landing and taxiing into position to take off.

She passed a grand piano – sadly there was no one playing it right now – and an oasis of small palm trees in giant clay urns with a trickling fountain in the middle. She noticed that the airport-wide Tannoy announcements didn't intrude into this quiet area. There were screens with boarding indicators here and there, and she suspected that if a guest was in danger of failing to notice their flight was ready, an Antoine in a gold-trimmed waistcoat would be on hand to gently remind them.

Boyd came to a halt outside a slate-covered door with a brass 3 on it. He rapped his knuckles loudly on it. 'Henry Sutton?'

The door cracked open and a slim man wearing a bathrobe appeared, busy towelling a mop of sandy hair. 'Yes?'

'Sussex CID. We have an appointment?'

The man frowned for a moment, then nodded. 'Ah, yes. Go grab a seat – I'll be out in a minute.'

The door closed and Boyd turned to a mortified-looking Antoine. 'Thanks, mate. We'll be sitting over there if there's a coffee going,' he said, pointing to some cane garden furniture framed by pots of pampas grass by the broad windows. '

Okeke caught up with them and Boyd led her over to the seats. 'Lord Muck will grace us with his presence in a minute,' he muttered under his breath.

They sat down, side by side, on a chaise longue.

'Well, this beats EasyJet,' said Okeke.

'They even have a spa in here – look.' Boyd pointed at a doorway flanked with folded towels and scented candles. 'Roman-emperor-level indulgence.'

'Did you expect anything different?' said Okeke.

Henry Sutton emerged from his private cabana, wearing a cream shirt and trousers and a dark-blue blazer; his tousled hair had been slicked back with a comb. He looked younger than his twenty-nine years, but his choice of couture made him look like a something out of the sixties – a poor man's Edward Fox. He spotted them and strode over.

'Hello,' he said, sitting down in a cane chair opposite them. 'I'm sorry but I won't have very long to chat.'

'I'm DCI Boyd and this is DC Okeke, Sussex CID,' Boyd said. 'So I presume you've been informed about your father?'

Henry nodded. 'Hermione emailed me. Ghastly news. Smoke inhalation, wasn't it?'

'Forensics are still investigating the cause of death, but it looks as though the fire was started deliberately,' Boyd said, 'and whoever did it knew with certainty that your father was inside at the time.'

Henry let out a low whistle. 'So murder, is it?' he said, seeming to Boyd more intrigued than upset. But then Hermione had said neither of them were close to their father.

'Mr Sutton,' said Boyd, 'I'm sure you'll understand our first priority is confirming where you've been for the last week and asking why it's been so difficult to get hold of you.'

'I've been with friends,' was his deadpan response.

'Where? Doing what?'

'I was entertaining some clients,' Henry said, looking amused. 'Surely you can't think that *I* did it?'

'We'll need your friends' names and contact details to verify this,' said Boyd. 'Just as a matter of routine.'

'Ah, the old alibi thing?' Henry nodded. 'Of course. Of

course. Well, to answer your question... I was grouse shooting with an old colleague and some clients, then humping.'

'Humping?'

'Yes, you know, into the wilderness, tent on your back, wind in your face, a bit of the ol' outdoors and back-to-nature sort of thing.'

'Were you with someone?' Boyd asked.

Sutton smiled. 'Yes. I was with several someones.'

Boyd pulled out a pen. 'Who?'

'A viscount and a couple of nice young princes from the Emirates.'

'And when did you get back?'

'Last night.' He glanced at Okeke. 'I picked up, I presume, all *your* messages to get in touch.'

Okeke nodded. 'And that, I *presume*, is when you learned about your father?'

'Yes. I picked up Hermione's email then too.'

'If you don't mind me saying... you don't seem that greatly affected by the news,' she said.

'Life goes on,' replied Sutton. 'Dad and I weren't close. But I'm sure you probably know that. He had his life... and we had ours.'

'Hermione said something along those lines,' said Okeke. 'She wasn't particularly broken up about the news either.'

Sutton nodded. 'Oh, she utterly despises him. She's definitely always been on Mum's side.'

'And you?'

'I spent my childhood at boarding school. I didn't really see what he did. She said he was a horrible man. I... only ever really knew an absent man. He was always out networking at dinners or fundraisers. He was very driven. And I don't blame him for that, given where he came from. Humble beginnings.'

Boyd nodded. 'He was a self-made man?'

'Well... yes, I suppose. Although that makes him sound like

a greengrocer who turned into a retail magnate,' he said with a wry smile. 'A Phillip Green. No... Dad, I think, was always aware that he hobnobbed with the rich and powerful at their discretion and that the doors could close on him at any moment. So he worked hard to keep them open.'

'Worked hard? In what way?' asked Boyd.

Henry shrugged. 'In the usual way. Making friends, alliances. Doing favours for favours.'

'Did he make any enemies doing that? Would anyone have had a grudge against him?'

'A grudge?' Henry smiled again. 'What is this... *Midsomer Murders*? How long have you got?' said Henry. 'I imagine every bloody Remoaner in the country had a grudge against him. Do you need me to go on?'

'We're thinking a bit closer to home,' said Okeke dryly. 'Colleagues? Acquaintances, friends... family? Your father did very well out of the divorce, according to Hermione.'

Henry sighed. 'He got half.'

'Hermione said that was your mothers' family's wealth?'

'It probably mostly was. But look – that's the way things go, right? Dad worked hard, that's all I remember... He was always working. Whether the money they had to their names when they separated was even or not, I don't think it's unfair that it went fifty–fifty.'

'Hermione does,' said Okeke.

'Well, like I said, she's always been very close to Mum.'

'Do you think your mother holds a grudge against your father?' asked Boyd.

Henry's face creased with incredulity. 'Do I think she had a grudge? Yes. Absolutely! But are you asking me if I think she had him *whacked*?'

Boyd shrugged. 'Do you?'

'No! Obviously. She hates him, I'm sure. But... you know,

something like that?' He laughed. 'It's a bit too *Eastenders* for her, I'd have thought.'

'What about business associates? Partners?'

Henry shrugged. 'He was in Westminster long enough to piss a few people off, I'm sure, but I don't think they're the kind to firebomb a man's home.'

'You'll benefit from his estate, won't you?' said Okeke.

'So will Hermione,' he replied. 'But most of all I suspect that Polish tart he's been shagging will.'

'Polish tart?' Okeke queried. 'I presume you're referring to his carer? Margot Bajek?'

'*Carer*, eh? There's a novel term for it. She's been gold-digging around him for a while now, hasn't she? Parasitic little Slavic...' He tailed off, looking furious.

'Are you aware your father was suffering from motor neurone disease?' asked Okeke.

Henry Sutton took a moment to respond to that. 'Yes, I knew.'

Boyd caught Okeke's eye. Hermione hadn't known.

'Dad was a proud man; you could even use the term *vain* if you want. He wouldn't have wanted people seeing him reduced to a wheelchair, losing control of his body. So, yeah, he kept it quiet.'

'What about your mother? Would she have known?'

Henry shook his head. 'I doubt Dad would have told her. But if Hermione knew, then... probably she would have shared it with Mum.' He looked at his watch. 'Look... I'm going to need to finish getting ready. My flight's going to be called soon.'

'Fine,' said Okeke. 'We'll need the names and contact details of who you were with this last week to –'

'Call my PA,' Henry interrupted. 'She'll give you all the details you need.'

'And where are you off to now?' asked Boyd.

'Monaco. I have some important investment meetings out there.'

'How long will you be gone?'

Henry shrugged. 'A few days. A week maybe? Depends how lucky I get over there. I'm chatting to several sweet old dears who have money to invest.' He smiled. 'Should be a like shooting fish in a barrel.' He got up. 'I'll say one thing about Dad. It was all about the image with him, the impression. That's how he talked himself from a housing estate into the cabinet. He brassed things out. The truth is... he was facing a few declining years in a wheelchair and that wasn't his style. I don't think he would have waited for the bitter end. I think he'd have wanted an out.'

28

'What did you make of that?' asked Boyd.

'Henry?' Okeke pulled out of the blue 'K' parking zone onto the feeder road. 'I think he sounded credible. I mean, I wasn't getting *liar, liar, pants on fire* from him.'

'He was quite blunt about Margot Bajek, wasn't he? Seeing her as a gold-digger.'

She nodded. '*Parasitic little Slavic*, I believe was the phrase he used. Nice.'

'I wonder if he sees her as a threat?' said Boyd. 'In terms of Sutton's estate, I mean.'

'Then you also have to wonder if his ex-wife is thinking the same thing?' added Okeke. 'That her family's long-held wealth – well, half of it anyway – could fall into Margot's family's hands.'

Boyd nodded. 'These things usually boil down to money... if there's enough of it at stake.'

'So we still think there's a motive there for Kate Munton-Jones and Henry Sutton?' Okeke said.

'Yup. Still in the frame. What about Hermione?' Boyd asked.

She pressed her lips. 'Possibly.'

'Or all three of them?'

She nodded. 'Shit. A family conspiracy to knock off Dad?'

Boyd leant forward to look out of her window as she waited for a gap to pull onto the roundabout. 'Hold on. Not yet... Not –'

Ignoring him, she lurched forward into the steady stream of traffic with plenty of room to spare. 'God, you can be an old woman sometimes, guv.'

He settled back in his seat, mulling things over as she took the exit for M25. 'Sutton's kind tend to settle inheritance grievances in court with expensive law firms. Not with scrotes-for-hire swinging cans of petrol around.'

'But if he was desperate?' she said. 'In debt, perhaps?'

Okeke had a point. He looked at her. 'You want to follow that up? See if he was?'

She grinned. 'With great pleasure.'

Boyd's work phone buzzed in his lap. It was an unknown number. He tapped the screen and held it to his ear. 'Hello, DCI Boyd speaking. Who is this?'

'Lena Bajek.'

'Is everything okay?' Boyd asked.

'No. Mama's condition is worse.'

'How do you mean? Lena?' He could hear her voice hitching. 'Lena?'

'I think she might be dying.'

Boyd found the ICU consultant dealing with Margot Bajek, but as soon as the doctor saw the warrant card and realised Boyd wasn't family he pointed both him and Okeke in the direction of the ward's head nurse and left her to bring them up to speed.

'Her lungs are filling up with fluid and she's showing signs of ventilator-associated tracheobronchitis. They're having to pull her out of the induced coma so they can remove the endotracheal tube and... well, hopefully she'll be able to breathe on her own.' She shook her head. 'I mean it's godawful that she's got to be brought round... but they've got no choice.'

'How serious is this?' asked Boyd.

'Very. If she can't breathe by herself, she could die of hypoxia. If they don't balance the barbiturates, she's going to be fully awake and in agony. And they can't leave her on mechanical ventilation because... of this, because of the build-up of fluid.'

'We won't be able to talk to her?' asked Boyd.

'No. No way. If she can breathe on her own, then they've got to make sure the air mix is getting enough oxygen into the system, then they've got to balance the meds, then they've got to deal with the infection. So no... not today.'

A phone rang. She looked at them apologetically and headed off to answer it. 'Her family?' Boyd called after her.

She pointed to the family room. Boyd could see through a small window in the door Lena Bajek talking to a much older woman in a wheelchair, presumably Margot's mother.

'Right then,' he said to Okeke. 'Are you okay staying here with them?'

'What? Because you're...?' She looked at him to complete the sentence.

'I'm heading back to the station,' he said. 'I want to check in on the others.'

She tipped her head to one side with her lips pursed, not breaking her hard stare.

'And you've established a connection with them,' he continued. 'And you're better at this kind of thing than I am.'

She narrowed her eyes suspiciously. 'This kind of thing?'

'People,' he replied. 'Look. There's no point us *both* sitting here. And if you've got the chance to talk to her daughter, her mother, well, maybe Henry was right... Maybe there was more than a carer–patient relationship developing. Maybe you'll be able to get the truth out of them.' Boyd smiled apologetically and looked down at his watch. 'Pick you up at half five?'

Okeke sighed. 'Don't worry, guv. I'll ask Jay to get me when I'm done.'

29

Boyd returned to the Incident Room to find Lane, Warren and Minter in a huddle around a monitor. O'Neal was on the phone.

Lane looked up and waved Boyd over, who circumnavigated the conference table to join them.

'What have you lot got there?' Boyd asked, peering at the screen.

'Public space CCTV for London Road,' said Warren. 'We think we've got our man.'

Minter made room for Boyd so that he would have a better view. 'Show the boss the previous file,' he said.

The screen was cluttered with opened AVI files showing frozen, grainy, pixelated images of Hastings by night. Warren found the first file and opened it.

'And maximise it,' said Lane.

The image filled the monitor. It showed a five-way junction with traffic lights. 'This is from the CCTV outside the Clarence pub in Silverhill,' said Warren. 'It's aimed across London Road and southwards.' Warren put a finger on the screen. 'That's the entrance to Eagle House.'

The two stone eagles were barely visible, almost lost amid the overgrown trees that spilled over the low flint wall.

'So this is the very end of the trail,' said Minter. 'Or the beginning, actually, since we're working backwards. That dark smudge there, beside the wall, is our man. Warren, hit play.'

The frozen video began to fidget as compression pixels jittered around the screen. 'Since it's not in the centre of town, it's a fixed camera,' said Warren.

'But luckily for us it's facing the right way,' added Lane.

The black smudge wasn't walking past the house. It had stopped. Boyd checked the timecode in the corner – 22:37.

'So, he lingers there for quite a while. Several cycles of the traffic lights, in fact,' said Minter.

'What's he doing?' asked Boyd.

'No idea. He's just waiting most of that time. I think he gets something out, lingers a bit longer... then wait for it...'

Boyd watched the dark shape – quite honestly, if he hadn't been aware of the scale of the wall, the figure could have passed for an urban fox standing on its hind legs to peer into the undergrowth. The figure was still as several cars passed by, winking red tail lights as they descended down the hill towards the front, then lurching quickly it was on top of the wall and disappeared into the foliage.

'Are you sure it's male? Please tell me you've managed to get better images.'

Warren looked up and grinned. 'Further down, there's CCTV from a camera mounted outside the Methodist church. He's definitely male, sir.' He clicked on another open media file and maximised the image. 'We're looking southwards and downhill again; this is two minutes earlier.' He pressed play.

Boyd could see another sodium-orange monochrome view of Hastings at night. On the far side of the road there was a row of shops: a betting shop, a plumbing supplies place and a kebab takeaway. On the nearside was a row of terraced houses.

The dark figure was on London Road walking towards the camera. 'There's our man again,' said Minter.

Other than the time sequence fitting – and Boyd presumed the three of them had verified that – the only thing this figure had in common with the other one was that he was clad in dark clothing.

'He's got a rucksack, or a shoulder bag,' said Lane. 'See?'

Boyd nodded. It was big enough to hold a container of fuel. 'Can you identify the petrol stations close by. We might catch footage of someone filling up a jerrycan or something,' said Boyd.

'O'Neal's on that now, boss,' Minter said.

The figure loomed closer into the shot, walking casually towards the camera seemingly without a care in the world, then, finally, was out of shot again.

'Have we got anything better further down into town?' Boyd asked.

'We're working our way through it,' said Lane. 'Hopefully we can timeline him all the way to a parked vehicle.'

'Wouldn't that be handy,' said Boyd. 'Excellent work, everyone. Well done.'

Warren and Minter high-fived. Boyd turned to head back to his desk and Lane came with him. 'How was your visit with Henry Sutton?' he asked.

'Interesting. He seems to be a chip off the old block.'

'How did he come across?'

'Apart from talking like a prize prick, you mean? He did seem concerned about Margot Bajek.'

'How so?'

'He says she's a gold-digger. He seemed wary that she was going to run off with all the family silverware.'

'They were close? I thought she was his housekeeper-slash-carer?' Lane said.

Boyd nodded. 'Well, I did too. I just hope she pulls through. She's our only potential witness to what happened in Sutton's house that night and, from the sounds of it, the only one likely to know why.'

30

Boyd was grabbing his car keys from the desk and his jacket from the back of his chair when his work phone buzzed. It was Okeke.

'Hello, is everything okay there?' he asked.

'Guv, it's touch and go. Margot's out of the induced coma, and the doctors are seeing whether she can breathe unassisted.'

'Well, that's good news, right? And can she?'

'At the moment... but that's likely to change over the next six hours. Look, I'm going to stay here this evening with the Bajeks. Margot's under sedation and pumped full of drugs, but the doctor says she'll be in and out of consciousness. They've allowed us to sit with her. If there's a moment or two, I could...'

'Right, got you,' Boyd said. 'Do what you can.'

'I'm thinking the best we're going to get is a yes/no answer. She won't be able to talk.'

Boyd saw that the others were getting ready to clock off for the day too. Lane was gathering his jacket and looking his way, tilting his hand to ask if Boyd was up for a pint.

Boyd held a finger up for him to hold on.

'You want me to think up a couple of questions?' he asked.

'Yeah. That'd be good. Thanks, guv.'

'It's the least I can do. Thanks, Okeke. I'll text you.'

He heard Okeke sigh. 'Right, I suppose I'd better let Jay know he's fending for himself tonight.'

'See you tomorrow. Keep in touch tonight and let me know when you head home.'

'Yeah. See you tomorrow, guv.' She hung up.

Lane came over. 'What's up?'

'Okeke's sitting with Margot Bajek tonight. It's touch and go there.'

'Right. Sad, but not unexpected. Poor thing.' He turned to look at Minter and the other two. 'They're off down to some place called O'Connors. There's a World Cup warm-up match with Poland this evening. You coming?'

Boyd shook his head. 'Football's never really been my thing. You'd think they'd have had enough of looking at a bloody screen today.'

Lane laughed. 'All right, then,' he said. 'See you in the morning.'

BOYD WAITED until the others had gone, then followed them out into the hall. He could still hear their voices echoing up the stairwell, O'Neal absolutely certain that England was going to thrash the Poles tonight.

He stepped out into another pleasant summer's evening. He had the car today, but actually rather fancied walking home along the beachfront as it was so nice.

Sod's law, he thought. If he left his car here – guaranteed – it'd be pissing down tomorrow morning.

On impulse, Boyd went out through the gates and looked up and down London Road. Downhill he could see his team on their way to wherever O'Connor's was. Uphill... Eagle House called softly to him.

Five minutes later, he was standing opposite the overgrown entrance. There was police tape across the driveway, running from one old eagle to the other. The smell of bonfire had finally faded. He looked around to where the CCTV footage had come from – on the wall outside the Clarence pub.

He carried on uphill for another fifty yards until he was outside the pub's entrance. A sign on a chalkboard advertised that there'd be a big TV screen in the beer garden for England versus Poland.

Boyd turned to look back down the road towards the two eagles. He had roughly the same view as the camera now – just lower down. He recalled the video; the black smudge had been about a dozen feet short of the entrance. He could see, where the figure had lingered, that the ivy that was spilling out from beneath the trees and completely obscured the old flint wall. Presumably that's why he'd chosen that spot.

Boyd walked back down to the place he'd picked out, past the two eagles.

'Evening, fellas,' he muttered.

He came to a halt at the point where the figure had disappeared into Sutton's hidden grounds.

The exposed flint wall was chest high and so easily scalable. It wasn't even a vertical wall; it had sagged back on itself over the centuries, almost as if recoiling at the prospect of bordering such a busy road. A person could scramble up it effortlessly. There were flint stones sticking out or missing from the old crumbling cement, creating footholds. But that wasn't the only thing that caught Boyd's attention.

It was the graffiti from the photo in the paper. A lazy loop in black spray with what looked like an inverted V inside it. Or it could as easily be an A without the cross bar. Like that anarchy sign from the 80s.

It didn't look old, but then he was no expert on graffiti lifespans. And it was sprayed right where that figure had been lingering.

Warren said it looked like he'd reached into a bag for something.

Boyd pulled out his work phone and took a picture of it. Then, after checking around for a few minutes for a forensic gift like a footprint (he found none), he headed back down to the station to get his car.

31

Okeke was the only person in the ICU room who was awake. It was gone eight o'clock and the muted small TV on the wall was showing Phil Mitchell scowling at someone across Albert Square.

Lena had her face buried in her knees, legs drawn up onto the bucket chair she was sitting on; her grandmother was sagging in her wheelchair like wilted broccoli. The beeping of the machines and the rustling of Margot's breath behind the oxygen mask had produced a soothing soundscape.

Fifteen minutes ago, the nurse had popped in to note down the readings on several of the screens and to offer Okeke a polite nod. Margot had been asleep.

But she was awake now.

xxy

Okeke stood up slowly so the movement wouldn't startle her. Above the pale-blue plastic rim of the oxygen mask, Margot was barely visible beneath the thick swirls of antiseptic and analgesic creams. There was no hair left on her head. The flames had all but destroyed her face. The only human features were two wide staring eyes, both of them settled on Okeke.

'Hey,' she said softly. 'Margot... it's okay. You're in hospital. Your daughter and mother are right here.'

I have no idea how good her English is. Okeke suspected she must speak some if she worked closely with Sutton. She couldn't imagine he'd taken the trouble to learn any Polish.

Margot tried to raise one of her mottled arms.

'No,' said Okeke. 'Please don't need to move. Stay still, Margot.'

Her steady breathing became erratic as she struggled to speak.

Okeke hastened over to her bedside. 'It's okay, it's okay. Shhhh.'

Margot's eyes fixed on her. From beneath the oxygen mask, there came a horrific gurgling sound.

'Matka?' Lena lurched in her chair. A split second later, she was right beside Okeke, looking down hopefully at her mother.

Margot tried to raise her arm again and Okeke was unsure whether to steer it gently back down. The gurgling grew louder, more insistent.

She's trying to say something.

Her arm raised again, it looked as though she was trying to indicate something.

'Mama, what is it?' said Lena. 'What do you need?'

Okeke could see the agony of the movement, the effort to talk was killing her. 'No. Please. Just relax, Margot. We can talk another time.'

'*Ah... Ah... Azzz...*' Her hand continued to waver uncertainly in the air.

The effort had triggered one of the machines, which was beeping insistently, and within seconds the nurse was back in the room, shouting, 'Back. Get back from her! Please!'

Okeke pulled Lena away from the bedside to give the nurse room to move around. He tapped on the screen of one of the units and then reached for a pager clipped to his breast pocket.

Margot's rasping voice was getting louder. '*Azzuh... Azzuh...*'

'Margot!'' said the nurse. 'We're going to raise the pain meds. Just hold on, love. Hold on!'

Another machine began to beep and the room, an oasis of calm barely a minute ago, was beginning to feel small, chaotic and loud.

'Mama!' Mama!' Lena was crying over Okeke's shoulder, squirming, to get round her and back to the bed.

'Lena! Come on! Let him do his job!'

Okeke steered, almost wrestled, the girl through the door and into the hallway as a consultant came running down.

'What's going on?'

'She's awake and in pain!' said Okeke as the doctor squeezed past her, disappearing into the room.

The door closed on the chaos, with Lena's grandma still inside. The old woman was calling out Margot's name, adding to the confusion.

'Lena... stay! I'll bring your grandma out.'

Okeke stepped back in, unlocked the wheels on the wheelchair and brought the old woman out, sobbing and distraught. Together they went down the hall to the family room.

'It's going to be okay,' Okeke said to Lena, who had started to cry. 'Her painkillers needed increasing, that's all. They're dealing with that right now. They'll sedate her again so she can rest.'

That wasn't all, though, was it?

Okeke was sure the woman had been trying to tell her something.

Between sobs, Lena was trying to explain to her grandma what Okeke had said, trying to calm her down, reassure her.

'Ask your grandma if she'd like a hot chocolate or tea. Or something to eat,' Okeke said.

'Yes. Hot chocolate, please,' Lena replied, wiping her eyes.

'Can I get you one?'

Lena nodded. Okeke left the room and headed down the hallway towards the Costa concession café on the ground floor, hoping it was still open while she went over what had just happened.

Margot had seen her – presumably worked out she was the police and had been trying desperately to tell her something. Okeke was sure about that. Az – something? She'd lifted her arm and Okeke thought she'd been trying to draw something in the air. Maybe the letter A? And doing that had cost her a lot in pain. It had been *that* important.

The café was closed, but she found a vending machine and returned to the family room with two paper cups of watery hot chocolate and a couple of Mars Bars in case either of them felt hungry.

She set them down on the table and waited until Lena had passed one to her grandmother.

'Lena?'

She looked up.

'Your mum... She was trying to say something to me. A word.'

'What word?'

'I don't know. It began with "Az" or maybe "Azsh"?'

Lena frowned, the little puzzle clearly a welcome distraction. 'Az...?' She pondered that for a moment, then shook her head. 'I don't know.'

Her grandma perked up and said something to her in Polish. Lena turned and then for the next minute there was rapid back and forth between them. Finally, Lena turned back to Okeke.

'Azor, Babcia thinks.'

'Azor?'

'It is a dog's name.'

'Why would your mother say a dog's name?'

'There is a dog in our kitchen. A porcelain one. It is

Babcia's. It is named after her old Alsatian back in Poland. Azor.'

Okeke felt the first tickle of adrenaline in her veins. 'That's a possession your mum would know about?'

'Yes. Of course.'

'Would she hide something behind it, maybe?'

'*In* it,' replied Lena. 'It is a cookie jar.'

Okeke leant forward. 'This is obviously something important to her. It must be.'

'Yes.' Lena's face lifted. It was something else to focus on. 'Perhaps this is true.'

'Look, your grandmother should stay here, you too... but there may be something in that jar that your mother wants. In your grandmother's house. Do you understand?'

'You want to go into our home?'

Okeke couldn't think of any better way. Both Lena and her grandmother needed to stay at the hospital in case Margot took a turn for the worse, and Okeke was now suddenly paranoid that there might be crucial evidence tucked away in the Bajeks' home that needed to be bagged and tagged – before anyone else got there.

She nodded. 'I can go and get this thing. Maybe it's just something she wants with her?'

Lena shrugged. 'Okay.' She pulled a key ring out from her jeans and passed it to Okeke.

'Is there anything else I can get? For you? Your grandma?'

Lena looked across at her grandmother. 'It is cold in this room. She has...' Lena mimed wrapping something over her shoulders.

'A shawl?'

'Yes. She wears this watching TV. It is in the lounge on her chair. You have our address?'

Okeke nodded; she had it in her notebook. 'I'll be as quick as I can.'

32

The Bajeks' home was a flat above a corner shop in Ore. The manager of the shop owned the whole building and had turned what had once been stockrooms into a barely habitable – and probably illegal – rental.

When Okeke flashed her warrant card at him, his eyes instantly widened into bloodshot ping-pong balls of panic.

'Is it just the old lady and granddaughter who live up there?' she asked.

'Yes,' he replied somewhat defensively.

'For how long?'

He seemed reluctant to answer. 'A little while.'

'How long?' she asked again, her voice hardening.

'Five years,' he mumbled.

She showed Lena's door key to him. 'I'm going in to get some things for them. If I don't find smoke alarms up there, you're going to get them put in the moment I leave, aren't you?'

She knew there wouldn't be any there. She'd been in enough bottom-of-the-barrel rentals while in uniform to know that every safety regulation in the book would have been flouted. The door to the flat, for example, was only accessible via the shop. Whether he was open twenty-four-seven, or whether there were times they simply weren't able to enter or leave their home, she wasn't sure.

The door was past the till in a corridor stacked with pallets of stock. Okeke unlocked it and flicked on a light switch to find herself beneath a bare bulb dangling from dusty flex, facing a wall with coat pegs on it, with a steep and narrow flight of wooden stairs to her right. How the hell Lena got her grandmother up and down those, she had no idea.

Okeke looked up. *No smoke alarm*, she noted.

She climbed the steps quickly, flicked on another light switch at the top and found herself looking into a space that just about met the bare minimum of standards to call itself a kitchen; there was a tiny sink and tap beneath a narrow sash window. A plug-in hob sat on a twin-kitchen unit carcass that had a length of faux-wood Formica resting on top of it.

The walls were lined with heavily laden shelves, which she presumed had either been put up by Lena and her mum, or had been there previously to stack boxes of crisps, chocolate bars and cans of no-brand lager. Now, they were laden with the accoutrements of cooking, mix-and-match crockery and jars of homemade preserves and pickles. The room had the faint smell of cabbage, garlic and caramelised onion, and the minty bouquet of caraway seeds.

The kitchen in Okeke's childhood home had had a very different palate of odours coming from much stronger spices, but the overall effect was the same – a warm cuddle of nostalgia. A place of home-cooking and steamed-up windows. She smiled.

Something brushed past her and she looked down to see a tabby cat, tail held aloft like the radio antenna on a remote-controlled car. It began to meow at her insistently. She saw two empty bowls on the floor.

'All right, let's get you something to eat and drink, sweetie,' she said as it arched its back and rubbed its side against her leg.

She filled one of the bowls with tap water, then looked around the busy shelves for some cat food. She found a box of Meow Mix dry food, which looked like the most budget of brands.

'So then, no dogs here, eh?' she said to the cat as she set down the bowl of Meow Mix in front of it.

On the shelves at eye level were family photographs that had faded from colour to almost black and white. She glimpsed background fragments that suggested a rural life, a farm, perhaps.

And, yes, a dog. An Alsatian. Azor – presumably.

Okeke got the sense that the Bajeks had seen better times and experienced better fortunes. It was difficult to piece together the framework of their family; there were a couple of men in the photos, but no men, it seemed, around any more.

She decided to grab Lena's grandmother's shawl before she forgot. She backed out of the kitchen and along a very short hall – three steps and you were done – and entered a room she deemed most likely to be the front room and flicked the light switch on.

The front room too was tiny. The limited space allowed for one armchair, a rocking chair and a TV perched on a kitchen stool. The walls were lined with vertical metal shelf struts, the brackets and shelves removed, and one small high-up window allowed the spill of some sickly sodium amber street light in but offered no view.

Okeke found the shawl on the back of the chair in front of the TV and returned to the kitchen to see if she could find this porcelain dog/cookie jar.

It took her some time to locate it because the shelves were so deep and cluttered, doing the work that wall units would have done if the landlord could have been arsed to put some in.

But at the back of one, hiding behind a row of coffee urns, there it was. A clumpy clay jug with lumps that suggested limbs and a head that seemed more like the wedge-shape of a bull terrier than the noble sharp angles of an Alsatian. She wondered if a much younger Lena had made it. Perhaps even Margot, for her mother.

Carefully, trying not to catch it on anything, Okeke eased it out from the back and set it down on the small picnic table in the kitchen. It was heavy enough that the table's metal legs creaked.

'Okay then,' she said softly. The weight was a little disconcerting, but, as she lifted the lid off – the dog's head – she realised the weight was in the jug itself; it wasn't the smooth slim shell of a pottery professional.

She peered inside to see it was empty apart from an envelope.

She was about to retrieve it, when her brain jolted awake and she mentally kicked herself. At least she'd stopped herself in time, she thought. She reached into her bag and pulled a pair of nitrile gloves out of the side pouch. She snapped them on, then carefully reached inside the cookie jar and lifted the envelope out.

Scrawled in handwriting that looked laboured and scratchy was: *To Margot Bajek.*

It wasn't sealed and she could tell that care had been taken to steam the flap open. Okeke teased the flap open once again to find a single folded sheet of paper inside. Gently, she shook the envelope until the page slid out onto the table.

It had been printed rather than handwritten. Flattening the page out, she could see why. There was a fair amount to read. At the bottom, though, was the same shaky handwriting again.

A signature and a date.

Sir Arthur Sutton's signature.

33

Sutton's house is pitifully easy to break into. It's old and quirky, like a Victorian folly designed by one of the Addams family. Its faux watchtower and bay windows, protrusions and nooks make a mockery of the 360-degree cover of his CCTV cameras.

The stalker enters the house with the ease of a serpent through a torn screen door.

Inside the house, fortunately, there is noise. Sutton has put on some music. It's something by Wagner – of course, it is – something swaggering and pompous.

The house is decorated inside in much the way one would expect. Dark brooding walls and high ceilings. Mahogany furniture and wood panelling. Sir Arthur has one of those drinks cabinets that sit inside an old cartographer's globe. That says it all.

He's a cliché – the gentleman adventurer and writer. A Richard Francis Burton of his time.

The woman needs to be dealt with first. Neutralised.

Then Sutton can be dealt with at leisure.

34

Day 7

'Right, everyone, settle down and pick a seat,' said Boyd. He looked around the table, aware that the face count was one short. 'Who's missing?'

'Lane,' said Warren. 'He just went up to get a coffee.'

'Bloody hell,' Boyd said, albeit mildly. 'I gave a five-minute warning!'

The door to the room opened and Lane entered sheepishly. 'Sorry, the queue was longer than I thought it would be.'

Boyd shook his head and gestured for him to sit down. 'Okay, top of this morning's agenda is this.' He waved a piece of paper in a plastic sleeve. 'A letter from Sutton from beyond the grave.'

He placed it on the table and slid it across the surface towards Okeke. 'Since you're the one who found it, do you want to read it out?'

'Not really, guv,' she said, sliding it back.

'Fine.' He took the piece of paper out of the sleeve. 'The original's with CSI right now; we're hoping to get print and DNA results later today to validate it. We're assuming for the moment, though, that it's genuine.' Boyd cleared his throat and began to read it out loud.

THIS IS FOR MY CHILDREN,

I know I have not been the most dutiful or attentive father, for this I am truly sorry, but it is my work that has kept me busy. You know well enough that I came from a humble background and I have had to fight my way, inch by inch, to provide you both with enough social elevation that doors of opportunity would await, open, for you. It is the best of fathers who take on that struggle and pass on a better start in life to their children than they inherited.

With that in mind, I write this memorandum of intent to supersede the directions of my will, last made seven years ago. After my death, my total estate including all present assets and future income from literary works will be adjusted from the present arrangement to the following:

Margot Bajek will receive sixty per cent.

Henry will receive thirty per cent.

Hermione will receive ten per cent.

These allocations have been assigned to reflect a complicated mixture of my gratitude and my affection, a recognition of ambition and achievement, and finally my parental responsibility. Let me address you individually.

Henry – your greater share than Hermione is to reward you in your efforts to forge your own path and make your own fortune. I know that in you my spirit lives on and I wish you good fortune.

Hermione – I know there is a great division between us and that you have sided with Kate. The lesser amount is not to punish you, but a recognition that she will undoubtedly favour you over Henry when her time comes.

Margot — the majority I give to you in gratitude for entering my life when I most needed you. And for all the help and support you have given in my final endeavour. You know by now that I have a morally compromised past, that I have done things of which I'm not proud. Our work these last few months and my gift to you of the majority of my estate is an attempt to balance the scales. You know there will be a reckoning in the wake of my death. Much will be said about me and the others. I ask that you only remember me as the man you met.

'THERE'S MORE, BUT…' Boyd set the photocopied letter on the table and looked at his team. 'Any thoughts on that?'

'Well, it's got to be all about the money, then, boss, hasn't it?' said Minter.

'Keep in mind we don't think either of his children know about this letter,' said Okeke. 'As far as they're concerned, they're his main beneficiaries.'

'But they must suspect he's giving some or all of it to the Polish lady,' O'Neal said.

'Margot Bajek,' replied Okeke. 'She does have a name.'

'I'm interested in that "there will be a reckoning" comment,' said Lane. 'Presumably that links to this "final endeavour" he mentioned.'

Boyd nodded. 'There's quite a bit to unpack there. "Morally compromised". "Much will be said". '

'And "the others"?' said Okeke. She looked around the room. 'Anyone else here thinking that sounds a little fucking creepy?'

'Aye,' said Lane. 'Very.'

'I'm sure I'm joining up all the wrong dots,' said Sully, 'but with this "final endeavour", the mention of "others", this business of balancing the scales, and the very nearly successful murder attempt on both of them, I can't help but think Sutton and Margot were working on exposing something that some-body didn't want exposed?'

'Agreed,' said Boyd. 'I'm beginning to think Sutton acquired a fair amount of compromising material over the years. What if his skillset included leverage as well as the gift of the gab?'

Boyd grabbed his whiteboard marker and wrote *Others* on the board and drew a loop around it. He drew a linking line and labelled it *Secrets*.

'You said there was a bit more, boss?' Minter nodded at the sheet of paper.

'Yeah,' said Boyd. 'It's some pseudo legal stuff about being of right mind and compos mentis, then his name and date.' He returned to the table. 'Warren... what's the latest on the CCTV Easter-egg hunt?'

'We've managed to patch together a cam trail on our man all the way back to White Rock Road. We lost him at the junc-tion outside White Rock Theatre. The public-space CCTV camera that looks south towards the pier was out of order that night; it still is. So we don't know whether he came up from the East Hill end of Hastings or down from Bexhill.'

'We also know he isn't local, then,' added Minter.

'How's that?' Boyd asked.

'If you're heading up to London Road from the Hastings side, you can carve off a whole chunk by walking up around Priory Meadow Shopping Centre and then Newgate Road. If he was local, he'd know that, boss,' Minter explained.

'And if he was coming from Bexhill?' Boyd prompted.

'Well, you wouldn't, see? Parking's too far away. Your nearest parking is Pelham.'

'All right, so you're going to need to canvas the pier and the theatre for private CCTV,' said Boyd. 'We need to know which way he came from. We don't want to waste time running through shop CCTV from the *wrong* side. O'Neal, you go and check the pier, and I'll drop into the theatre.'

'Yes, chief,' said O'Neal with a nod.

'Sully?'

'My turn?'

'Yup. Where are we on Sutton's Facebook access and iCloud storage?'

'The Facebook request has been approved. They're going to send a ninety-day activity dump for us to trawl through. Apple's going to be a little tougher on cloud storage. I've logged a request and their legal eagles are looking it over.'

'Minter?'

'Sutton's phone network provider has given us the multilateration data from their towers going back two months. So we've got a pretty decent patchwork of his movements to pick through.'

'Right,' said Boyd. 'I want an itinerary of Sutton's movements going back to... let's start with his last week.'

'Righto, boss.'

'Also check Margot Bajek's phone network. If she's been assisting Sutton in getting around, her movements should match; if she's got a different network provider, she may ink in any tower blanks for you.'

'On it.'

'Okay,' said Boyd. 'One last thing...' He pulled out his work phone and swiped at the screen to bring up his recent photos – and there it was, the last picture he'd taken. He studied it for a few moments, then drew the graffiti symbol on the whiteboard.

HE TURNED BACK to face his team. 'Anyone know what this is?'

'Anarchy sign?' suggested Sully.

Warren shook his head. 'No... the A's middle bar is missing. And anyway the A extends outside the circle.'

'Where's that come from?' asked Lane.

'It was scrawled on Sutton's front wall. At the point where the intruder was lingering on the pub's CCTV footage.' He showed them his phone screen. 'It looks like relatively recent graffiti. I think our chap might have been lingering to scrawl that. So, Lane... here's a task for you, if you want? See if you can work out if this means anything.'

'Semiology?' Lane smiled. 'Interesting. I'll have that.'

Boyd was about to wrap up the meeting when he noticed Okeke was staring at the symbol on the whiteboard, frowning, her eyes narrowed.

'Okeke?'

She pressed her lips together. 'It's nothing, guv.'

'Are you sure?' he queried.

'Sure,' she replied.

'Right. Final thing, everyone. The gardening-party-slash-barbecue-slash-piss-up at mine on Sunday. Do I have any takers?'

The room fell silent.

'I'll be there,' said Okeke eventually. 'And Jay.'

'Excellent.' Boyd smiled, relieved that at least it wouldn't be a complete no-show. 'Anyone else?'

The collective murmur from the others, as they stood up and shoved their chairs under the table, could, at best, be described as lukewarm.

'Okeke, wait a second,' said Boyd. She lingered beside the conference table. 'How's Margot Bajek doing?'

'I called Lena this morning,' she replied. 'Her mother's stable for now, but still critical. If her lungs become infected it's... well, it's all over for her.' She paused. 'Guv, that thing you drew on the whiteboard?'

'Yup? The graffiti?'

'Last night – I told you this already – when Margot was trying to communicate with me, she raised her arm – perhaps to draw an A. I thought she was trying to air-spell that dog's name at the time, but maybe...'

'She was drawing that shape?' he completed.

Okeke nodded.

Boyd took a moment to consider the implications of that. If there was a link – and that was a bit of a leap, to be fair – then it would have to suggest that she knew the same piece of information that the killer did. And what did that mean?

His eyes settled on the small pile of newspapers spread across the conference table. He looked thoughtfully at the picture of the fire engine, next to the overgrown wall, the faint outline of the symbol sprayed across the flint wall.

'Okay,' he said. 'Maybe there's something in that.'

35

He squinted at the picture on his laptop screen: the *Mail Online*'s news landing page. His eyesight wasn't great these days. The online versions of the red tops often didn't insert images that could be enlarged into their articles. It was the size it was on the screen and no more. Something to do with preventing cut-n-paste journalism. He'd been in the business back when actual journalists did actual digging, rather than just scanning and copy and pasting press handouts.

The image was of the rear of a fire engine poking out onto a road from an overgrown driveway. A fireman was coiling a hose, or uncoiling it, from a compartment at the back, and over his shoulder was a low wall, dapple-shadowed by leaves and branches. Leaning in closer... it was undeniable. His skin prickled with goosebumps. It was the same symbol. The same message.

Don't make the same mistake as Sutton.

He sat back in his chair and scratched absently at his bare feet. The anxiety was making his psoriasis flare up badly. It was a torturous condition he'd been struggling with since his nervous breakdown and the short spell in prison. Recently he'd managed to wear socks and shoes once again, but, since learning about Sir Arthur Sutton's death, the condition had returned with a snarling vengeance. He scratched at the red blotchy skin between his toes until the dry skin and the scabs were gone, leaving damp welts.

They'll be coming for me next.

36

Boyd wandered downhill from the station along Bohemia Road. By the time he was standing beside the entrance to the White Rock Theatre he was sweating. He gazed out at the pier and the beach for a moment, enjoying the view. He took off his jacket, slung it over his arm, took the steps up to the entrance portico and pushed the glass door.

It was even warmer in the foyer – the building was all glass doors and no breeze. It was like a greenhouse. He approached the box-office counter, currently un-manned, hoping to see Charlotte.

'Hello there.'

He spun round to see her head poking out of a doorway.

'Sorry,' said Charlotte, smiling. 'I didn't mean to startle you. I saw you enter on the CCTV.'

'Right,' he said, smiling back. 'How're *you* doing?' He winced. He'd made that sound very Joey from *Friends*. He took a couple of steps towards her.

'Um, I'm very well, thank you,' she said. 'To what do I owe the pleasure, Bill?'

'Uh...' *Oh, for fuck's sake. Get a grip and stop mumbling like a bloody idiot!* 'It's work related, I'm afraid,' he said.

He wasn't sure, but he thought her shoulders sagged slightly.

'It's to do with a case I'm investigating,' he explained.

'I should hope so,' she said, though still smiling. 'Taxpayer's money and all that.'

'It's to do with your CCTV, actually. You've got a camera out there under the entrance roof, haven't you?'

'We've got two of them out front,' she said.

'Are they static or panned?' Boyd asked.

'Sorry?'

'Are they fixed in one direction or –'

'Oh, fixed,' she said. 'One's aimed at the doors. The other points down White Rock Road.'

'Which way does it look?' he asked.

'Towards Pelham.'

'Right. And for how long do your cameras store data?'

She shrugged. 'I have absolutely no idea. Do you want me to find out?' she said, stepping back into the office and waving at him to follow her in.

It was even warmer in here. Three tall bay windows made the small space feel like the lantern room of a lighthouse. One of them was open, he noticed with relief, allowing in the lightest puff of breeze.

There was a desk by the windows, cluttered with paperwork and a monitor. Opposite were another small desk, a floor-standing safe and half a dozen small CCTV monitors showing jerky two-frame-a-second footage. Boyd wandered over to them and pointed at the screen showing the portico and the one showing the road heading east along the front. 'Cameras three and four are the ones I'm interested in,' he said. 'I'm keeping my fingers crossed that you've got data stored from a week ago.'

'Let me call our security manager and find out.' She picked

up her mobile phone and gestured at her seat at the bay window. 'Sit down, enjoy the view. I'll be back in a minute.'

Boyd watched her go, then crossed the room and sat down in her office chair. He looked at her monitor and saw that Gmail was up, several emails open on a discussion about ticket takings over the last quarter.

The screen glare was unbearable. He wondered that her face wasn't permanently crinkled with frown lines.

'So, it's a fortnight that we keep backed up,' she said, re-entering the office and making him jump, guiltily.

Boyd joined her back at the monitors.

'And he said that they each have a USB stick beside the screen and it's all stored on that. I'm not sure how...'

Boyd leant forward. 'You just push it in and they eject. Voila.' He retrieved the memory sticks from both cameras.

She smiled. 'Ahh, I can see you've done this before.'

'Many times,' he said. 'Look, can I borrow these for a couple of hours? Download the contents and then drop them back after lunch?'

'Sure. You can drop them back *for* lunch... if you like?'

He looked down at the memory sticks in his palm, sliding them one over the other with his thumb absently. 'Okay, sounds nice. But I insist on paying this time.'

'I didn't pay last time,' she confessed with a guilty bite on her lip. 'Staff perk. So let me "buy", all right?'

'Deal.' He dropped the memory sticks into an evidence bag. 'Right then.'

'Right then,' she echoed.

'See you up in the...'

'*Titanic?*' she said with a smile.

He laughed. She'd remembered his comment about the café looking like the gallery deck of an old cruise ship. 'See you later. One-ish sound okay?'

She nodded. 'See you then.'

Boyd returned at one o'clock on the dot, with the memory sticks, and found Charlotte sitting at a table beside one of the tall windows in the café.

'I see you're a big sun fan,' he said as he pulled out a chair.

'Oh, yes, particularly after such a grey year thus far.' She got up. 'I better get us some food. What do you fancy?'

'Cup of coffee, and... I dunno, a sandwich?'

'Let's see if we can narrow that down, shall we?'

He smiled. 'It's before two, so black, no sugar. And... egg and cress?'

She gave him a quizzical look. 'Certainly.'

He watched her go, wondering why the hell he'd asked for an egg and cress sandwich. Maybe it was the vibe of the place. It had a Betty's Tea Room feel to it. Or maybe it was Charlotte herself, the way she spoke, her old-fashioned mannerisms. He was going to feel an utter berk if she came back with half a pint of lager and a quarter-pounder for herself.

I like her.

The thought came to him unbidden. It was a strange feeling. He glanced out of the window and saw several of his team waiting to cross the road to grab chips-and-whatever from the café on the pier. DI Lane was with them, chatting animatedly with Warren and O'Neal. The two young lads seemed drawn to him and were hanging on to his every word.

He watched them until they reached the café; cigarettes were ditched and they disappeared inside from view. Then his gaze rested absently on the hovering gulls and the lazy waves rolling up the shingle, the sun making the Channel look invitingly blue for once, lost in his own thoughts until...

'Lunch is served.'

Charlotte set the tray down and he helped her transfer the contents onto their table.

She'd ordered herself a fish-finger sandwich. So much for old fashioned, he thought, eyeing it enviously.

'So, what's the investigation all about?' she asked, pouring her tea.

'Do you know Eagle House?'

Charlotte nodded. 'That's the one that burned down the other day, isn't it? Some ex-politician, I think, died in the fire?'

'Arthur Sutton,' Boyd said.

'Oh, that's right, he writes those... thrillers, doesn't he?'

'You're not a fan?'

She pressed her lips. 'Not really my cup of tea. I'm more your Truman Capote type of reader.'

'Truman Capote?' There was a name he'd not heard in a while. He only knew the writer because... 'My wife used to read his short stories.'

There was an uncomfortable silence.

'Used to?' Charlotte saved them both from it. 'You're separated?'

'Widowed,' Boyd replied.

'Oh, I'm so very sorry,' she said. And she really did look sad. That was one of the things he liked about her. She seemed open and genuine.

Boyd waved his hand as if to banish any awkwardness. 'It happened a few years ago. My wife and my son died in a car accident.'

'Oh gosh,' she said. 'What happened?'

'It went down as a DIC – drunk in charge...' he explained, taking in her baffled look. 'She wasn't *drunk*... by the way, barely a unit over. And it wasn't her fault.' He didn't know why he was telling Charlotte this and he really didn't want to get into how he blamed himself. He didn't want to talk about the fact that their car had actually been stationary when the distracted – entirely sober – truck driver piled into the back of her.

'It's how we police write things up,' he added. 'Everything reduced to a three-letter acronym.'

Charlotte shook her head. 'That's truly awful.'

'Yeah, it is. But –' he picked up his coffee and took a sip – 'I'm in a better place now.' He could see she desperately wanted to ask but wasn't going to. 'Her name was Julia. My son was Noah. He was four. Just starting to get to know the little rascal, really.' He could feel the emotions racing up on him from behind like an ambulance. 'Anyway, enough wallowing. So, what about you? Your other half never seems to bother walking the dog.'

He took a large bite out of his sandwich.

'Oh, there's no other half.' She laughed and shook her head. 'Oh, God, no. Never. I'm far too old and difficult to be married to.'

He nodded. 'Get into your forties and you're unlikely to change for someone else, right?'

'Forties?' She smiled. 'That's awfully kind of you.'

Boyd, who had actually been talking about himself, realised he'd accidentally complemented her. She *looked* like she was in her early to mid forties but, judging by the smile on her face, she was hinting she was a little older.

'I'm a little past my mid forties too,' he said. 'Getting to be a grumpy old man.'

She looked at him, surprised. 'Mid forties? You've done jolly well, then.'

'I'm trying to keep desk-based flab from overwhelming me,' he said, patting his stomach. 'I'm not sure I'm winning, though.'

'It *is* difficult, isn't it? Walking Mia twice a day and dancing twice a week seems to be just about enough to allow me a naughty lunch every now and then.'

'Dancing?' Boyd was intrigued. 'What kind?'

'Jazz and swing.'

He had no idea what that even looked like.

'It's a good way to meet other lonely people,' she said, before she took a delicate bite out of her sandwich.

Lonely? That surprised him. He'd thought of her as confident and friendly, the bright-'n'-breezy type at a gathering who collected phone numbers and lunch dates with thoughtless ease.

He took another large bite from his egg-and-cress sandwich.

'What about you?' she asked.

'Oh, I think I've met too many bloody people recently,' he said, mouth full. 'Present company excepted, of course.'

She laughed. 'No, I mean... exercise? Are you a gym man, or a running man?'

He washed his sandwich down with a swig of coffee. 'Oh, I'm a spaniel man, these days. Walking Ozzie up and down East Hill every day and chasing after scrotes... sorry, *suspects* is enough for me.'

Her eyes rounded comically. 'Scrotes?'

'Sorry.' He grinned. 'Police speak – it's all a bit vulgar and salty in the office.'

Talk of the devils – he spotted some of his team wandering back across the road with their half-eaten bags of fish and chips. He'd need to head back soon.

She noticed him watching them. 'Are they your colleagues? Gosh, they all look so young.'

He nodded. Standing beside them, he often wondered if he looked like someone's dad. 'Doesn't everyone look young when you're our age?' he said, turning to look at her.

'I'm fifty,' she clarified. 'Before you ask.'

'No.'

'Yes.' She smiled again. 'Since a couple of months ago, actually. In fact, the night we bumped into each other in the pub.' She took another bite, then shook her head. 'That was me celebrating the big five-oh.'

'*Alone?*'

'With a lady from work. But... yes, I suppose I was the last to leave.' She shrugged it away. 'It's only a number really. Not worth a big fuss, I don't think.'

'Well, maybe you'd like to celebrate it again with a barbeque at mine?' The words tumbled out of his mouth without warning.

Her own mouth dropped a little open.

You've gone and done it now, mate. He blundered on: 'This Sunday. I'm having a bit of a garden-clearing party. A few work friends are coming over to help. It's nothing much, but you're welcome to come if you like.'

She looked away awkwardly, her cheeks flushing slightly. He felt like a lumbering elephant for being so leaden-footed and inappropriately forward. 'Only if you're at a loose end, or something.' He finished off his sandwich and shrugged. 'I mean, it *is* basically unpaid labour on a Sunday. Rewarded only with a burnt burger in a bap.'

'That would be very nice,' she said quickly. 'Thank you.'

'Whuh?'

'I'll bring my gardening gloves.'

'Oh, right. Good.' He felt his own face warming slightly, and thanked God that at least some of it was hidden behind bristles.

'What time?' she asked, 'and can I bring anything?' She spread her hands. 'It'll either be a cake or a rake?'

He laughed a little too eagerly. 'The afternoon. One onwards, I guess. No need to bring anything.' He checked his watch and swilled down the last of his coffee. 'Look, I'd better get going, otherwise the kids will get unruly. Thanks for lunch, Charlotte.'

'My pleasure,' she said.

'Sunday then?' He bent over the table and offered a hand – a halfway house between a handshake and a polite Edwardian kiss. Charlotte, unsure what exactly it was that he was attempting to do, settled on lightly holding one of his fingers like he was King Kong.

'I'll be there on one condition,' she said as he went to leave.

Boyd turned back to look at her.

'You'll need to give me your address.'

BOYD WALKED up the hill towards the station, eye-rolling at his own lack of judgement. He'd invited a rather lovely lady, who looked as though she'd just stepped out of Downton Abbey, to an afternoon of gruelling manual labour, or, worse-case scenario, if they all turned up armed with six-packs... a loud and leery piss-up.

'Nice one, numbnuts,' he muttered.

37

'Hey, boss?'

Boyd looked up from his monitor at a solid wall of Welsh muscle clad in a figure-hugging waistcoat.

'Yup?'

'I've been working on the data sent by Sutton's phone network provider.'

'Anything interesting?' Boyd asked.

'Well...' Minter pulled up a chair, sat down and wheeled it around the desk to sit beside him. 'The triangulation data for the last week before his death shows us that he was mostly located in his London home.'

'Shit, which reminds me...' Boyd scribbled a note down to remind himself to ask Okeke to contact the Met's CSI people for the SOC report on the Chancery Lane flat. 'Go on.'

'So, mostly at his London home – but, four days before Sutton came back down to Hastings, he took a trip out to Little Horshall. And spent an afternoon there before going home.'

'Right. Do we know what or who's out there?'

'Well, see, I took a look at the place where he was lingering for the afternoon and it's an address.' Minter checked his notepad. 'Bumble House, Number Fifteen, The Green, Little Horshall. The person who lives there is an M. Webster.'

'And who is he to Sutton?' Boyd asked.

'I don't know, boss. A friend maybe? The address is all I could get off LEDS.'

'And a phone number, I hope?'

'It's right here, boss,' Minter said, tapping his waistcoat pocket. 'Want me to give him a call?'

Boyd fancied a gear change; he was fed up staring at the screen in front of him. 'No, I'll do it,' he said. 'Were there any other interesting detours?'

'Just his trip back home to Hastings, boss. And then... well... that's it.'

'Right, nice one, Minty. Cheers.'

Minter rolled the chair back around the desk and got up. 'I'm going to check on the lads to see how the CCTV breadcrumb trail is going,' he said, as he handed Boyd a folded piece of paper.

Boyd unfolded it and looked at the number. It was a landline number. He toyed with a quick request to see whether it was a business number or a private one, but decided the quicker thing was to go old school and just bloody dial it and see.

After several rings, a woman with a deep smoker's voice answered. 'Maria Webster.'

'Ah, hello, I'm Detective Chief Inspector Boyd from Sussex Police CID. Have you got a moment or two?'

She was silent. 'Yes?' she replied eventually. 'I have a moment.'

'I don't know if you're aware that a man called Arthur Sutton died in a fire last week...' Boyd began.

'*Sir...* Arthur, yes, I know,' she interrupted tersely. Her crusty voice reminded him of Dot Cotton.

'Did you know him, then, Ms Webster?'

'Not particularly well, but he's a client of mine. Or he *was*. I'm his literary agent.'

'Ah, I see,' Boyd replied. 'I'm not particularly up to speed on the world of book publishing, I presume that's what... a sort of advocacy role? Contracts? Management?'

'I read his first drafts, for my sins. I provide early feedback, I negotiate contracts. I listen to my clients moan about their publishers. I provide tea biscuits and sympathy... and only charge fifteen per cent commission for it all,' she informed him.

'So it's what... a remote working relationship? Emails? Phone calls?'

'Emails in the main.'

'May I ask when was the last time the two of you met face to face?'

Maria Webster's reply was slow in coming. *Now... is she going to tell me a porkie?*

'A while ago,' she replied. 'I'd need to check my diary.'

'Roughly?'

'Months, I think.'

Tsk. Tsk.

'Ah, about that...' Boyd cut in. 'His mobile-phone data indicates he was actually at your house last week for several hours. Does that help?'

There was another pause. He could hear her nose breathing into the handset.

'Yes,' she replied finally. 'He did drop by, as I recall now.'

Oh, now you remember. Hmmm?

Boyd realised he was quite enjoying himself. It was always satisfying, catching people in an outright lie.

'May I ask what that was about Ms Webster?' he asked.

'Not really,' she replied. 'It's client confidentiality. I take that part of my job very seriously.'

'Right. But we are in fact investigating the fire as a murder case. Which means I'm afraid that you will have to tell me.'

'It was more of a social call than a meeting. Tea and cakes. You know.'

'I thought you said you didn't know him particularly well?' Boyd shook his head. Some people were born to be liars, but others? Well... 'I wonder if I could pop over and have a chat with you about Sir Arthur?'

'Let's see... That's... difficult. I'm rather busy today,' she said, sounding flustered.

'How does tomorrow sound?' Boyd asked calmly. 'In the afternoon? I'm sure we won't be long. It'll just be a few routine questions, nothing to worry about.'

'Fine,' she replied. 'Tomorrow. Two. Don't be late. I have a three o'clock.' With that, she hung up.

'Charming,' he said as he noted down the details. Then Boyd realised that Lane was standing behind him.

'Minter asked me to give you a heads-up on the CCTV work.'

'Ah, how's that going?'

'It looks like we've tracked our man. We think we've got him parking in that seafront car park.'

'Pelham?'

'Yes. And then heading into the old part of town.'

'What time?'

'Late afternoon. About five.'

'So, he was lingering around Hastings for a number of hours, then?'

'Seems that way,' said Lane. 'Probably doing a bit of sight-seeing first.' He nodded at the phone. 'Who was so charming, by the way?'

'Sutton's literary agent. I'm going over to speak with her tomorrow. Know anything about literary agents?'

'Didn't Frank Sinatra once say that hell hath no fury like a hustler with a literary agent?'

'Did he?' Boyd smiled. 'Well, your knowledge of them

clearly outweighs mine. Fancy a trip out in the sun?'

Lane nodded. 'Pub lunch on the way?'

Boyd grimaced. 'You can be the one who tells my Emma about that. She'll blame you as the bad influence, you know?'

Lane laughed. 'Maybe not, then. Where does this agent live?'

'Little Horshall, not far from Guildford.'

'Perfect. It's Friday tomorrow. You could drop me at the station to head back into London after. If that's okay?'

Boyd nodded. 'Ah, yes... So it's a no for my barbeque, then?"

'Sorry, Boyd... My boy?'

Boyd shook his head. 'No problem, mate. You should get back to him. If I can get you home an hour or two earlier, then that's a win, right?'

'Yes, it is.' Lane nodded. 'Thanks.'

38

The woman who cares for Sir Arthur Sutton is surprisingly strong for her diminutive size. She puts up a heroic fight until she suddenly feels the point of the knife against her throbbing carotid artery, then she is very still... and very happy to follow instructions. Which involve going into the pantry, lying face down and not making a sound as her hands are tied behind her back and her ankles roped in and cinched tight, so that she's hogtied and resting on her belly.

The rag in her mouth is enough to reduce her whimpering to something almost unheard, and with Sutton's Wagner playing so loudly it's not really a great concern.

When diesel is poured over her back and head, she screams into the rag... Then she is warned that if there is one single noise coming from the pantry there'll be a return visit – with a match.

Compliance... That's always their downfall, isn't it? Assure them that if they simply follow instructions everything will work out fine. 'No one needs to get hurt.' If they only knew that their chances of survival would increase from nothing to... something had they tried to fight back the first time they heard those words.

The woman is dealt with.
Now it's Sutton's turn.

39

DAY 8

Maria Webster lived in a Tudor-era, or at least Tudor-styled, house in the centre of a cosy little village with a green, one pub and one post office. The front garden looked out onto the modest village green with a single willow tree lapping water in a duck pond.

'See? This is what you get moving out of London,' said Boyd.

'I would if I could,' said Lane. 'Trust me.'

Boyd parked the car outside her garden gate, bang on two o'clock as requested. He could see a woman had opened the front door and was waiting on the doorstep for them.

'Ms Webster?' he called out as he opened the gate and walked down the short path.

'Detective Boyd?'

Close enough.

'Yes. And this chap is DI Lane.'

Lane nodded politely.

Maria Webster wasn't at all as Boyd had imagined her. He'd

expected a brittle-faced twig of a woman with a severe greying bob and don't-screw-with-me trouser suit. She was the opposite in every way – she had a sort of Edina from *Ab Fab* look going on.

'You're punctual, very good,' she said. 'Come on in.'

She led them inside where they were greeted by a blond Lab that barked so loudly and repeatedly that any further conversation was pointless.

Lane squatted to pet it.

'I wouldn't do that,' said Maria. 'Molly's a bit reactive...'

He ignored the warning and ruffled her head, shutting the Lab up immediately. 'I'm good with dogs,' said Lane. 'The sooner you rule yourself out as a threat, the happier they are.'

Maria nodded, impressed. 'Let's go and talk in my study,' she said, leading them into a room off the hallway. The study was *exactly* what Boyd was expecting. Books lined the walls and in the few spaces on the shelves that weren't spines stood glass awards and photographs of Maria in evening wear. He spotted her standing beside a few famous faces. Sir Arthur Sutton was one of them.

So much for not really knowing him, he thought.

'Take a seat, gentlemen,' she said, gesturing to a pair of winged-back leather chairs that faced her desk.

They sat down. Boyd noticed her window looked out onto the village green. It really was very pretty here.

'So, you would like to talk about Sir Arthur,' she said.

'Yes,' Boyd replied. 'As I said on the phone, we know he came here recently and spent a few hours with you.'

'Good grief, the Orwellian surveillance state has finally arrived,' she said.

'It's just the connection data on his phone,' said Boyd. 'If you want to go off grid, you only need to switch your phone off.'

Maria looked sceptical. 'Or so you say.'

'Anyway,' he continued, 'we know he was with you for a few hours. Can you tell us what that was about?'

'As I explained to you yesterday, agent–writer conversations tend to be private affairs, because often we're discussing matters like contracts and book proposals... or bitching about other writers and agents.' She gave him a tight-lipped smile.

'I understand. But, as I explained to *you* yesterday, this is a murder inquiry. So... can you tell us what Sutton came to talk to you about?'

Maria still seemed reluctant to answer.

'Look,' Boyd said. 'At this stage it's just an informal chat, but, if necessary, we can make it more formal and take it to the station.'

'I'd rather you didn't.' Maria leant forward and rested her forearms on the desk. 'He came to see me about a book proposal.'

'Another one of his thrillers?' asked Lane.

She shook her head. 'Something quite different. It was another novel, but –' she took in a deep breath – 'he was really pushing his luck with it.'

'How do you mean?' asked Boyd, glancing at Lane.

'His book proposal was a political thriller, but very much grounded in reality. Identities disguised, of course, but not really that much. You could guess who the characters were meant to be.'

Boyd tried a disarming smile. 'Anyone we'd know?'

Maria shook her head. 'I'm not saying any names, but they're certainly very recognisable faces in Westminster.'

'I'm guessing you advised against it?' said Lane.

'Damned right, I did. Changing a few letters in the spelling of a character's name does not protect you from a libel claim.'

'And what was Sir Arthur's response to that?' asked Boyd.

'He was angry with me!' She sat back in her chair. 'Did you know he was dying?'

Boyd nodded. 'MND.'

'Yes, well, he wanted to write a Fuck-You book to go out on. He had a number of – shall we say – 'big scalps' that he wanted to take down. Big names. Powerful people,' she added. 'And, no, I'm not saying who.'

'But you know.' Lane said.

She looked at him. 'Yes.'

'Had he started work on it?' he asked.

'He was nearly done on it, actually. A first draft at least.'

'Did you read it? Did he leave it with you?' Boyd asked hopefully.

'No and no. He pitched it... and I said no way. Not in a million bloody years would I touch it!'

'Because of legal action?' asked Boyd.

She hesitated. 'My answer to him was a flat *no*. I wasn't going to take it on and, if he pushed any further with it, I wasn't going represent him either. And that's pretty much how our conversation ended.'

'Was anyone else with him?' asked Lane.

'A Polish lady. His assistant or something.'

'Margot Bajek?' said Boyd.

She nodded. 'I think that was the name, yes.'

'And that was it?'

She nodded again. 'Apart from him telling me I was a spineless old bitch on his way out of the front door, yes. That was it.'

'Okay,' said Boyd. 'Did this book have a title?'

She shrugged. 'I suppose I can tell you that... It doesn't give much away. It was called *A Burning Truth*.'

~

'WELL, what did you make of that?' asked Boyd. He indicated right and waited for a gap in both directions to line up so that he could turn onto the A3 heading to Guildford.

'I think the theory that Sutton wanted to go down, guns blazing, is sounding more and more convincing.'

A gap appeared in the traffic and Boyd lurched forward to the far side of the road with the engine screaming.

'Very smoothly done,' said Lane dryly.

'Sorry about that,' Boyd said a few moments later, after he'd found the right gear and dialled the revs down. 'I'm a bit heavy on the clutch sometimes.'

'Didn't do the advance driving course when you were in uniform, then?'

Boyd looked at him. 'I did, actually.' They picked up speed and ended up falling into line behind a truck. 'Didn't pass it, though.'

Lane laughed. 'So it seems Sutton *did* have some dirt,' he said.

Boyd cast his mind back to what he knew about Sutton's career. He'd been an MP for a while and a cabinet member for an even shorter time. Undoubtedly he had a few salacious titbits on some powerful people, but would they be bad enough that they'd have him 'dealt with'? He found that hard to believe. This wasn't some emirate with princes jockeying for power, having each other whacked. Assassinations in the UK tended to be of the character variety. The British equivalent of a hitman was usually a tabloid editor or a talk-show host.

'Not very British, is it?' said Lane.

It was Boyd's turn to laugh. 'I was thinking the exact same thing.'

They drove in silence into Guildford, and Boyd eventually managed to nudge his way through the mid-afternoon traffic to the station. He dropped Lane off at the taxi rank.

'Thanks for that, Boyd. Sorry I won't be there to help on Sunday.'

'No problem. Kids come first, right? You give that little rascal of yours some quality father time.'

'I certainly will. See you Monday.' Lane swung the door shut and tapped the roof as the car pulled away.

DI Douglas Lane, Boyd realised, was someone who'd clearly managed to figure out his priorities early on.

Something which Boyd had left too long and too late to do for his own boy.

40

Sutton is sitting in the drawing room, his back to the double doors, his eyes on the muted TV screen while Wagner blares out from a teak cabinet where presumably his hi-fi is kept.

He is watching the nine o'clock news with subtitles on while he sips his tea.

'Margot!' he calls out. He presumes she's in the kitchen putting supper together for him. 'Margot!' he calls again irritably.

Perhaps the music is too loud for her to hear him. He twists painfully in his seat for the remote control – damned this disease – and in his peripheral vision he sees the dark-clad figure looming over him.

'Who the hell are you–' is all he manages to say.

41

Day 10

Sunday morning, Boyd was deeply relieved when Okeke and Jay turned up outside the house in Jay's van. So not a complete no-show from his team then, thank God. Mind you, this whole thing had been Okeke's suggestion. Jay had brought a keg of beer and some tools, including a traditional garden sickle, its large crescent-shaped blade freshly sharpened.

'Good God,' said Boyd. 'That'll take someone's head off!'

'It works way better than any of those crappy B&Q power tools, boss,' Jay said.

'I'm not your boss, Jay,' Boyd reminded him for the umpteenth time. Ever since Jay had saved Boyd's life during an off-the-books op to find the killer of Gerald Nix, he'd insisted on referring to him that way.

Okeke grinned at Boyd behind her boyfriend's back as Jay took the tools out of the van.

Minter was next to arrive, a quarter of an hour later, and looking like an advert for Australian lager with a crate of beer under one arm and a bottle of cheap sparkly 'for the ladies' in the other.

It took all of five minutes in the sun for both Jay and Minter to shed their shirts and bare their tattooed chests. Emma's eyes popped at the sight of so much muscle in one place, while Daniel seemed to visibly shrink to the size of a drinking straw.

It was sunny this afternoon, but not exactly Ibiza hot.

Boyd shook his head. *Any bloody excuse to bare their pecs.*

O'Neal turned up in a battered Saab with his girlfriend, Lorna, and Warren tucked into the back seat like their toddler. They'd brought more beer and a quiche.

As Boyd ushered them into his house and Lorna cooed at the sheer size of it, Sully rolled up on foot, sweating profusely from his ascent up Ashburnham Road. He was wearing a white panama hat, a lemon-coloured blazer, burgundy cargo pants and flip-flops.

'Now there's a bold fashion statement,' said Boyd.

'I do believe the saying is "Go large or go home",' Sully replied, breezing past him.

Boyd introduced Lorna to everyone in the backyard and left Ozzie – clunking around with his cone of shame – to make his own introductions as he wandered from person to person and evaluated them for treats.

Emma took charge of the growing workforce while Daniel began to set up the barbecue, with Sully providing back-seat advice on how to stack the charcoal briquettes for maximum thermal efficiency.

Boyd busied himself in the kitchen, removing meat in various forms from plastic and Styrofoam packets, then hacking away at an iceberg lettuce to produce a salad.

'Let me do that,' said Okeke. 'You're actually killing it.'

He handed her the knife. 'Thanks.' He looked at her. 'Is this your doing?' he asked.

'What?' she replied innocently.

'The full team turning out?' From the muted response around the conference table the other day he'd assumed this afternoon was going to be tumbleweed.

'I might have given them a little kick up the arse on Friday night,' she confessed.

'Well, thanks, Okeke. I appreciate it,' Boyd said, moving on to mixing the fruit punch. There were, after all, drivers out in the garden and work tomorrow morning, where clear heads would be needed.

Someone had put the music on. It sounded to Boyd like a playlist Emma would have put together: energetic stuff to get the workers out there stoked up to properly flatten his jungle. He glanced at his watch. It was nearly half past one and there was no sign of Charlotte so far.

Maybe she isn't coming?

If he was completely honest, a part of him was a little relieved. With all the beer that had turned up, this afternoon was in danger of becoming a bit laddish. *Some worlds should never be allowed to collide*, he thought. Throwing someone like Charlotte – a woman he really didn't know that well – into a backyard full glistening chest tattoos and locker-room banter, fuelled by ice-cold export lagers, probably wasn't the smartest idea he'd ever had.

On the other hand, he also realised he felt a little stung that she'd decided to give it a pass. She'd probably had no intention of coming along and was just being polite at the café. He'd forgotten to get her number, or give his. So perhaps she'd decided it wasn't a serious invitation after all.

He could smell the charcoal going already and could hear them outside cheering on Minter and Jay as they beat paths into the wilderness like lost Victorian explorers. He finished pouring in the orange juice and lemonade, then tipped some orange slices and apple chunks he'd chopped earlier into the punch bowl.

'Aren't you going to put a little something in there for the grown-ups?' asked Okeke.

'Absolutely not. This is to mitigate all that beer,' he said.

She shrugged. 'And that's very sensible of you.'

'Well, I might *say* it's got a little alcohol in to entice them into drinking it,' he said with a grin. 'So keep shtum!'

THE MAIN PART of the marathon gardening task was completed surprisingly quickly. By three o'clock, Minter and Jay, with a little help from Warren and O'Neal (both of them shamed by Lorna into picking up a garden tool to at least give them the impression they'd done something) had made his forty foot-by-forty-foot garden look as though a Brazilian logging company had been through it.

The ground was a battlefield of slaughtered stems, branches and upended roots. A couple of discoveries had been made during the process too: they'd uncovered an old stone fountain, that Jay had offered to load into the back of his van and take away, and a sinister-looking pile of old plastic dolls that Sully had enjoyed making tasteless, but funny, forensic-themed quips about.

'We'll gather up the brown-bin stuff, boss,' said Jay, 'and might as well bonfire the lot.'

Minter nodded. 'There's way too much to fit into a wheelie bin.'

'Thanks, guys,' said Boyd, surveying the wasteland. 'I just need Charlie Dimmock to come in and pretty it up.'

'She your type, then, is she, Boyd?' asked Sully. Emma snorted into her drink.

Five minutes later, a small bonfire was going halfway down the garden and Warren and O'Neal were feeding it branches and twigs one-handed while they smoked.

Work stopped for food. Boyd laid everything out on the dining-room table and pulled all the chairs outside for folks to sit on and eat off their laps.

The team queued up to fill their plates and refresh their beers and came out to sit in a contented circle in the afternoon sun.

'Thanks for coming, everyone,' said Boyd as the tailenders emerged with laden plates. 'That garden would have taken me days.'

'Or never at all,' added Emma.

'Well...' He shrugged. 'Yeah. Probably.'

'No probs,' said Jay. 'It was good to see you getting your hands dirty with that salad too, boss.'

The workers laughed and raised their beers. There was a chorus of 'yeah's and 'we noticed'.

Okeke nudged her boyfriend. 'He's not your boss.'

Jay shucked his huge shoulders. 'He's the Big Man. The Chief.'

She laughed. 'Yeah, but not *yours*.'

'Today, I'm not anyone's boss,' said Boyd. 'We're off the clock, folks. Eat, drink, enjoy.'

'Hey, Chie– Boyd?' started O'Neal. 'Why've you got such a big house? I mean, it's just you, the dog and Emma, right?'

'I picked it initially,' answered Emma. 'We wanted something that contrasted with the last place. Big rooms, high ceilings and stuff.'

Before Boyd could add to that, Daniel emerged from the kitchen doorway. 'You've got another guest,' he said, throwing the group a big comedy wink.

Charlotte walked out behind him. She had a large summer fruit Pavlova in one hand and a bottle of Pimms in the other. She Pavlova cotton dress and a broad-brimmed sun hat, and Boyd thought she looked perfect.

42

'Uh, good afternoon... *everyone*,' she said politely.

'Charlotte!' Boyd said, getting up quickly. 'I... thought...'

'Well, I wasn't sure what time you... wanted me here. So...'

He must've forgotten to give her a time too. 'Oh, fuck, I'm sorry. Didn't I say?'

'Dad?' said Emma with a friendly warning tone. 'Language?'

Boyd walked over to Charlotte and held his hand out for the Pavlova. 'Let's put that in the fridge and... get you something to eat and drink.'

THEY DISAPPEARED INTO THE HOUSE, leaving the garden silent for a moment.

Okeke turned to Emma. 'So... your dad has a lady friend?'

Emma looked at her, Okeke's brows arched with intrigue. 'Apparently so.'

'You've not met her?'

Emma shook her head. 'Nope. I have absolutely no idea who –'

'Good for him,' said Jay, quickly glancing from Okeke to Emma to check he hadn't just said the wrong thing.

Emma nodded. 'No, you're right. Good for him. It's about bloody time.'

∾

INSIDE, Boyd led Charlotte to the dining table, which looked as though a tornado had swept across it.

'I'm so sorry,' he said. 'I thought you weren't coming, otherwise I'd have held back feeding time.'

'Oh, that's all right,' she said. 'I wasn't sure if it was an invitation for lunch or tea. So I aimed for somewhere in the middle.'

'Ah, my bad. I messed up.'

She patted his arm lightly. 'Not at all. So...' She nodded through the dining-room window at everyone gathered outside. 'Are they your police force?'

'Yeah, they're my team,' he replied. He pointed out Emma. 'That's my daughter, Emma, and her boyfriend Dan. The rest of them may not look like it, but they're all detectives. Except for that odd one with the plum trousers. He's a forensic pathologist.'

'Gosh,' she said, gazing out at them.

He took that moment to study her face surreptitiously and realised just how pretty she was. Her auburn hair with a few early strands of grey was pinned up into a forties style. He caught a glimpse of her slender neck and angular jawline. Her eyes were dark brown, to the point of blending with her pupils, and the gentle flare of crow's feet and the pencil-line crease either side of her lips told him she was a habitual smiler.

He picked up a clean plate and piled it with salad, garlic

bread, a jacket potato and a couple of crispy-black sausages. She looked at the plate full of food. 'Oh, gosh! That's more than enough, thanks.'

'Can I get you a drink?' he asked.

'Just something soft to start with,' she said. 'I'd hate to make a fool of myself in front of your colleagues.'

'Oh, don't worry about them,' he said. 'Despite me telling them otherwise, they're all on their best behaviour.'

He served her some punch and then, carrying her plate, led her outside to meet the others. After a round of polite nods, Boyd gave up his empty seat and found some loose bricks to stack into a low stool beside her. The playlist had ended and the garden was quiet save for the sound of the parrot next door whistling away to himself and the crackle of the bonfire.

'So how do you and Dad know each other, Charlotte?' asked Emma.

She explained Ozzie's toilet infractions down on the beach and Boyd coming to the theatre for CCTV footage.

'Ahh.' Emma smiled at him. 'So he *can* make friends with people outside the office then?'

'As opposed to getting involved in punch-ups with them,' offered Sully.

The others laughed as Charlotte's eyes widened.

'Ignore him,' said Boyd. 'There's always a bit of argy-bargy with fieldwork. It goes with the job, I'm afraid.'

'What... punching?' she asked, frowning.

'Well, in my case, being punched mostly,' he said as the others laughed again.

Jay was about to speak, but Okeke nudged him discreetly.

Emma got up. 'I'm just going to put some more music on. Charlotte, do you have any favourites?'

'Oh.' She pursed her lips. 'I'm rather partial to a little Erik Satie, or umm... William Byrd on a day like this, but, honestly, don't mind me. Whatever everyone else wants to listen to.'

'The Manics for me,' Minter said to Emma, 'although you millennials are probably too young to remember them.'

Daniel smiled. 'Oh, we know the Manics,' he said. 'They're rock legends.'

'Nothing too blarey, Ems,' Boyd called out after her. Given Charlotte's suggestions, he didn't want the peace in the back garden being shattered by Nine Inch Nails or the Chemical Brothers.

Warren got up. 'Can I go get some more food, sir?'

'Bloody hell, Warren. Are you *still* hungry?' Boyd said, incredulous. Warren had been to the table several times already.

'I'm starving,' he said.

Boyd wafted his hand in the direction of the door. 'Fill your boots.'

'Me too,' said O'Neal, getting up and following him. Ozzie and his cone bashed their way to the front, helpfully showing both lads the way.

'Actually, I'm still a little peckish,' said Sully, hurrying after them.

Jay looked at Boyd. 'Mind if I...?'

Boyd nodded. He had been hoping he'd have a week full of fridge-cold leftovers to work through, but it seemed as though the table was going to be cleaned.

'I'm glad you brought a pudding,' Boyd said to Charlotte.

He looked around and saw that Minter was feeding the bonfire, Lorna standing beside him having a smoke and not too subtly admiring his bare back.

Okeke finally stood up. 'I'd better go in and make sure the kids don't squabble over seconds,' she said.

Boyd and Charlotte were left with a circle of five empty dining chairs and Daniel perched on a stool and intently scrutinising something on his phone.

Charlotte smiled. 'Was it something I said?'

He chuckled and sipped his beer. 'Bunch of gannets.' Although, to be fair, he was still feeling a little bit peckish too. 'I thought you might have had a change of mind?' he said.

Charlotte gave up trying to balance the plate on her lap while using cutlery and picked up one of the sausages in her fingers. 'On the contrary... I've been looking forward to it.' She took a delicate bite and began to chew it cautiously. She swallowed her mouthful and looked at him. 'These are delicious! What's in them?'

'Err... they're just Tesco's regular pork sausages,' he replied.

'Oh,' she said, 'well, they're utterly scrummy.'

Warren returned a minute later with an almost completely refilled plate. Then O'Neal, who was also clutching another beer.

'Who's your nominated driver?' asked Boyd.

O'Neal nodded at his girlfriend. 'Lorna.'

Lorna had a bottle of Stella in one hand, but it looked as if it was the very same one she'd been handed earlier. Anyway, she seemed far more interested in pointing out and discussing Minter's various tattoos with him than drinking.

Stormzy blared out from the dining room. It was hardly the chilled Sunday afternoon playlist Boyd had been hoping Emma would put on.

'Well, this is a very *cool* garden party,' Charlotte offered sincerely. 'The kind I've been to in the past have been all blazers, cricket jumpers and cucumber sandwiches.'

'What sort of –'

'You know, church fetes, work dos. Local charity things.' She grinned. 'Certainly no Stormzy playing.'

He did a double take. 'You know who this is?'

She winked at him. 'Maybe I'm younger than I said.' She got up. 'I might grab a naughty beer. Do you want one?'

He nodded, watching her as she walked towards the house. There was the slightest swagger in her hips, which contrasted with the hesitant little steps she'd taken into the back garden earlier. He wondered if Emma or Okeke had sneaked something extra into the mostly-non-alcoholic punch.

Daniel got up from his stool, his eyes still glued to his phone.

'You okay, mate?' Boyd asked.

He nodded absently as he headed off the uneven cobbled patio and onto the flattened wilderness towards Minter and Lorna. Minter had just dumped another armful of foliage on the fire and a cloud of white smoke billowed upwards into the blue sky.

Boyd shifted his bum from the improvised brick stool and onto the ground. He settled back against an old vinyl beanbag that he'd dug out of one of the back rooms. He wriggled until he was comfy and folded his arms up behind his head. After all that haring around this morning to Tesco and Homebase to buy briquettes, firelighters and food, he realised he was beginning to feel pleasantly chilled. He'd only had one beer so far, obviously a little stronger than his usual brand, but then he wasn't driving anywhere later. Another would be nice.

He looked up at the clear sky and the circling seagulls high above and even felt a bizarre neutrality towards them – for today, and today only, there was a negotiated truce between them, as long as they stayed in the sky and didn't start dive-bombing his garden for snacks.

He felt... good. *Really* good. When was the last time he'd felt this chilled and content? Years? Decades?

Charlotte appeared over him with a bottle of beer in each hand, the brim of her sun hat catching the sun and making the light flicker in his eyes.

'You look rather comfy down there, Mr Boyd,' she said, taking a swig from her bottle.

He started to get up. 'Do you want to...'

'No. No. You stay put,' she said, handing him his beer. 'Is there room for another, do you think? If I perch on the edge?'

'Uhh... sure,' he said, scooting over slightly.

She made an attempt to descend gracefully to the beanbag, but its apparent bulk was deceptive and she sank deep into it, ending up wedged against him.

'Ooops,' she said, giggling. 'I think that punch has got a little *goodness* in it somewhere. I'm feeling a little tiddly and I've only just sipped this beer.'

She pulled off her sun hat and removed a hairclip from the back of her head, quite literally letting her hair down. 'Oh, now... this takes me back.'

'To what?' he enquired.

She cocked her head as she tried to pinpoint exactly what and when. 'To my music college days,' she said. 'A whole lifetime ago.'

'Music college?' he asked, curious.

She nodded. 'I used to play the flute.'

The rest of the team began to drift back into the garden. Boyd decided to not mention the Pavlova in the fridge quite yet. After the vultures had been through that, they'd be down to just crisps and biscuits.

The playlist had moved on to Nile Rodgers and Chic, giving the garden a chilled festival vibe. Sully, of all people, had started dad dancing on the scorched ground beside the bonfire, beer bottle in one hand, waving his straw hat around in the other, his supernaturally pale skin beginning to redden in the sun.

'Do you and your colleagues party like this often?' asked Charlotte.

Boyd emptied his bottle with one long chug. 'It's the first time actually.'

He watched Okeke get up, dragging Jay over to the bonfire to join Sully who was dancing to Le Freak. It was soon evident that Jay's lumbering top-heavy bulk was completely unsuited to the activity.

He looked around and saw Emma chatting with the 'boys'. It seemed bizarre that his little girl was – give or take a couple of years – pretty much the same age as Warren and O'Neal. A couple of lads with the authority to arrest, charge and interview, looking right now like a couple of mischievous scallywags.

Daniel was squatting beyond the bonfire, still with his phone in his hands, Ozzie peering curiously over his shoulder. It seemed as though he was taking photographs of the trampled garden for some reason.

'I like this song,' said Charlotte. 'Fancy a dance?'

'What?'

'Come on,' she said, getting up off the beanbag. 'Stop acting ten years older than you are.' She grabbed his wrist firmly and pulled him up to his feet with all the grace and effort of a ship being launched from dry dock.

She led him to the trampled flora that had become this afternoon's improvised dance floor and – with Okeke's help, whooping and egging him on, and Jay, bare-chested and punching the air like some vast Nordic warrior celebrating a famous raid – Charlotte finally managed to get Boyd to swing his booty.

Boyd saw off the last of his CID team in yet another Uber cab at about ten. Ashburnham Road was going to have to play host to their various vehicles overnight since no one was anywhere close to being able to drive home.

Not only was everyone way over the legal alcohol limit, if they'd been pulled over they'd probably have tested positive for drugs. Now that he knew precisely why the party had become so lively – and, admittedly, so much fun – he couldn't help but detect that herbal, woody smell of weed everywhere.

Daniel, hero of the evening (or villain, depending on one's point of view), had spotted a cannabis leaf amid the mound of foliage that had been raked up, ready to go on the bonfire.

Boyd and his team had unknowingly harvested and lit up a king-sized joint of epic proportions in his back garden. Apparently there'd been a fair number of hardy *Cannabis ruderali* plants scattered among the brambles and the undergrowth. As a collective patch, Minter would have surely recognised what they were, but dotted around amid the nettles they'd been just been more jungle to hack.

Boyd went back inside the house and stepped over Ozzie, who was lying sparked out on the cool wooden floor in the hallway, another innocent victim of the collateral narcotics. In the lounge, he found Daniel and Emma tangled sleepily on the sofa, only half-watching Ben Fogle roughing it in some bitterly cold wilderness with yet another frazzled-looking survival nut.

And… there was Charlotte. Slumped in the armchair and completely out for the count. With her muddy bare feet dangling over one arm of the chair and her long frizzy auburn hair tumbling over the other, she looked like some hippy wild child recently returned from a week-long acid trip.

43

He lies defenceless on the snooker table, spreadeagled like a frog pinned out and waiting to be dissected.

'P-Please... please...'

The intruder raises a finger to his lips. Wagner is still playing loudly in the drawing room, but it seems that Sutton is hopeful his screams will be heard.

'No one can hear you, Arthur. No one's coming to help.'

'Who... who are y-you?'

'Joe,' is the reply.

'J-Joe?.... Joe who?'

'Stephen,' he says. 'George, Nigel... yes, call me Nigel if you like. My name really isn't that important, Arthur. Let's leave the asking of questions to me, eh? I'm in a better position to do so.'

Sir Arthur Sutton is absolutely terrified, but he's trying to maintain his pompous swagger. 'If you l-let me go... I won't go to... to the police! I –'

Sutton needs a little more convincing that this is serious. 'Nigel' leans over him and slices off the tip of his nose.

Sutton's scream is all but lost in the soaring operatic notes of Wagner's Die Walküre.

'So now, Arthur, here's my first question. Do you know why I'm here?'

Sutton shakes his head. 'If y-you want m-money, I keep s-some upstairs in –'

'Shhhh.' Nigel pulls up a stool and sits down beside the snooker table. 'It's not money. Try again. I'm almost certain you do know.'

'No... I... no... I... r-really –'

'All right, too difficult.' Nigel playfully slaps his cheek. 'Maybe I'll answer for you.' He winks at the old man. 'It's going to be quicker to get going that way, I think. I'm here because of your vanity project. Your book.'

The old man's face stretches with fear.

'Are you surprised you were found out? What did you think would happen, Arthur? Wandering around from one old club member to the next, waving it in their faces. People talk, you pompous idiot.'

Sir Arthur Sutton tries to spit defiantly in his face, but only manages to dribble onto his own cheek. 'I'm... a d-dead man anyway,' he rasps. 'I... I'm not scared of you.'

'This I heard. Motor neurone disease. Very nasty.'

'I'm... I'm not scared of you, you bastard! What have you done to Margot?'

'She's tied and gagged so we've got this precious time to ourselves.'

'If you've hurt her...!'

'Be quiet!' Nigel slaps his cheek hard. 'Now listen – we've got all night, and I will use that time to search every room in this house thoroughly. And once I'm satisfied I've got what I came for –' Nigel smiles – 'we'll be done.'

'What... what are you after?'

'Every single draft and page of this book of yours. Your notes. Your synopsis. Printed and digital. Notebooks, idea pads. We're going to make this book completely disappear tonight. Is that perfectly clear?'

Sutton nods.

'*Good. We're going to start with the digital stuff. Your computer password, please...*'

44

Day 11

Charlotte emerged from the guest bedroom and appeared downstairs in the dining room as Boyd was making coffee. She looked ashen-faced.

'What in God's name happened yesterday?' she asked, not meeting his eyes.

'We all got a bit accidentally stoned; some of us drunk *and* accidentally stoned,' Boyd said, pouring coffee into two mugs.

Charlotte groaned.

'It's okay. Everyone's in the same boat,' said Boyd. 'Would you like some coffee?'

'I...' Charlotte shook her head. 'I can't remember anything!'

She frowned. Quite beautifully, in fact, Boyd thought.

'Come and sit down before you keel over,' he said.

She took a seat at the table, then let her face fall into her hands. 'Oh, God... was I dancing? Dancing around a bonfire?'

He smiled. 'Barefoot.'

Charlotte looked down at her almost completely blackened feet, dark with soot and ashes. 'Oh my God!' She paused, trying to remember what else she'd done. 'So how did I get like that?' she asked eventually. 'Was it the punch? Was something put in my drink?'

'It was the bonfire actually,' Boyd explained. 'It seems that there were a bunch of cannabis plants in my garden, which were then burnt, by accident, on the bonfire.'

Charlotte shook her head. 'I've never done drugs. Ever.'

Boyd wished he could claim the same. He pushed her coffee towards her, and she lifted her head at the welcome smell.

'I've got to be off in fifteen minutes,' he said. 'Work.'

'Work?' Her eyes bulged. 'Oh, crap. I thought today was Sunday!'

EITHER BOYD HAD A STRONGER constitution than the rest of his team – which he very much doubted – or he'd had less to drink. After dropping Charlotte off at the White Rock Theatre and grabbing another black coffee from the CID kitchenette, he felt fine.

Almost.

The same couldn't be said for the rest of them as they washed up into the Incident Room like sorry pieces of cargo spill.

'We'll postpone the nine o'clock meeting to nine thirty,' announced Boyd. 'Go and get what you need from the canteen, everyone. And back here in twenty.'

He was greeted with a chorus of grateful moans.

He'd had a text from DI Lane to say that his train was delayed, and that he would get in to Hastings at about twenty past and grab a taxi from the station. So a half-hour delay seemed like the best outcome all round.

Left alone in the Incident Room, and having finally swapped numbers, he dialled Charlotte. She answered on the first ring.

'How are you doing?' he asked.

'My office is spinning,' she replied. 'I can't even bear to look at my monitor.'

'Well, if it's any consolation my crew are all pretty much the same way.'

'Bill? You must tell me. Did I do anything embarrassing? I simply can't remember anything after we started dancing around the fire like wild savages!'

He couldn't remember much either. Just fragments. Chances were that no one was likely to recall much, looking at the state of them this morning. 'No, I think we all just had a jolly good time,' he said, in what he hoped was a reassuring voice.

'I am so sorry,' she said.

'For what?'

'For my behaviour, the dancing, the... whatever I did or said.'

Boyd laughed. He had fleeting memories of Charlotte's hair flying Kate Bush-style as she pirouetted in the dirt like some wild first-year student at freshers' week. 'I think you're okay,' he said. 'But look – I should apologise. I had absolutely no idea about the cannabis plants.'

'Shhh,' she said. 'Won't you get into trouble?' She lowered her voice to a whisper. 'Honestly, I'm completely mortified, but I suspect I had more fun than I've had in a long time...'

LANE TURNED up just after half past nine, dragging his wheelie suitcase behind him. He took one look at the walking wounded around the conference table and grinned at Boyd. 'It's like a triage ward in here. Is this because of your barbeque?'

Boyd nodded. 'It's a long story and, trust me, you're better off not knowing.'

Lane appeared intrigued.

Boyd rapped his knuckles on the conference table. 'Okay, everyone, grab your notes and coffees and pull yourselves together.'

The door opened and Sully strode in, looking fresh as a daisy and dressed in his usual dark office trousers and pale-blue collared shirt. 'Why the delay? I was ready to start at nine.'

'We delayed for Lane,' said Boyd. 'His train was late.'

Sully's lips pursed into a Cupid's bow of scepticism as he regarded Warren, forehead flat down on the conference table. 'Of course you did.'

While Boyd was impressed with the CSI manager's recovery, he didn't think he could manage a duelling session with his chirpy, acerbic banter this morning. 'Take a seat, Sully,' he said wearily.

Sully pulled out a chair next to Lane. 'Looks like we're the only two compos mentis this morning,' he observed.

'Right then,' Boyd said. 'Hangovers to one side... please.'

'And the rest,' grumbled Okeke.

'Let's get this update started. We're on day eleven and Her Madge will be wanting a summary of progress on her desk by mid-morning, so let's get cracking. Minter, you've got more info on Sutton's activity in the days before his death?'

'Right, boss,' Minter said, making a Herculean effort to pull himself together. 'He made a couple of calls while he was still at his London place. I've traced the numbers. One is a company called Jupiter Books; that's a publishing company. The other is to a private residence –' Minter checked his notes – 'of one Elaine Lewis.' He looked up. 'If that name's familiar, it's because she's the wife of that MP who was killed in a hit-and-run four years ago.'

Boyd remembered it vaguely. There had been talk at the time that it was a hate crime. Chris Lewis was Green Party had been campaigning against the HS2 project.

Sully looked surprised at that. 'Sutton was talking to someone on the other side?'

'It happens,' said Lane. 'But usually only when they're up to something.'

'All right, Minter. Follow those up with a tactful call and see what Sutton was –'

'Excuse me?' Lane interrupted. 'This is where I'll have to step in.' He looked at Boyd. 'If this is parliamentary business.'

'And get your big black redacting pen out, huh?' said Okeke.

Lane's face twitched slightly with irritation, but he was quick to cover it with a patient smile for her. 'Hopefully not, but... Sutton does seem to have been evidencing erratic behaviour in his last few days. I've got to make sure he wasn't blabbering about material from confidential cabinet meetings.'

'*Old* meetings,' Sully replied.

'Yes, but still confidential old meetings.'

'I'll make the calls,' said Boyd. 'How's that? You can sit in and interrupt if you think we're stepping onto confidential turf.'

Lane nodded. 'Fair enough.'

'Okeke, anything on the SOC report from London?'

'Yes, guv.' She picked up a printed report from a file, several sections of which were marked with a highlighter. 'It was forced entry, but we knew that anyway. Fingerprints and DNA samples from the loft apartment match Sutton and Margot Bajek. The intruder obviously wore gloves and made a conscious effort not to lick anything.'

Sully chortled.

'Any indications on the purpose of the break-in?' Boyd asked.

'It still looks like an attempt to find something,' Okeke replied. 'Sutton's writing desk and filing cabinet at the flat were forced open. Some of his wall paintings were wonky, suggesting someone had had a look behind them, and, of course, the safe was open.' She paused. 'I'd say they were looking for something, rather than looking for Sutton.'

Boyd nodded. 'Which might fit with what we got from his literary agent on Friday.' He explained the purpose of Sutton's visit, to have her land his final book with a willing publisher.

'Is it possible that Sutton's book was simply too shit for her to want to be involved with it?' asked Sully.

'She hadn't read it. He'd only pitched it to her,' Boyd replied.

'She said she turned it down because it was potentially libellous,' Lane added. 'He apparently used barely fictional names, but was recounting allegedly real events. Using near-miss or made-up names would still be breaching the Official Secrets Act.'

'So what was the book about?' asked O'Neal.

Boyd shrugged. 'We don't know.'

'Who knows what old skeletons are lying in government cupboards?' said Sully. 'Sutton was in the cabinet in 2015 to 2016.' He glanced to Lane for confirmation. 'That overlaps the Brexit campaign, Russian money being pumped into various campaign fund accounts.'

Lane nodded. 'And much as I'd like to expose all that gerrymandering –' he shrugged – 'my job is to keep all conversations and communications made under the blanket protection of the Official Secrets Act redacted, I'm afraid.'

Boyd sighed. 'Right.' He turned to Warren and O'Neal. O'Neal was in better shape to deliver an update. 'How are we doing with our mystery man?'

'It looks like one of the public CCTV cameras caught him after he'd been into a shop, sir.'

'Which shop?' Boyd asked.

'We don't know,' O'Neal replied. 'He's carrying a shopping bag for about a hundred metres down the street and then he ditches it. The thing is... he got out of his car without one.'

'Do we have a reg' for the car?'

'No, the car park was old school,' said O'Neal. 'Pay and display.'

'Bollocks,' said Boyd. He turned to Lane. 'Pelham parking is pay and display only.' He turned back to O'Neal. 'Okay, so this bag?'

'We're going to try and ID the shop this morning, sir, aren't we?' O'Neal nudged Warren, who groaned and nodded.

'Good. ASAP, please. If we get a shop, we may get a decent internal cam image, maybe even a credit card transaction.'

'Want me to help them?' asked Lane. 'That seems like our best lead so far.'

'Yeah, do that. I want as many eyeballs on that as we can. Sully? Any luck with social media?'

'The activity log from Facebook came in this morning. It's a rather dense forty-page PDF that shows every link that Sutton clicked in the last ninety days, complete with unique follow-on trackers.'

'Meaning?' asked Boyd.

'Basically where he looked next.'

'How detailed are we talking?'

'It's just that, essentially the next thing he clicked on. Nothing more. Where he used his iPhone or any other iOS product, is blocked, but his laptop or Mac...'

'What about access to his iCloud storage?' asked Lane.

Sully shook his head. 'Still waiting on their legal people to grant us a password. Apple are extremely tight on this sort of thing.'

'Okay, well, share that Facebook PDF with Okeke. Two pairs of eyes should make shorter work of it.'

Boyd looked around at his team. They weren't exactly on top form this morning. There wouldn't be much in the way of insightful speculation going on, that was for sure. 'Right, you all have tasks,' he said. 'Crack on. Minter?'

'Boss?'

'Can you give me those two phone numbers and details, please?'

45

'This is Matthew Berringer. How can I help?' The man sounded as if he'd just drifted back from a leisurely lunch break at some private member's club.

'This is Detective Chief Inspector Boyd, Sussex Police CID. May I speak to you about your recent conversation with Sir Arthur Sutton?'

The prolonged pause was more than a giveaway. Boyd had the conversation on speakerphone, and he and Lane were alone in the spare meeting room. Lane nodded at Boyd. He was obviously thinking the same thing.

'You spoke with Sir Arthur Sutton days ago,' prompted Boyd. 'What was the conversation about?'

'Can I ask why you want to know?' Berringer replied finally.

'Are you aware that he's dead?' Boyd asked.

'Yes. I saw it on the news the other day. Awful news about the house fire.'

'Murder, in point of fact,' added Boyd conversationally. 'He was tied down, tortured and then burned alive.'

'Good God!' To Boyd's ear, the alarm in his voice sounded genuine. 'Are you...? Jesus! Are you sure?'

'Oh yes, we're sure. And, from Sir Arthur's phone data, we know that he spoke to you a few days before his death. Can you tell us what that call was about?'

There was another telling pause. 'He... well, the chap was trying to pull in a favour.'

'What favour?' asked Boyd.

'To publish a book. I should hasten to add that we're not his regular publisher. Hardline normally put out his stuff.'

'But he chose you for this one. Why?'

Boyd could hear the tension in Berringer's voice. 'I... I don't know. But I said it wasn't for us.'

'I'm presuming he came to you because this was a different kind of book. Did he explain any of its contents to you?' Boyd asked.

'What? No. Absolutely not!'

'Then how would you have known it's not for you?'

'Look. Lloyd, is it?'

'Boyd.'

'Boyd, Sutton was not a close friend of mine. I didn't particularly like the man, nor his books for that matter. And I really didn't appreciate him sidestepping our normal manuscript submission process to speak directly with me. That's not how publishing is done.'

Boyd suspected that that was probably exactly how it was done for those with connections. 'His literary agent, Maria Webster, spoke to him a day before you,' Boyd continued. 'She said his book was controversial and potentially libellous against some senior political figures.'

'Well, I don't know,' Berringer said firmly. 'Like I said he didn't get as far as telling me anything about its contents.'

'She said she wouldn't touch it for fear of legal action,' Boyd said.

'As I said... I wouldn't know.'

'Or worse...'

Boyd could hear a flutter in the man's breath. The rustle of air caught and amplified.

He's scared. Genuinely scared.

'Mr Berringer, is there something in Sutton's book that we need to know?' Boyd wondered if the man was spooked enough to roll over for him. 'He told you what his book was all about, didn't he? And I'm guessing you decided you wanted nothing to do with it? Isn't *that* what happened?'

'No. That isn't what happened. And I'm done talking with you. Please don't call this number again.' Matthew Berringer hung up.

Boyd looked at Lane. 'What do you think?' he asked.

'I think he knows what's in the book. And I think he sounds fucking terrified.'

Boyd nodded. That was exactly what he thought too. He looked at the other number. The one for Elaine Lewis, the wife of Chris Lewis, ex-Green Party MP for Norwich South.

Lane watched as a couple of uniformed PCs walked past the interview-room window. 'Sutton talking to the wife of an opposition MP... That wasn't like him,' said Lane.

'You knew him well?'

'No... but he was a career boy, wasn't he? Keep the party whip happy, say all the correct party soundbites on *Question Time* or *Marr*. I didn't think he was a troublemaker.'

Boyd dialled the number and the phone range half a dozen times before going to voicemail. He left his number and hung up. 'Well, I guess we'll have to wait and see what that was all about.'

'So what the hell do you think happened with Sutton?' asked Lane. 'What's your gut instinct?'

Boyd crossed his arms and sat back. He sighed deeply. 'I think it's probably quite simple. He had something he wanted to spill before he died. He tried and now he's dead.'

'It must be one helluva secret,' said Lane. 'Which really begs another question.'

'What?' Boyd asked.

'If you find out what it is... is *your* life going to be in danger too?'

Boyd looked at his phone, dark-screened on the table. 'Look, I'm just after the bloke who killed Sutton and very nearly killed Bajek. I'm more than happy *not* to get involved in some shady conspiracy.'

46

B oyd got his return call twenty minutes later on his way back from the toilet. He stopped in the hallway to answer it.

'Hello, I'm returning your call?' It was a woman's voice. She had a flat, lifeless tone.

'Mrs Lewis?'

'Yes, Elaine Lewis,' she confirmed.

'Thanks for returning my call,' Boyd said.

'Is this about Chris? About what happened to Chris?' she asked.

'I believe he died in an accident,' said Boyd. 'A hit-and-run?'

'It wasn't an accident,' she spat. 'He was assassinated. Murdered. *Some* of the papers implied that; the rest said he'd been drunk and just stepped in front of a car. I'm sure you can guess which papers were which.'

'*Murdered.*' He said the word evenly. Not in a questioning tone, but not a statement either. 'What makes you so sure?'

'Because he wasn't afraid to be a *proper* journalist. To tell the truth.'

'He was an MP, wasn't he?' Boyd said, momentarily confused.

'Yes. He was,' she said. 'But he also followed and wrote up stories.'

'For who?'

'He was freelance. Some of his articles ended up in the *Independent* or the *Guardian*. But mostly he blogged. Most of his stuff was too... *much*, even for the papers.'

'What kinds of things did he write about?' Boyd asked.

'Corruption. Cronyism.' She laughed gently. 'He'd have had a field day if he'd been alive to write about all those Covid PPE contracts.'

'Was he working on one of these corruption-type stories when he died?'

'No. I don't think so, anyway,' she said.

'Can you remember what he was up to?'

He heard her sigh. 'He was at Westminster all day. Then he rang me to say he was meeting someone at the pub on his way home.'

'Who? Another MP?' Boyd asked.

'I don't know.'

'Did he give you a name?' he pressed.

'Oh, yeah. I always wrote down in our diary who he was seeing. As a habit.' She sneezed. 'Excuse me. Yes, it was a Darren *something*. I didn't write down a surname,' she replied.

'Do you think it was social?' asked Boyd. 'Or did this Darren have something?'

'I don't know. I never got to speak to Chris again.' She sniffed. 'What's this about? Has something new come up?'

'Were you contacted by Sir Arthur Sutton recently?'

'The MP who died in a house fire? Yes. He wanted to know if he could have access to the archive for Chris's old blog. I told him he couldn't, obviously.'

'Did he say anything else?'

'No. It was brief.' He heard her take a sharp intake of breath. 'And now he's dead too.'

'We're investigating the fire,' Boyd said.

'Do you think his death could be related to Chris's?' she asked.

'That's something we're trying to work out, Mrs Lewis,' Boyd replied.

BOYD HAD JUST STARTED READING up on Chris Lewis, MP, when the tail end of his hangover hit and the page of Wikipedia text started to make him feel queasy. He stepped out of the Incident Room, went down the hallway and took the stairs to the entrance lobby, hurrying out into the sunshine to catch some fresh air.

'Finally hitting you, is it, guv?' Okeke was leaning against her car and enjoying the heat from the bonnet and the rays as she smoked.

He wandered over, careful not to get too close; the last thing he wanted to inhale right now was cigarette smoke.

'Oh, guv,' she said. 'We've found something that might be worth flagging.'

'What?' he asked.

'Sully and I started picking through Sutton's activity log and, apart from clicking on the usual clickbait articles and liking the usual memes, he accepted a friend request. He doesn't seem to have accepted many, but he did accept this person. The day before his death.'

Boyd raised his eyebrows. 'Was there any communication?'

'Facebook don't share message exchanges. But, yes, there's a marker indicating that communication was established.'

'You got a name for me?' he asked.

'Darren Jacobs.'

'Riiight,' he said slowly, pulling out his phone.

'Guv?'

Boyd hit redial.

'Hello?' It was Elaine Lewis.

'Hello, Mrs Lewis. It's DCI Boyd again. That person your husband saw for a pint the night he was killed? Does the name Darren *Jacobs* ring a bell?'

'Yes,' she replied. 'Yes, that was it.'

'Thank you,' he said. 'I'll be in touch again if there are any further developments.' He hung up and looked at Okeke. 'Finish your fag. We've got some googling to do.'

47

Boyd made the coffee while Okeke logged into LEDS and pulled up a Google search on her phone.

His personal phone buzzed with a text. It was from Charlotte.

How are you doing? I think I might die

He was about to ping back a reply when Lane came into the kitchenette looking to make himself a fresh coffee. 'Aye, Okeke said you'd be in here. Something come up?'

'Yeah. I think we may have something.'

'What?'

Boyd spooned granules into his and Okeke's mugs. 'A name that links Sutton to the murdered MP Chris Lewis.'

Lane's brows lifted.

'Don't get too excited yet,' Boyd replied. 'But he could be a person of interest.' He poured the water into the two mugs, then waved the kettle Lane's way. 'Want some?'

Lane nodded. 'Boyd, mind if I huddle in with you and Okeke?'

'There's no point until we know if it's something or nothing,' said Boyd. 'The CCTV trail is still our best shot at getting a close-up or even a transaction. I want you to keep on it with Warren and O'Neal; hopefully we'll meet in the middle with enough evidence to make an arrest and talk to him at leisure.'

Lane looked unhappy. 'But if there's anything –'

'If there's something that looks anything like an official secret, I'll call you over so you can tell us to forget all about it, okay?'

Lane's face flexed with irritation. Then he managed a smile. 'Sure. Whatever you say.'

Boyd returned to Okeke with two mugs of steaming coffee. He placed them on her desk, pulled up an orphaned office chair and sat down beside her. 'Right, what have you got for me so far?'

'You've only been gone five minutes,' she said, laughing. 'You're obviously feeling better.' She pointed to her phone. 'Darren Jacobs – he's a bit of an East End wide boy, an ex-freelance journo, mostly for the *News of the World*. One of the low-scoring scalps taken during Operation Weeting, the phone-hacking inquiry. He got fifteen months inside for his part in it.' She gestured to the monitor. 'Since then, he set up as a PI, but that seems to be a very murky shop window.'

'What do you mean?'

She shrugged. 'A man-for-hire who knows how to find out things. Break into phones, accounts, computers... A general shithead for hire.'

'A hack in more ways than one,' muttered Boyd. 'Elaine Lewis thought it *might* be "business" over a pint.'

'Elaine Lewis?'

He explained... and as he did he realised they'd gone from a random Facebook friend request to a potential suspect within the space of an hour.

'Any recent form?' he asked.

'Nothing since he was busted during Weeting. He's obviously been a lot more careful since. Or got a lot better at doing what he does.'

'Okay,' Boyd said. 'Find an address for him. We're going to pay the slippery bugger a visit.'

48

'Here you go, Boyd.' Lane handed him a bacon roll and a large paper cup. 'It's the best cure for a hangover: a bacon butty and builder's tea. Learned that in the army.'

Boyd had asked for black coffee.

'It's tea, mate.' Lane saw him looking sceptically down at it. 'Honestly. You don't want black coffee. Tea rehydrates you.'

'Thanks,' said Boyd. 'In full disclosure mode, I'm going to have to admit this is also a weed hangover.'

Lane wide-eyed him.

'It was a case of accidental second-hand smoking.' He explained what had happened.

Lane shook his head and laughed. 'The whole ruddy team?'

Boyd nodded as he took a bite from the bacon roll. 'Let's just hope Her Madge doesn't choose today to drop an RRT on us.'

'Or a bleep test,' said Lane. 'By the state of him, I don't think even Minter would pass it.'

Boyd took a slurp of tea. It had been sugared generously

and was surprisingly refreshing. 'Thanks for dragging me outside,' he said to Lane.

'It was that or a mercy killing,' Lane replied, laughing.

'So, how was *your* weekend?' Boyd asked.

Lane sucked in the fresh salty air and gazed out at the sea. 'It could've been better,' he said. 'Joshua took a bad turn.'

'What happened?'

'He's... well, he's basically very sick.'

Boyd brushed away the last trace of his hangover self-pity. 'Jesus. What's wrong?'

'He has infantile Batten disease. It's not that common. It's um... it's not too dissimilar to what the late Mr Sutton had. It's a progressive neurodegenerative thing,' Lane said.

'My God, I'm... Jesus... I'm so sorry, mate.'

Lane shook his head. 'It's very early stages, and I'll get another ten years with him. That's something. But it's one long, downward slope.' He sipped his tea. 'The worst part is that it was a gift from me.' He turned to Boyd. 'It's congenital. I've got it and handed it down to my son. That's where my epilepsy comes from,' he added.

'Ah, shit.'

'It's mild in adults. Occasional seizures, a higher risk of dementia in later years, but... yeah, not terminal. Not like the infantile variant.'

Boyd experienced a strong wave of an emotion he couldn't put a label on. Guilt? Pity? Remorse? Maybe it was all three. He'd been dragging around his own burden of grief for three years, lost in his own self-pity, from which he was only now emerging – while the man leaning on the rail next to him was staring down the barrel of ten years of heartache... before the grief even started.

Christ. Life's crap didn't come down as a fine rain that dampened everyone evenly; for some it came down like a fucking meteorite. Boyd couldn't begin to imagine what it must be like for Lane, stuck alone in that shitty B&B room every night and yearning to spend that limited invaluable time with his son.

'Lane... why the bloody hell did they send you down here?' he asked.

'Like I said, I'm not match-fit for close protection work any more. I didn't really have a choice.'

'Look, stay at my house,' Boyd said. 'Until this is done. You'll get to carpool with me, you lucky bastard, and there's a free dog thrown in.'

Lane laughed. 'No. That's really kind, mate... but I'm good. I get to Skype him to sleep every night. And, to be honest, after that I'm done in. Bed and a book is the most interaction I can manage.'

'Well, the offer's there. Any night. Okay?'

Lane nodded. 'Thanks, Boyd.'

The pier was busier today than it usually was. A week's worth of warm, sunny days seemed to have convinced everyone that summer was finally going to stick around for a while.

'Boyd, you're a good man. Can I give you a word of advice?' Lane said.

Boyd looked at him. 'I'm listening.'

'Just be careful.'

Lane had said that before. And Hatcher had too for that matter. 'What is it that I don't know?' Boyd asked. 'Why is everyone telling me to be careful?'

'I'm just saying you could be pulled into the orbit of some very influential people. Sutton was very well connected.'

'Yes, I know that.' He could see Lane was picking his words carefully.

'He ate at the *top table*, you know... if you get what I'm saying?'

Boyd shook his head 'Not exactly, no.'

'I'm saying... if Sutton had some compromising material on

someone and that's how he ended up ...' Lane left the end of his sentence hanging in the air.

Something about Lane's words felt deliberately nuanced to Boyd. 'Is that advice... or a warning?'

'It's advice, mate. I've done enough close protection in my time to overhear some hair-raising one-sided conversations.'

'Such as?'

Lane shook his head. 'You know I can't.' He sipped his tea. 'All I'm saying is, let's find Sutton's killer. But let's not go *twanging* the threads of some large spider's web.'

49

'So, guv, this Darren Jacobs is a bit of a hard one to get hold of,' said Okeke. 'I've tried his mobile number and it keeps going to voicemail. I've tried the website that advertises his PI services. No luck. I've had Met uniforms knocking on the address he lists. No answer.'

'His home address?' Boyd asked.

She shrugged. 'They've gone there too and there was no answer either.'

'Christ.' Lane's caution was still ringing in his ears.

This Jacobs, as far as Boyd was concerned, was now part of Sutton's case and potentially also that of Chris Lewis. Perhaps he was their killer, or – more worryingly... since they couldn't get hold of him – maybe another victim.

'All right. Well, he's now earned himself my full attention,' Boyd said. 'He's who I want to speak to ASAP. Jacob's number appeared on Sutton's call logs. So can we get Jacobs' call log? Find out who his provider is.'

'Will do,' said Okeke, jogging back to her desk.

'Minter?'

'Boss?'

'Dig up what you can on Chris Lewis. The investigation into his death. Any leads, friends, associates, especially anyone called Darren or Jacobs.'

'Righto.'

'Warren? O'Neal?'

Both detectives looked his way. Boyd beckoned to them and they came over to join him. Warren was still looking green around the gills.

'Where are we at with the CCTV?'

'We've ID'ed the row of shops that the guy must have gone into, chief,' replied O'Neal. 'We're going down there tomorrow to check out their in-store cameras.'

'Is there a reason you can't go right now?'

They glanced at each other, then shook their heads. Boyd spread his hands. 'Then why am I still looking at you? Off you go! Run!'

Jesus. He realised Lane's friendly lunchtime advice had actually shaken his cage. On Friday afternoon, this had felt like a murder: plain and simple. Someone with a grudge, somebody Sutton had fucked over. Perhaps even – though, having met them, admittedly a bit of a stretch – Henry Sutton after his dad's money or Hermione Sutton out to settle a score for her mother. But, since talking to Elaine Lewis, Boyd had a strong feeling he'd been looking very carefully in the wrong direction all along.

And Darren Jacobs... Wherever you are, sunshine, we will find you.

On a whim, he called the IC ward at Conquest Hospital, hoping that the news on Margot Bajek was going to be better. If she could talk, then they might be able to get a description, perhaps even a half-decent identikit image of her assailant to compare against the last photo of Jacobs. But the news wasn't promising. She was back on a ventilator and, of course, sedated.

It wasn't until gone four in the afternoon that Boyd

suddenly remembered he hadn't replied to Charlotte's text. He dialled her number and after several rings she answered.

'Hullo,' she replied warily.

'Sorry, Charlotte. I've only just got your message. It's been a bit busy here this afternoon. Are you okay?'

There was a pause. 'My head is pounding,' she said eventually.

'Yeah, I'm not feeling so clever either,' he confessed.

'Poor Mia was starving hungry when I got back this morning and not at all happy. I took her for a quick walk on the beach and she seemed better after that.'

'You've been home?' he said, surprised.

'Yes. I had to for Mia,' she explained. 'But also, Bill, I stink of... drugs! I'm sure my colleagues think I'm a... a complete pothead or whatever the term is.' She chuckled. 'Plus, my feet were still dirty. I turned up to work late, looking like someone raised by wolves. I didn't explain why I had to go – I just said I had to pop home for a bit.'

Lane drifted past Boyd's desk, pulling his wheelie suitcase behind him.

'One second,' said Boyd. He covered the mouthpiece. 'What's up?' he asked Lane.

'I'm off. I need to check in. I want to make sure I can get my delightful B&B room back,' said Lane. 'See you in the morning.'

Boyd nodded and waved him off.

'Sorry about that,' he said, returning to his call with Charlotte.

'That's okay. Sounds like you're still busy there,' she said.

'We are. It's typical, isn't it? It's right near the end of the day and things in the case have dialled up a notch.'

Okeke had got out of her chair and was heading his way. She looked as though she had a bee in her bonnet over something.

'Look, Charlotte, I'm sorry. Can I call you back? Something's –'

'That's fine,' she said quickly. 'I'll speak to you soon.'

'See you on the beach,' he said, and hung up.

See you on the beach? He winced. He'd meant it to sound funny – but feared that this time it had come out sounding more like a 'see you around' or worse: 'Don't call me...'

'Guv,' Okeke blurted out. 'I've found Darren Jacobs.'

'*What?* Where?' Boyd stood up.

'I filed a DPA request form against Jacob's number before lunch and just received the data. They were super quick.' She placed a printed page on his desk. 'He'd turned his phone on and made a short call this morning.'

Boyd looked at the printout. Jacobs had made a call that had lasted a little over a minute at 11:17. Beneath the logged call was map indicating a triangular area of overlapping signal-collation rings and a red dot in the middle.

'Where's that?'

'Cobham Services. It's a Days Inn hotel.'

'Shit.'

'Yes, and it's okay, guv. I've called there already. He's booked in tonight, until the end of the week. In fact, he was booked in for all of last week too.'

'Under his own name?' he asked.

She nodded. 'I presume he's on some PI job.'

'Or in hiding?' he said.

'Well, he's doing a rubbish job if he checked in without using an alias,' she pointed out.

Boyd looked across the room. Minter was chatting with Warren and O'Neal about their errand; they were pulling on their jackets and listening avidly to Minter's, no doubt sage, advice.

He grabbed his phone and pulled up Maps. 'Cobham

Services, eh? We could be knocking on his door in an hour and twenty minutes,' he said quietly.

Okeke took the last steps towards him. 'Guv? You sure?'

Lane's earlier advice about not twanging the threads of a spider's web was still troubling him. All the same...

'Yeah, I'm sure. Let's go.'

50

O'Neal insisted on taking a pool car, since his was still parked outside the guv's place.

'We could have walked,' said Warren. He'd actually been looking forward to some fresh air.

'Right – we could have, or we can drive, mate.' O'Neal glanced at Warren as he signalled left and swung onto the seafront main road. 'Don't forget we'd have to walk all the way back to the station before clocking off. And you don't exactly look A game.'

'I've never felt so shit,' Warren conceded.

O'Neal shook his head and chuckled. 'You seriously telling me you've never done weed before?'

Warren shook his head. Nor was he ever likely to again after today's ordeal.

'What you're experiencing, young padawan, is just the booze hangover. Don't blame the weed.' O'Neal grinned. 'We sank quite a few brewskies as well yesterday. Anyway,' he pointed out, 'the day's nearly over and you can die quietly at home while your mum gets your dinner.'

Warren groaned. O'Neal's boy-racer driving wasn't helping matters.

O'Neal signalled right, swung into Pelham car park and headed left towards the arcade and the pitch and putt, finding a space and quickly zipping into it before anyone else could take it.

Warren climbed out of the cool car into the late afternoon warmth – only to be greeted by the smell of frying doughnuts coming from the arcade, and frying fish from the chippy over the road. Not exactly the kind of fresh air he'd been hoping for.

'You're such a drugs noob,' said O'Neal with cheeky wink.

Warren looked at him. 'You actually smoke that stuff outside work?'

'Well, obviously not these days, mate, but yeah... I've rolled a few in my time back in my party days.' He steered Warren towards the nearest zebra crossing. 'Right, game faces on,' he said as he scanned the tired old seafront apartments above the shopfronts for any useful cameras.

Across the road were the shops they were canvassing: a mixture that included chippies, souvenir shops, ice-cream parlours, a corner shop and a café. Warren readied himself for the onslaught of foody odours soon to be coming his way.

As usual, Okeke drove while Boyd pondered. The northbound A21 was still relatively empty, but the other side was starting to show signs of the homeward-bound commuter herd.

'So let me get this straight,' she said. 'We're door-knocking some old hack who may have killed Sutton and this other MP guy?'

'He's an ex-journo, not a hitman,' replied Boyd. 'Plus, he's in a Day's Inn, not some remote campsite.'

'Yeah, see...' Okeke said, 'I was going to mention the camp-site. You don't learn from your mistakes, do you, guv?'

'At least I didn't go alone,' he said, grinning guiltily.

'If you'd gone to see Nix alone, you'd have been dead, guv. Thank God my Jay was there to save you from them.'

Boyd nodded; that was a debt of gratitude he'd yet to prop-erly settle.

'Speaking of them...' she said.

By '*them*', Boyd knew she meant the Russians.

'What are you going to do with their little gift? It's in your safe still, I presume?'

'It's evidence; we may have need to use it sometime,' he said.

'*Sometime* being when exactly?'

He turned to look at her. 'What if ten years from now some-one's trying to build a case against Rovshan Salikov and his dirty millions?'

'You'd actually whistle-blow? On a Russian crime boss?'

Boyd shrugged. 'If I've still got the evidence, I've got the option. And don't forget Her Madge. I mean, if she decides I know too much, or decides I'm a problem –'

'You still think the Chief Super's bent?'

'I don't know, Okeke,' he said, sighing, 'but, if she's not, she was definitely leaned on by someone higher up. Either way, there may come a time when she's looking for someone to throw under a bus. If she picks me, I want something I can use as leverage.'

51

Warren chose the souvenir shop because the thought of stepping into either Sid's Seafront Chips or Meg's Happy Baps filled him with the dread that he might hurl his lunch halfway through an interview.

The shop dinged old-style as he entered and it was mercifully cool inside. Plastic buckets and spades, cheap bath robes and T-shirts filled the windows, but inside it was essentially a corner shop with papers and magazines, snacks and booze.

The shop was busy with teenagers clasping cans of energy drinks while browsing a pick-and-mix display. Warren weaved his way through them to the counter.

'Excuse me?'

The woman sitting on a stool behind it didn't look up from her phone. 'Can I help you, love?'

He pulled out his warrant card and she glanced his way, then suddenly sat up straight. 'No,' she said quickly, 'we don't sell cigarettes or drinks without ID. I promise.' There'd been a crackdown last month, particularly among the shops along the seafront. Flack's county lines operation had flagged up the issue of young drug runners who were, it seemed, feeling ballsy enough to swagger in and ask for alcohol and packs of twenty.

'I'm here about something else,' said Warren. He cleared his throat to make his voice sound a little deeper and more commanding. 'There was a serious crime recently in the Silverhill area. We believe the suspect may have entered one of the shops along the seafront prior to the crime. I presume you have internal CCTV?'

The woman turned round and pointed to a camera above and behind her. 'That's the only one inside, love.'

'Right. Well, we're gathering the data stored from just over a week ago. Do you mind if I have a look at your camera feed?'

'Sorry, I don't know anything about them, love. Should I call my manager?'

Warren, a little annoyed by her constant 'love's, kept his mouth shut and nodded.

The woman dialled a number on her mobile and listened to a brief, pretty much one-sided conversation. Then she hung up. 'He's coming down, sweetheart. He'll be here in half an hour.'

Warren managed to supress an eye-roll, but not a tired sigh. 'All right,' he said. 'I'll be back in half an hour.'

Next door was a traditional tobacconist. The shop windows were obscured with a green sign like a bookie's: *Mallard's Traditional Pipes and Smoking Products*. As Warren entered, he was greeted by the smell of turpentine and the sickly tang of finely blended tobacco. He wondered if the odour was somehow faked, to induce the right ambience inside the gloomy shop. It had the look of a seedy gentleman's club, or at least what Warren imagined one would look like.

He approached the counter and found himself facing an old man who looked very much like a part of the shop itself. 'Yes, sir?'

Warren repeated his spiel.

'Yes, now, we do have one of those close-circuit camera

devices installed. Let me go and find the manual for it.' He smiled. 'I haven't actually bothered to look at what it films since I had the thing put in. You say it *stores* it all?'

Warren smiled. 'Yes, that's right.'

'Like a... like one of those video-tape recorders?'

'Yes, digitally. Typically on site. There's usually a removable storage platform.'

The old man's watery red eyes widened with this new-found knowledge. 'Well, I never. How very clever.'

OKEKE PULLED off the motorway slip road and took the first exit off the roundabout, into the confusing, multiple-choice of access lanes to the parking area for Cobham Services.

She found a parking spot in front of the cheerful sky-blue front of the Days Inn hotel. It was twenty past five and the service station was busy with commuters stopping on their way home, and tired-looking travelling sales executives with jackets over their arms and loosened shirt collars, resigned to their fate of a service-station dinner and a Netflix series on their tablets.

Boyd had brought up a picture of Darren Jacobs on his phone. It was a picture taken from 2013, when a non-descript Andy Coulson and the flame-haired Rebekah Brooks were walked into court accompanied by a phalanx of Murdoch-hired legal heavyweights.

Jacobs had been one of the many hacks caught up in the phone-hacking scandal. Though he'd been too low down the food chain to have any particular mention in the newspaper reports, nevertheless he'd been one of the surly faces going to court to receive their verdicts and sentences.

'It's from about ten years ago,' he said, showing her the picture.

'Nothing more recent?'

He shook his head. 'No. But it's more recent than the one on LEDS. Either he's doing his best to stay off the radar or he's not learned about flattering Instagram filters.'

Okeke grimaced at the picture. Jacobs was never going to be a poster child for anything. He had a boxer's nose – one that looked like it had been slammed into a wall a number of times – and a protruding Punch-and-Judy-like chin. The flattened nose, unkindly, served to make the chin look even more pronounced.

'Even if he's put weight on, I suspect we're still going to recognise him,' said Boyd.

'You're not kidding.'

He took his seatbelt off and opened the door. 'Let's try the hotel first. If he's not in his room, then he's probably lurking somewhere in the service station.'

Boyd led the way into the Days Inn and flashed his warrant card at the receptionist. 'You've got a Mr D. Jacobs staying here. Which room is he in, please?'

'Fifteen,' she said almost immediately.

'You didn't have to look that up?' said Boyd. 'I'm impressed.'

'He's been with us for ten days now,' she replied. 'Our residents are usually never more than one night.' She looked at Boyd, then Okeke. 'Is he a terrorist or something?'

Boyd shook his head. 'No. We just need to ask him a couple of questions.'

'Fifteen's through those double doors,' she said, pointing them out. 'Halfway along on your left.'

'Thank you,' Okeke said, heading towards them.

'Do I need to do anything?' the woman asked. 'Call a manager?'

Boyd shook his head. 'No – it's all fine. You've been very helpful. Thank you.'

They went through the swing doors and down the carpeted corridor, passing wafer-thin plywood doors that leaked out the theme tune of *The Chase*, one door after the other. They stopped outside room fifteen, and Boyd pressed one ear to the door.

'Anything?' whispered Okeke.

He shook his head. Gone were the days when one could peer or listen through a keyhole. It was one of those card-swipe doors. 'Nothing.'

He knocked on the door gently and nodded at Okeke to say something. She frowned with confusion. 'What?' she whispered.

He mouthed what he wanted her to say. She pulled a snarky face at him, but did what he wanted all the same.

'Room cleaning, sir? Is it okay to come in?'

They waited for a response. Still nothing.

'All right,' said Boyd. 'The service station it is, then.'

52

D arren Jacobs recalled how scared the young girl had been. And how brave. Or perhaps how naive she'd been to come and tell him what she knew.

'They did something to her, those bastards. Amy thought she was going to a posh ball.' The girl who'd spoken to him was Laura, Amy's best friend. *'She said it was going to be tuxedos and ball gowns. She'd been so excited.'*

'Who invited her?' he'd asked.

Laura shook her head. 'She didn't tell me his name. Only that his family were really wealthy and he was good looking.'

'Did you meet him?'

'No.'

'But you think something happened to her at the party?'

Laura had nodded. 'And I think they covered it up.'

He never had managed to follow up on Laura's story. The shit had hit the fan with the Leveson inquiry and *News of the World* the following week and soon after he'd found himself serving time.

He'd come across poor Laura again years later, hanging from an overpass. And even then he'd thought it too crazy, too ridiculous to be a part of her conspiracy theory. The post-mortem had found her to be intoxicated. Years of crying wolf for her dead friend had taken its toll, he'd thought. Nothing to see here, people, move along.

Now here I am, shitting myself in a fucking Days Inn.

He should never have taken that fucking phone call from Sutton. His psoriasis had flared up again with the stress, and his feet were scab-covered and raw with the endless scratching.

Sutton – dead. Shit.

And if they checked Sutton's phone... They'd know he'd called.

They'd know that I know what happened.

He reached down and scratched at his bare feet again.

53

'Hold on a flipping moment,' said Okeke. 'Isn't *that* him?'

She pointed through the plate-glass window to a smokers' area outside. Boyd had been busy studying the Starbucks and Burger King queues, having scanned the indoor eating area with no luck so far.

She punched his arm to get him to look the other way. 'Over there! Outside!'

Boyd turned to see a sad-looking picnic table and bench surrounded by discarded cigarette butts and an overflowing cigarette bin. There were two men smoking there: one standing and chatting animatedly on his phone in a work suit, that end-of-the-day look about him – his tie hanging loose around his unbuttoned collar.

The other was sitting down and staring out at the parked cars. He had a khaki canvas fisherman's hat on that looked naked without an array of fishing tackle, a red-and-white polka-dot short-sleeved shirt and a pair of baggy tracksuit bottoms. He was fidgeting, one hand vigorously scratching at one of his flip-flop-clad feet, the other holding a cigarette to his lips. He was sucking, puffing, sucking, puffing clouds of smoke like a diesel train ready to set off.

He turned his head slightly and Boyd got a better look at his face – that distinctive boxer's nose. He'd grown a thick dark beard over his Punchinello chin, though.

'That's him,' confirmed Boyd.

'So what now?'

'Gently, gently. He looks about ready to jump out of his skin.' He suspected if they approached him together looking exactly the way they did, like two plain-clothes coppers on a mission, he'd bolt like a rabbit.

'Go out there,' Boyd said. 'Light up, share the table. Chat him up.'

'*What?*' Okeke yelped.

'I mean, just chat. *Nice day, mate? Lovely weather we're having* – that sort of thing.'

'And what are *you* going to do?'

'I'll approach from behind. When I'm close enough, you can – very unthreateningly – introduce yourself. If he runs, hopefully he'll run right into me.'

Her expression relaxed. 'He doesn't look like the hitman type, does he?'

'Not even close,' replied Boyd.

Okeke emerged from the service-station concourse and pulled out her packet of Berkeley Blues. She slowed down to a casual amble as she neared the table where Jacobs was sitting.

'Mind if I...?'

He looked up at her and shrugged absently.

She sat down on the bench just as the man on the phone finished his cigarette and tossed it away, all the while 'yup-yup-yupping' on his phone.

Jacobs looked as though he'd forgotten he had a cigarette between his fingers; the ash had built up and was drooping forlornly.

'Oh, shit,' said Okeke suddenly. 'You got a light, mate?'

Jacobs stirred from his thoughts and patted his pockets. 'Uh, yeah.' He passed her his lighter.

'Thanks,' she said. She lit up and took a couple of eager puffs – and that wasn't acting, she was busting for a smoke. She handed it back. 'Thanks. You're a lifesaver.'

'No probs.'

Okeke noticed Boyd making his way towards a different exit and then lost sight of him.

'Are you all right?' she said.

He glanced at her. 'What?'

'I said, are you okay?' She wondered for a second if she'd buggered this up by being too forward.

'Yeah, fine,' he answered, finally waking up to the fact his fag had nearly burnt down to his knuckles. He took a pull, then tossed away what was left.

Shit. He's finished.

'Only...' Okeke continued quickly, unsure what was going to come out of her mouth next. 'You look really stressed out.'

He shot her a suspicious look. Okeke nodded down at her feet and did a little tip-tap with her shoes on the ground.

'I'm fine. I've got things on my mind.'

'Ah.' She nodded and smiled. 'Fair enough. A fag's a good way to clear your head, right?'

'Right,' He nodded in return, then made to get up from the table.

Shit. Come on, Boyd!

'I've got problems,' she blurted. Jacobs didn't appear to acknowledge her. 'I think someone's...' she began.

And now Jacobs stopped. Bitten by curiosity. 'Someone's what?'

'Someone...' She had no idea what to follow that with, then decided a version of the truth might work. 'Someone's after me.'

His frown deepened as he remained poised to stand up.

'My husband. If he finds me...' She realised she'd better push some emotion into the words. 'I-I think he m-might hurt me.'

Jacobs shrugged. Curiosity satisfied. He got up.

'Please!' Okeke managed to whimper. 'Don't go.'

'I've got my own shit to deal with,' he replied.

'Then just –' she grabbed her packet of cigarettes – 'have a cig with me. Please?' Okeke was surprised at her performance. 'I... just for a minute or two. You don't need to talk to me. Just...'

Jacobs tilted his head, evaluating something. He sat back down. 'Okay. For a couple of minutes. Then I've gotta go.'

Okeke smiled gratefully. She pulled one of her Berkleys out for him.

'No, I'm good,' he said, waving it away. 'I'm smoked out.'

She finally spotted Boyd approaching casually from behind – although his idea of casual seemed to be an unconvincing pantomime of whistling tunelessly, hands shoved in both pockets.

'So... is your fella here?' asked Jacobs. 'At this service station?'

She needed to spin this out for a few moments longer. 'I... I left him this morning. But... I know he'll follow me.'

'You got a smartphone?' he asked.

She nodded. 'An iPhone.'

'Then you should probably set your Location Services to off,' he said. 'Otherwise you might as well be leaving a trail of signal flares behind you.'

She nodded, acting shocked. 'Oh my God... you're right.' She pulled her phone out and pretended to swipe away at the screen.

'It's under Privacy,' he explained.

'Right. Yeah. Thank you. Oh my God.' She fiddled with it for another few seconds, then looked up. 'Thank you!'

Over his shoulder, she could see Boyd was now dawdling barely ten feet away, looking as innocuous and invisible as the Angel of the North. He took his final steps to the picnic table and sat down on the same bench as Jacobs. Jacobs lurched at the jarring weight landing beside him.

'Hello, Darren,' Boyd said quietly.

Jacobs' eyes suddenly bulged with fear. He scrambled to get up, but Boyd grabbed his wrist firmly. 'It's okay, mate. We're police.'

'Sorry,' said Okeke. 'I was distracting you.'

Jacobs spun round, looking for signs of anybody else closing in on him.

'It's just us,' said Boyd calmly. 'If you call out or struggle, then you're going to attract more attention: security, uniformed cops and comms traffic. I'm thinking you don't want that, right?'

Jacobs shook his head. 'Who... who sent you?'

'No one. We're investigating a murder,' replied Okeke. 'Your name came up.'

Jacobs looked at her. 'Sutton's murder. Right?'

She nodded.

He turned to look at Boyd. His eyes rounded. 'You don't think it was me, do you?'

'No,' said Boyd. 'I don't. But I think *you* might have an idea as to who it was.'

'We know Sutton reached out to you, not long before his death,' added Okeke. 'You got a reason why that might be?'

Jacobs' eyes were almost comically wide, swivelling between her and Boyd.

'He... he was ready to talk to me,' said Jacobs.

'Jesus Christ.' Boyd sighed, exasperated. 'Talk about *what*?'

That question and the frustrated way in which he said it seemed to relax Jacobs a little. 'Promise me. You really are just coppers?'

54

Warren and O'Neal returned to the Incident Room with a number of small evidence bags containing a variety of memory sticks. It was half five and DS Minter was on his way to the kitchenette with his dirty mug.

'Evenin', lads. You were gone awhile.'

O'Neal lifted the bags. 'Shop CCTV footage. What do I do with them, sarge?'

'You mean... can I dump them on the desk and register them as evidence tomorrow cos I want to knock off?'

O'Neal nodded sheepishly.

'No such luck, sunshine. You need to enter them in the evidence log, and then drop them into Sully's office, or whoever's on duty, for them to extract the files?'

'First thing tomorrow?' O'Neal tried again hopefully.

Minter shook his head. 'Evidence chain, O'Neal, isn't it? You know that. You and the boy wonder get it done, and *then* you can bugger off home.'

O'Neal sighed. 'Oh, come on.'

'Whose name is filled in on the bags?'

Warren showed Minter. 'O'Neal's.'

'Ah, well, it's got to be you, then. Hasn't it, O'Neal?' He smiled at Warren. 'You on the other hand are free to go.'

'Oh, for fuck's sake!' O'Neal looked at Minter. 'It's only my name because I was holding the Sharpie!'

'Fancy a quick pint at the pier? Seeing as we're both off duty...' Minter asked Warren.

Warren grinned. 'Yeah, actually. Sounds good.'

'Oh, piss off,' said O'Neal. 'The pair of you.'

55

Jacobs opened the door to his hotel room and waved them both in. Boyd wrinkled his nose at the stale odour filling the room. He could see pants and balled-up socks on the floor and a couple of KFC cartons on the side table.

'Not expecting guests, I see,' he said drily.

'I've been extending my stay every day,' said Jacobs. 'Sorry about the mess – I've not let the cleaners in for a couple of days.' He pushed some dirty clothes off the end of his bed and snatched up his underwear, tossing it into an open overnight bag. 'Sit. Sit.'

Boyd sat on the end of the bed. Okeke took the chair beside the small desk.

'You want tea? Coffee?'

Okeke looked at the kettle and the plastic tray it sat on, surrounded by torn open and empty coffee and sweetener sachets. 'No, we're good, thanks.'

Boyd gestured for Jacobs to take a seat too. He looked as though he wanted to stay on his feet, ready to run. 'Please,' said Boyd. 'Just sit down, take a breath and *calm down*.'

Jacobs relented and finally let himself sag down into a chair.

'Right, that's better,' said Boyd. 'Now, this isn't a formal police interview. I'll start by saying we're not after you as a suspect, okay? We just need to know what's going on.'

'I need protection!' said Jacobs quickly. 'They'll come for me next. I know it!'

'Okay, well, let's begin with that. Who are *they*?'

'The Lambda Club.'

'And who's that?' prompted Boyd.

Jacobs dropped his head and laughed despairingly into his lap. 'A dining club.'

'A *dining club*?' Boyd repeated, not sure he'd heard that right.

'It was an Oxford dining club,' said Jacobs. 'For rich boys who liked to party.' He leant to one side and dug into his overnight bag, pulling out a tattered blue cardboard folder. 'I presume you've heard of the Bullingdon Club?'

Okeke shook her head. Boyd had a vague recollection, but since Jacobs had started talking he wasn't going to interrupt.

'It's a rich boys' dining club at Oxford. Eton, Harrow, Charterhouse old boys only. You must have seen that famous photo? The one of a young Boris, a young Cameron, a young Gideon Osbourne – all posing in tailored cavalry-style evening jackets?'

That was as much as Boyd knew, other than that they had a habit of smashing up the restaurants they frequented.

'Well, the Lambda Club was the same kind of thing. Another private club for well-connected young prats. They also liked to call themselves the "Oxford Spartans".' Jacobs shook his head. 'They saw themselves as the elite. The crème de le crème.'

'Right,' said Okeke. 'Charming.'

'I didn't know anything about them until I started to dig into Laura Khan's death in 2017.'

'Who's she?' Okeke asked.

The name sounded familiar to Boyd. He vaguely recalled a suicide.

'We'll get to her,' replied Jacobs. 'Let's start with the Lambda Club. They had these once-a-year initiation parties for new members. Like that old Bullingdon thing of sticking your cock in a dead pig's mouth for shits and giggles. But, you see, initiation nights aren't really about the piss-up and laughs.'

Boyd thought that was exactly what they were about – drunk young brats arsing around. He shrugged. 'So what are they about, then?'

'They actually have a more serious purpose,' Jacob's said. 'They're about creating a bond, a code of silence. It's about forcing everyone present to partake in some act that could, in the wrong hands, be compromising, reputation-ruining. Shagging a dead pig's head is exactly the kind of old-boy nonsense they indulged in to ensure a code of silence, to ensure a "*you scratch my back and I'll scratch yours*" arrangement exists between members of the group. That's what Initiation Night is all about.'

'So... the Lambda lot had their very own version of the pig's head thing, did they?' Boyd asked.

Jacobs scratched absently at his left foot. For the first time Boyd noticed how sore and scabbed they were. As he scratched, flakes of dry skin cascaded onto the carpet.

'So?' prompted Okeke.

Jacobs sighed. 'So... on this one Initiation Night, something happened. Things went too far.' He reached into his folder and pulled out a photograph of a young woman. 'This is Amy Cheetham.' He handed it to Okeke, since she was closest. 'She was a first-year student at Oxford. She was invited as a plus-one and had no idea what kind of party it was.'

Okeke passed the photo to Boyd. He found himself looking at a girl only a couple of years younger than Emma. A girl who beamed a smile at the camera that spoke of a travel bag full of big dreams and plans for the future.

'She never came back to her halls. She went missing,' Jacobs said.

'And no body?' asked Boyd.

Jacobs shook his head.

'Was there an investigation?' Okeke asked.

'Of course not. None. It remained a missing persons case until it quietly dropped off the radar.'

56

'I reached out to Sutton about five years ago. I knew he was a member of the Lambda Club at about the same time that Amy Cheetham went missing,' said Jacobs. 'I managed to doorstep him with that question. Face to face is always the best way.' He shrugged. 'If you don't get an answer, you can still get a cheeky reaction photo.'

'And?' Okeke pressed him.

'He looked like he'd shit himself right there on the doorstep. Didn't tell me anything – but he took my card.'

'Okay,' said Boyd, 'and we've got Sutton's phone record that shows he rang you very recently.'

'He did. Yes.'

'Why? Why after all this time?' asked Okeke.

'He was ready to spill everything,' Jacobs said.

'We'll get to that in a minute,' said Boyd. 'I want to know how Chris Lewis fits into this. I spoke to his wife and she said that he went to have a drink with you the night he was killed.'

Jacobs nodded. 'I wanted Chris to partner up with me on the story. He had credibility. I, being a convicted *News of the World* hack, *didn't*, obviously. I told him my suspicions, which weren't much to go on, to be honest – but it was enough to bring him in.'

'Someone must have been watching you,' said Boyd.

'Yeah. When I found out the next morning that Chris was dead –' he reached down and scrubbed vigorously at the heel of his foot – 'it scared the fucking shit out of me.'

'So what did you do with the story?' asked Okeke. 'Over the last five years, I mean.'

'Absolutely nothing,' Jacobs replied. 'Zero. I was petrified to go near it. Then Sutton rings me up, out of the blue, discloses the whole bloody thing, and tells me to get it into the papers if something happens to him.' Jacob's grin turned into a jittering laugh. 'And look what happened to him.'

Jacobs pulled out a newspaper cutting from his cardboard folder. Boyd recognised it as the *Mirror*. The picture was the one of the fire engine's rear sticking out of the driveway, the two stone eagles and the low flint wall.

He laid the cutting on the writing table, then reached into his folder and took out a glossy photograph of a motorway overpass, which he placed next to it.

'This is where Laura Kahn supposedly hung herself,' he said. 'I'll explain who she was in a minute. I took this picture right after the police managed to cut her down.'

Boyd stared at the two images sitting side by side. 'Shit,' he murmured.

'You see it?' Jacobs said.

Boyd pointed to the overpass. Barely detectable among the other graffiti tags was the same inverted 'V' symbol that had been sprayed on Sutton's wall. He picked up the images for a closer look.

'The Greek lambda symbol,' Jacobs said, nodding. 'The symbol the ancient Spartan warriors used to have on their shields.'

'The Spartans,' muttered Boyd.

'But why would they do that?' asked Okeke. 'Why indicate they were involved?'

'It's a warning, isn't it?' Jacobs replied. 'One hidden in plain sight. A reminder to past members that what happens in the club stays in the club.' He scratched at the thick thatch of dark bristles covering his chin. 'Or else...'

'That's crazy,' said Okeke. 'It's right there, for everyone to see!'

'Indeed.' Jacobs held his hand out, and Boyd passed the photo and the cutting back to him. 'For everyone to see and yet not see. But for those in the club... it's like a huge fucking burning cross. A reminder. *Keep. Your. Mouth. Shut.*'

Boyd was beginning to get goosebumps. 'So you said Sutton told you everything?'

Jacobs nodded. 'He was there. On that Initiation Night. And he gave me a list of names of the other members who were there too.'

'The night Amy Cheetham went missing?'

'Yes.' Jacobs nodded again. 'That poor girl, Amy Cheetham, *was* the initiation ritual. And Laura Kahn was her best friend.'

57

'There, there, Sir Arthur... It's all done. It's all deleted and burned. That wasn't so bad, was it?'

He studies the pitiful man cable-tied to the snooker table. Stripped naked. He's a deplorable specimen of a man to have once considered himself 'a Spartan'.

'Your memoir is against club rules. You know the deal. What happens in the club stays in the club.'

'It... it's a... just a novel,' Sir Arthur Sutton whimpers. 'You bastard...'

'It was a novel. Now it's nothing.'

'Nigel' sits on the corner of the table. It's gone two in the morning. He's been here for over six hours. Pushing his luck, dawdling. But he's curious...

'What did you think was going to happen when you started running around with it? Did you honestly think they were going to let you blast it all out there?'

Sir Arthur shakes his head. 'I made a mistake...'

'Oh, you really did.' Nigel leans over him. 'You thought, I'm dying, so what the hell can they do to me? Yes?'

Sir Arthur licks his lips. 'I... I'm sorry... I...'

'Well, this is what happens. They send for me. And here's the thing. My job isn't just about silencing telltales; it's about convincing everyone else to keep their mouths shut too.'

'What... what are you... please? It's done. I won't...'

'Shhhh.' He puts a finger to Sir Arthur's lips. 'I know what your plans are. You're planning to go to Switzerland, to Dignitas. End things before it gets unpleasant.' He smiles down at the man. 'I know all your plans.'

'Then... then you... you d-don't have to kill me! I'll be dead s-soon.'

'Yes, I know. But there's many a slip 'twixt cup and lip, as they say. A last-moment confessional? Can't have that. No... I'm afraid tonight's your night.'

He can see that Sir Arthur's trying to muster some fuck-you courage, but it's pitiful. Really pitiful. He's pissing himself a little as he pleads, 'Do it, then, you b-bastard. Put a f-fucking bullet in me!'

'Well, that's the thing. I can't make this too easy. The others have to know... that it's an awful way to go. You know... if you talk.'

He stands up, goes to his rucksack and pulls out a red plastic twenty-litre jerrycan. The petrol inside sloshes around near the top.

'Oh... God... no! Please!! PLEASE!'

He uncaps the jerrycan as he approaches the old man on the table and sloshes some over his naked body. The man's pompous bluster has completely vanished now.

58

The Duck and Pike was one of those pubs in the middle of nowhere along a nondescript section of A road, with no homes close enough to call it their local. The kind of pub that countless thousands have driven past over the years and idly wondered how the hell they've managed to stay in business.

It was the perfect pub, therefore, to meet in.

He pulled into the car park and saw only one other car. A Jaguar. *So much for being discreet.*

He entered the pub's side door to the sounds of Tammy Wynette playing softly on the pub speakers and the howls of a bloodhound that seemed to have free roam of the place.

It was empty save for a young woman behind the bar, counting bottles of something, and a lone customer, a distinguished-looking man in a dark-blue suit. He was sipping a gin and tonic beside a crackling fire.

He approached the man. 'Hello, George.'

George looked up and smiled. 'What are you having?' he asked.

'Nothing. I'm driving,' he replied pointedly.

'Very sensible.' He set his drink down on the small table beside him. 'So, we should talk, T.P.'

T.P. sat down on the other side of the table. 'I'm concerned, George.'

'Well, we *all* are. We all are,' George said.

'There has to have been a better way to silence Arthur. I mean... burning his house down?'

'Our chap had to,' George replied, picking his drink up again. 'There's no knowing how many hard drives or notebooks he had hidden away in the nooks and crannies of that monstrosity of a house.'

'It's attracted far too much attention,' T.P. said.

'It'll settle down. Yesterday's fish-and-chip paper, you'll see.'

'Sussex Police have put a murder squad on this, George.'

'Well, of course they have. It was clearly arson. But look – I've put in a gentle little word to hobble the investigation and I'm sure something far more newsworthy will pop into the headlines soon enough.' George smiled. 'There's nothing quite like a timely distraction, right?'

'I don't like it,' T.P. said.

George's patient smile faded. 'Perhaps if they could teach a little *self-restraint* in the cloisters, common rooms and class-rooms of your expensive schools... we wouldn't have awful bloody messes like this to tidy up?' he pointed out.

T.P. nodded. 'I was very young, George.'

'Yes, you were,' he replied. 'A stupid, arrogant, entitled boy who couldn't keep his dick in his pants.'

'Now listen...'

'No. *You* listen!' George snarled softly. 'This *will* be tidied up. And you will have me to thank for the rest of your political career. And you *will* do as you're told for as long as you're useful to the party. Then, when we decide it's time for you to bow out, you'll do it gracefully. Is that understood?'

T.P. nodded. He *was* grateful to George. The Chief Whip

was very much like a party concierge – a Winston Wolf character, there to pick up the pieces. To keep things tidy.

'What're you going to do now?' T.P. asked.

'The less you know, the better it is for all of us,' George replied. 'Go home to your wife. Put this out of your mind. Concentrate on your career... Do what we say and all will be well.'

59

Boyd and Okeke headed back down to Hastings. Most of the M25 they spent in thoughtful silence, then as they headed southwards on the A21 Okeke finally spoke.

'Guv... We're fucked.'

'*We're* not fucked,' he replied stonily. '*They* are fucked. Their reputations will be fucked, and if there's any bloody justice a fair number of them will end up inside for conspiracy to murder.'

'Jesus, though...' she whispered. 'There's a serving cabinet minister in that list...'

Boyd glanced at her. He wasn't sure how many names on that list she recognised, but the Defence Minister was the biggest one. Not being a keen follower of politics, there were other names he *vaguely* recognised: a member of the House of Lords, several Commons backbenchers – one of them he was sure had been caught out in the PPE procurement scandal post-Covid.

Jacobs' scribbled list of names was a sobering roll call of establishment figures. It was incendiary. And he'd refused to hand it over to them until they promised to help protect him.

They'd moved him to another hotel, a Travelodge nearby, and, while Okeke booked him in under a pseudonym, Boyd bought a cheap pay-as-you-go phone for him to use. For a man who'd weaselled the secrets out of dozens of celebrity phones, he'd been appallingly lax with his.

'So what's the next step?' she asked.

'Well, *he's* safe for the moment, but... I dunno. I'm not sure what *we* do next.'

'The team?'

Yes. He trusted Minter, Sully, the lads. But the more people they shared Jacob's story with, the greater the chance it would spill into hearing range of someone less helpful. Of course, there was a flipside to that argument: to go large and take it to a whole load of international news agencies.

But then he was pretty sure one of the names on the list was the senior editor for the BBC's news department, though he wasn't certain about the others. Between them, how many other media outlets did they own shares in, sit on boards of? It would make sense for them to do their homework first.

'Let's sit tight on this for tonight. I need to think about how we go forward,' he said at last.

'Guv?' She glanced sideways at him. 'We've got a list on us of a bunch of powerful, influential men who are complicit in the murder of two women and two men!'

'Allegedly,' Boyd said. 'And the second they realise they're on a list, they'll be hiring legal counsel and flying abroad. Or worse.' He didn't need to remind her about Sutton.

'My God,' she whispered. 'Is this really how things work now? But we're being careful, right?' she said.

'Very,' he replied.

'No one else, then?' she said.

'Agreed. Let's both sleep on it.'

'That includes Emma, by the way,' she pointed out.

He looked at her. 'And Jay.'

'Deal,' she replied.

Great, he thought. Another bloody secret to tuck into his proverbial safe.

~

HE GOT HOME at nine to find Emma bubbling with excitement. She waited until he'd ditched his jacket over the back of a chair and plonked himself down on the sofa next to Ozzie.

'I've got a new job,' she said.

'Oh, yeah?'

'Yeah, at the Lansdowne Hotel. Bookings and reception.'

'That's great, Ems,' he replied absently.

'Yay, me,' she said, deflated by his lack of enthusiasm.

'Sorry, Ems,' he said. 'It's been a bloody long day.' He got up, crossed the lounge and gave her a bear hug. He felt her release the hold, but he wasn't done yet. 'I'm so proud of you, Emma.'

'Oka-a-ay, Dad, no need to go all mushy. It's just a job.'

He let her go and returned to the sofa. 'Yeah, well. You'll smash it. When do you start?'

'Tomorrow, actually.'

'Wow, that's quick.'

'I walked in this morning and asked if they had any vacancies...' She grinned. 'Five minutes later I'm doing a frickin' interview.'

'What time do you start?'

'Seven. Which reminds me...' She looked at Ozzie. 'What are we going to do about Oz Bear?'

'Well, how long's your shift?'

'Six hours. I finish at one. So, it kind of means leaving him alone at home for the mornings. Do you reckon he'll be okay?'

Boyd looked at him. Ozzie was sparked out across two of the three cushions, head hidden by his cone of shame, paws twitching as he pursued and dismembered something in his sleep. 'I think he'll be fine. I get the impression he spends most of the morning on here, looking out of the window and keeping an eye on who's doing what.'

She nodded. 'Pretty much. He's a very good neighbourhood watch.'

'If I leave for work at half eight, he won't be alone for too long.' Now they had cleared the back yard, he could see their garden was contained within a high brick wall at the back and two robust fences either side. 'Maybe we can see if Parrot Lady next door will let him out into the garden for a bit.'

'On nice days,' she agreed. 'Not when it's raining, though, right?'

'Let's see how it goes, I guess.' He yawned. He wasn't tired; in fact, he was almost trembling with the adrenaline still tumbling around in his blood. He desperately needed an early night. He needed to run Jacob's revelations through his head to try to work out what the hell he and Okeke should do next.

'Look, I'm knackered,' he said apologetically. 'I'm going to hit the sack.'

'Oh, okay,' she said.

He noticed a bottle of Malbec and two glasses on the side table. 'Sorry, Ems, I'm really flat out.'

'Sure,' she said, smiling. 'No probs.'

'And if you're getting up at sparrow-fart o'clock –' he nodded at the bottle – 'you'll probably want a clear head. What if we have a pub dinner tomorrow night to celebrate?'

'That sounds good,' she said more cheerfully.

He was lying in bed ten minutes later, alone. Ozzie had elected to stay put on the sofa.

'Julia?' he whispered to the vacant pillow beside his. She was the only person he could admit this to. The only person to whom he could permit every façade to peel away.

'I'm fucking scared.'

60

Day 12

Chief Superintendent Hatcher encountered him in the canteen. As far as Boyd was aware, she *never* used the canteen. Which could only mean that she'd come up here to find him.

She tapped his arm gently and spoke quietly. 'My office... five minutes?'

'Ma'am.'

Five minutes later, he knocked on the door to her office and entered. It was just the two of them this morning. Sutherland was presumably still off work.

'Sit down,' she said.

He closed the door and took one of the seats in front of her desk.

'Can I see your private phone and your work phone?' she asked.

Boyd shrugged and dug them out. She took them from him

and carried them over to a display cabinet, slid the glass door to one side and put them inside, next to a crystal trophy of some sort. She dug out her own phone and put that in too, alongside his, and slid the glass door shut.

She returned to her desk and very deliberately unplugged her desk phone and closed the lid of her laptop so that it went into sleep mode.

'Boyd. You and I are going to talk very candidly. And entirely off the record. All right?'

'Ma'am?' Well, this wasn't how he'd envisioned his start to the day.

'And this is going to be a conversation between two private citizens, not two police officers, okay?'

He nodded.

She smiled. 'So you can drop the "Ma'am" for the next five minutes.'

'Okay.'

Hatcher sat back at her desk and took a deep breath. 'I'm being leaned on to hinder your investigation into Sir Arthur Sutton's death. There's no other way of putting it. Someone up top wants a very specific conclusion to this case. An act of aggravated burglary that led to a brutal assault and manslaughter, which the perpetrator then attempted to cover up with a fire.' She straightened a fountain pen lying on her ink-blotter.

Boyd was stunned into silence by her candour.

'I need you to acknowledge that you heard what I said and understood me,' she said, looking straight at him.

'Um, yeah, I... understand,' was all he could manage.

'Good.'

'But... I can't just...'

She nodded. 'I know.' She pushed the pen across the blotter. 'We're in a difficult position, you and I. Potentially career damaging. I know you have... questions... about my integrity...'

'Ma'am, I haven't –'

She raised a hand to stop him. 'We don't have time for this, so let's cut the bullshit. You think I steered the Nix investigation into the long grass. Right?'

He nodded.

'Okay. And I happen to know *they* sent you a warning. So...' She spread her hands. 'We have each other over a barrel, so to speak.'

He was reluctant to acknowledge that verbally. *Is she recording this conversation?* He gave her the slightest nod instead.

'I'm going to admit to you that I was ordered to deflect the Nix case. And I did.' She sat back. 'There! I've said it. All right? If I'm recording this conversation, I've just admitted knowingly perverting the course of justice. So, for God's sake, can we both speak plainly *now*?'

Boyd took a deep breath. 'All right.'

'Good.' She let out a deep sigh. 'It'll make what I have to say, a lot easier.' She sat forward. 'I'm going to phrase it this way... We're in a transition period between the old guard and the new guard,' she began. 'It's a difficult time – a transition like this. You want to make sure you stay on the good side with whomever is taking over.'

'Taking over what?'

'The establishment.'

'I'm not sure I understand,' Boyd said.

'You're not an idiot. I think you do. Old Money is being replaced by New Money. We opened a Pandora's box in recent years, opened our doors to a lot of very rich and very dirty people.'

'You're talking about... *Brexit*?'

'I'm talking in broad terms, Boyd. We're a little island out on its own now. To paraphrase someone else's metaphor: a lamb has separated from its flock... and the wolves are hungry.'

'By the wolves... you mean?' asked Boyd, not entirely sure he was keeping up.

'Laundered money. Dirty money. And much of it is Russian. England has become a haven for grey currency. That's what's keeping this country running now, like it or not.

The money's coming in fast. It's buying influence and, to be blunt, its outbidding old influence.'

'Old influence being?'

'You know exactly who I mean. The old boy network. The charming, bumbling public school elites who have been running the show since...' She paused, laughing bitterly. 'Well, I suppose since William the Conqueror.'

'History isn't one of my strong subjects,' said Boyd.

'Well, it is mine. I did a degree in it. And it's a subject that illuminates the future as much as it does the past. Things are changing here, and changing fast. We have a new elite setting up home. And they have more money and more influence than the old boys.'

'So we're swapping one set of bastards for another, then? Is that what you're saying?'

She smiled. 'It's a lot easier talking plainly, isn't it?'

'It helps,' he admitted.

'So... all that said, I'm being politely asked, by the old guard, to influence the outcome of this particular investigation.'

'Just like the Nix case.'

'Yes, only, unlike the Nix case, I'm inclined to ignore this request.'

He hadn't been expecting that. 'What?'

'Follow this case wherever it goes, Boyd. If it leads to the front door of some Knight of the Garter or some House of Lords grandee, I don't care. I'm not going to stop you nor pull you off the case.'

Boyd stared at her, unsure as to how to respond.

'Don't look so shocked, Boyd,' she said. 'What you need to

understand is that at my rank and upwards, *neutrality* isn't an available option. You are part of a solution or part of a problem. You're on one side or the other.' She was fiddling with the fountain pen again. 'There is a changing of the guard, Boyd. The old Junta is being replaced with the new... and the best way to demonstrate one's allegiance to the new ones is to help put the old ones to the sword. And this is not a hill that I'm prepared to make a last stand on. Fuck them.'

So... she sat back. 'How is the investigation going?'

Just like that? From casually admitting to gross misconduct, to asking for an update within thirty seconds?

'We have a potential lead, a journalist,' he said cautiously.

'With a story, I presume?'

'Yeah. In a nutshell – a rich boys' initiation party. A female student was drugged and raped by a number of them. She died from a combination of the narcotics and alcohol.'

Her mouth dropped open as he explained most of what Darren Jacobs had told them yesterday – holding back his name and where precisely they'd stashed him.

'My God,' she said. 'The *haute monde*, they can't help themselves, can they?'

'Sorry?' he said, wishing she'd stick to English.

'Those *born* into it.' She shook her head, looking genuinely disgusted. 'The "little people" mean nothing to them. I want you to nail those bastards, Boyd.'

On that point, it seemed, they were in total agreement.

'So this informant, Boyd, is he safe?' she asked.

He nodded. 'For the moment.'

'Will he interview willingly?'

'I think so. If he's protected.'

'Well then, for goodness' sake, bring him in!' She got up and rounded the desk. 'And, for the love of Christ, do it *now* and do it *discreetly*.'

She went over to the cabinet where she'd placed his

phones. 'Take DI Lane with you. He's trained in close protection. Just in case.'

'Can... he be trusted?'

She turned to look back at him. 'What do you think? You've been working with him.'

'He seems straight,' he said.

'Okay. Well, don't make a big fuss about it. You and Lane go and get him.' She looked at her watch. 'And you'll be back for lunch.'

'Yes, ma'am.'

She returned his phones to him. 'Plain talking.' She managed a faint smile. 'It's rather refreshing, isn't it?'

'Yes, it is.'

'Good, well... hopefully that's the last time we'll need to have a conversation like that. Now let's get your informant here asap.'

61

'Not that I mind being whipped off my feet and whisked away to some surprise spa retreat, but...' Lane turned to look at Boyd as he drove past the eagles standing guard to Sutton's ruins and headed up London Road and out of town. 'Where are we going?'

'We got a lead yesterday after you left to check into your B&B,' Boyd replied.

'And?'

Boyd found himself evaluating on the fly. *How much to share?* There was no reason not to trust Lane, but at this stage all he needed to know was that they were picking up someone who might be useful to the investigation.

'Someone came forward with new information on Sutton.'

'Oh, yeah?'

Boyd nodded.

'What was he doing – drug dealing or something?' joked Lane. 'Home-cooking meth?'

'He had compromising material.'

'On who?' Lane asked.

'We're bringing him in to interview. Hopefully we'll get some names,' Boyd said.

'Who's the informant?'

Boyd glanced his way. 'Lane... I don't want to sound like an arse, okay. But I'm keeping names out of it until we get him safely to Hastings.'

Lane raised his hands in supplication. 'That's fine. I get it.'

'I brought you along because you're trained in close protection.'

Lane's brows raised. 'Seriously? Are you actually expecting trouble?'

'Not expecting it, exactly, but, you know... It's always best to be prepared, right?'

'Christ,' Lane muttered. 'It's all got very serious all of a sudden.'

Boyd cleared Hastings and they travelled up a relatively empty A21, listening to Radio 4.

'*...the prime minister's pre-election cabinet pick. It's thought that he'll be looking to give the cabinet a few long-serving familiar faces from the back benches to reassure the party and the public alike that wiser, older minds are steering Britain into the turbulent future...*'

'Jobs for the old boys,' said Lane. He looked at Boyd. 'But in the end they're all the same.... aren't they?'

'Politicians?'

'I was going to say the Eton lot and the like. Groomed from birth to be either ministers or board members, moving from one easy gig to the next... and all the time privately patting themselves on the back.'

'Christ, you sound like Emma.' *And Hatcher*, Boyd thought.

'Doesn't that bug you, Boyd?'

'A little. Not enough to vote Labour if that's where you're going.'

'Who would you vote for?' Lane asked.

'None of the above.'

Lane shrugged. 'Well, there you go... That's why the old boys network is so entrenched.'

They drove on in silence for a while, the radio talking for them.

'So... whose job do you think is safe in the cabinet, Laura?'

'Well, it does seem that Tim Portman is a very popular choice within the party. He's been a stoic supporter of the PM through the recent difficult times. He performs well on camera, and he has the advantage of being quite charming and debonair. Some are likening him to David Owen. So a future PM perhaps? A fresh face for the party and a chance to rebrand their image after all the sleaze and cronyism allegations...'

Boyd reached out and switched to Radio Two.

62

Okeke arrived at work an hour late. She'd got home at nine last night. In any case, she was certain Sutherland would rather she flexed her hours than log overtime.

Plus, last night had been sleepless. Her mind had been racing in tear-arsing circles with Darren Jacobs' story. And then, when she'd finally dropped off at whatever o'clock and woke up this morning, the whole thing was beginning to sound a little like a paranoid conspiracy theory.

Maybe... this girl, Amy Cheetham, did go missing after some Oxford freshers party? That was something she was going to check on LEDS first thing this morning. But... her friend Laura Khan being murdered in such a public way ten years later? Then the MP Chris Lewis? And someone as well known as Sir Arthur Sutton?

It struck her that a group of rich, now middle-aged men – who shared a secret from their past that would destroy them if it came out – would be somewhat more circumspect and cautious about how they covered it up.

She entered the Incident Room and noticed it was down a

couple of people. 'Where's the guv?'

'He nipped out with Lane,' said Minter. 'Didn't really catch where they were off to, to be honest.'

'How long ago?'

Minter checked his watch. 'Three quarters of an hour ago, or thereabouts.'

She hadn't seen Boyd's Renault in the staff car park. She'd presumed he hadn't walked into work today, because, in all likelihood, the first order of business would probably have been to bring Jacobs into the station.

He's gone to get him... with Lane. Jacobs was *her* discovery. Not Lane's. The conclusion stung more than a little. She hung her jacket over the back of her chair, switched on her PC, then wandered into the kitchenette and slapped the kettle on.

It's not fucking fair. While she waited for it to boil, she went over to see how Warren and O'Neal were doing.

'How's the CCTV going?'

O'Neal answered. 'We're just going through a bunch from the shops by Pelham Arcade.'

'Rather you than me.'

'You could help?' said Minter, looking up from his screen. She gave him a sharp glance, and he shrugged. 'Many hands make light work, Okeke?'

'Yes, *sarge*,' she replied sarcastically. She had been going to offer to make a brew, but that ship had sailed. She went back to her desk and logged on.

She navigated to their team's shared storage area to find that the CCTV footage had been dumped into folders named by the shops they'd come from.

'Who's on what?' she asked.

'I'm on Chappy's Chippy,' said O'Neal.

'I'm doing the café right now,' said Minter.

'The corner shop's been done. And I'm doing the tobacconists at the moment,' said Warren.

She sighed. 'All right... Seaside Gifts is mine, I guess.'

~

BOYD PULLED into the Travelodge's car park and found a space tucked away in a discreet corner.

'Good thinking,' said Lane. 'Away from the reception cams. We should sneak him out of a side exit rather than reception, if that's possible.'

Boyd nodded. 'Are your bodyguard superpowers tingling yet?'

Lane looked around the car park. 'There's nothing here that looks like goons-in-waiting.'

'All right, then.' Boyed pulled out his phone and dialled the number for Jacobs' new pay-as-you-go. It rang a dozen times before going to answerphone. He glanced at Lane and dialled again.

There was still no answer.

'Boyd,' said Lane. 'We going in?'

He took a deep breath. 'Yes. Let's go.'

They made their way to the reception.

'Morning,' Boyd said to the receptionist. 'We've come to collect one of your guests. It's a Mr Jay Turner. I believe he's in room twenty-three.'

She checked her screen. 'Yes, yes he is.'

'Great, can you buzz us through and we'll go knock on his door?' He pulled out his warrant card. 'Police,' he added.

'Oh. Are you arresting someone?' she asked.

'No, just collecting. May we...?'

She buzzed the door to the rooms and Boyd pushed it open. 'It's up the stairs on your right,' she called out as they stepped through.

'Boyd, wait,' said Lane after the glass door swung shut behind them. He seemed to Boyd to be taking this a little more seriously now. 'Let me take point.' He pulled his jacket aside to show a discreet shoulder holster.

'Jesus, Lane! Is that logged out from London?'

'It's unofficial,' he replied. 'If it turns out there's no problem here, can we say you didn't see it?'

'Shit.' Boyd nodded. 'Have you been wearing that since you joined us?'

He shrugged. 'Most days.'

Boyd shook his head. 'Jesus Christ, Lane.'

'I'm licenced to carry,' he pointed out.

Boyd sighed. 'Provided you don't bring it into the bloody office again, I guess I can have *not* glimpsed it just now.'

'Deal.' Lane stepped round Boyd and led the way up the stairs. At the top they picked out room twenty-three and cautiously approached it. Boyd leant close to the door and listened. He could hear that the TV in the room was on.

'Telly's on,' Boyd whispered. He dialled Jacobs' phone again and leant in to listen once more. After a few seconds he heard its ringtone.

Lane could hear it too. 'That's not promising,' he said.

Boyd was about to hang up when the call was answered. 'Yes? Who is this?'

'Jacobs?' he replied.

There was a long pause, then: 'Is that you, DCI Boyd?'

He felt a surge of relief. 'I'm outside your hotel-room door.'

A moment later, the door clicked open and Darren Jacobs' dark beard and battered nose appeared in the gap. His small sleepy eyes squinted suspiciously out at Lane. 'Who's this?'

'This is DI Lane. He's one of my team. We've come to bring you in. We're going to take your statement down in Hastings. Then sort you out with witness protection. Are you ready?'

'Oh, thank fuck,' Jacobs said, visibly relieved, and beckoned them in.

63

Warren quickly realised that the entire day was going to be devoted to watching CCTV on his monitor. Of the nine seafront businesses from which they'd acquired footage yesterday, only one of them had a modern motion-sensor-activated camera. The rest were five or ten years old: cameras that recorded at a rate of two frames a second. Their jerky images gave him a stress headache in much the same way as watching a film that was having buffering issues. He'd already spent an eye-watering hour watching stop-motion kids and mums come and go from the corner shop. Another hour of that and he was going to need a lie-down.

He opened the folder for the old-fashioned tobacconist's shop, fully expecting a stop-motion migraine for the next hour, but was relieved to discover that the folder was full of lots of little AVI files instead of a single twenty-hour file.

Thank fuck.

He remembered now that the old man in the shop had said he'd only had his CCTV installed a year or so ago. The files – there were three hundred and two of them – were all small, and mercifully named with a timestamp. Looking at the dates, the oldest was a fortnight ago; they'd been lucky to pick them up when they did. Another couple of days and, starting with the oldest, they'd have been deleted.

Warren scrolled down the list of files until he reached the date of the Eagle House fire, then continued through that day until 5.45 p.m., the time at which the mystery figure had been spotted emerging from Pelham car park and crossing the road.

He double-clicked the first of six recordings that had occurred during that hour. The first AVI file opened to show a view from the corner of the shop that took in the shop's door and most of its small interior including, nearest to camera, the edge of the counter. He watched the back of the old man, as he wandered over to the door, opened it and looked out.

'Slow day, eh?' muttered Warren. He watched to the end of the clip and sighed. He'd just spent forty-seven seconds watching the old man standing in his doorway. The good news was that half a dozen figures had passed his door in that time and, although none of them were their man, the image quality was good enough, and in colour, to be sure of that.

He double-clicked on the next file. The same view appeared on the screen, this time with a customer entering the shop. Warren lurched forward in his seat.

The figure entering the tobacconists was darkly clad, with a bulky rucksack on his back and wearing a dark-blue baseball cap.

'Shit.'

The man wandered over towards the counter. His free hand was gesturing slightly; he was asking something. The back of the old man's head was in shot as he turned round and pointed at something behind him.

Baseball Cap Man removed the rucksack and set it down on the floor. To Warren's eyes, it looked heavy. The man seemed relieved to offload it as he leant on the glass counter and pointed at something. His face, most of it anyway, was obscured by the peak of the cap. Warren could see his mouth moving, though.

The old man pulled something from the shelf behind him and showed it to his customer. It looked like a pack of cigarettes.

Baseball Cap Man nodded, then pointed again. Warren thought he could guess what he was saying, or thereabouts. *'Yeah, mate... Those are the ones. Gimme another pack, could you?'*

The old man produced a second box and set it on the counter.

Warren leaned closer to the screen. *Come on. Come on.* The holy grail moment, that's what he was waiting for, hoping for... *Pull out a card reader...*

Baseball Cap Man reached into his back pocket and took something out. As he passed it over the counter, Warren's heart sank.

Cash.

'Oh, for fuck's sake,' he hissed.

'You all right there, Warren?' called out Minter.

Warren answered without taking his eyes off the screen. 'I think I've got him!'

64

'All right,' said Lane, peering out into the corridor. 'The coast is clear.'

He led the way to the stairs; Jacobs followed, with Boyd bringing up the rear.

Jacobs had hastily dressed in the first clothes he could grab: a floral short-sleeved shirt, dark tracksuit bottoms and a pair of sandals.

When Boyd suggested he wear something more practical, he pointed at the flaky rash across his feet. 'I've got psoriasis in case you hadn't noticed. I need air on my feet otherwise I get –'

'Fine. Fine.' Boyd didn't want a detailed account. 'Sandals are fine, mate, honestly. But let's get a move on.'

At the rear, Boyd couldn't help a quick glance down at Jacobs' feet. They were raw and red from being scratched, and had been dusted with a coating of talcum powder that was leaving a pitiful trail in his wake.

Downstairs, Lane steered right, away from reception and towards a fire door at the end of the corridor.

'Where are we going?' asked Jacobs.

'We're taking the discreet exit,' said Lane. He turned to look at Jacobs. 'You're lying low for a good reason, right?'

Jacobs nodded.

'Well, the fire door, it is.'

'Won't it be alarmed?'

'Possibly, but hopefully it's not on camera. Come on.'

They reached the end of the corridor and Lane shook his head and smiled.

'What?' asked Boyd.

He pointed to a small white box beside the door and an LED light that was dark. 'The battery's flat. I wonder when that was last checked. Health and safety, eh?'

He pushed the locking bar, the door swung open and they stepped out into the sunshine. Lane scanned the busy car park.

'What are you looking for?' asked Jacobs.

'Spooky-looking men sitting in a spooky-looking van,' he said. He continued a quick sweep then nodded. 'I think we're good.'

They hurried across the car park to the quiet corner where Boyd had parked. 'Back seat, please, Jacobs,' said Lane. 'And until we're on the motorway you'd better lie down. Avoid the ANPR cams.'

Jacobs bundled himself in and lay down as Boyd started up the car. 'It feels like we've been a touch overdramatic here,' he muttered.

'Well, *you* brought *me* along, Boyd,' replied Lane, smiling. 'This is how *I* do it.'

'Fair enough,' said Boyd as he headed for the exit.

'Go back to the beginning,' said Minter.

Warren rewound the clip and set it playing again.

'Fuck me,' said O'Neal. 'That's him!'

Minter leant in. 'That's our man, all right. Does he use a card?'

Warren shook his head. 'It's cash.'

'Bloody cash,' Minter grumbled. Okeke had joined them, and they huddled together, crowding around Warren's desk.

'He's got a baseball cap on,' she said. 'Please tell me he takes it off now he's inside?'

Warren shook his head again.

They observed the man approaching the counter, then talking to the shopkeeper. 'He looks up a bit, though,' said Warren.

They watched in silence as he pointed at the display case behind the counter. The old man turned to look –

'Wait!' Okeke reached out and grabbed the mouse.

'Hey!' Warren protested. 'What are you doing? There's nothing there.'

She paused the video, then rewound it a couple of seconds.

The man in the baseball cap rolled his head around, as if his neck was stiff, and she stabbed the pause button. They stared at the man's fully revealed face. The image was blurred, the resolution somewhat pixelated.

While everyone else's eyes were on the man's face, Warren's were on the pack of cigarettes frozen in place as the old man slid them across the counter. He knew that logo – that red circle, the figure smoking a peace pipe. He'd seen that before. Very recently.

'I know that,' he said. 'Those ciggies...' He looked up at the others around him. 'American Spirit. Lane smokes those.'

'Shit,' said Okeke.

The blurry face had seemed vaguely familiar, but she couldn't quite place it. Now the pixels coalesced into a very familiar face.

65

Boyd was heartily wishing he'd brought Okeke along to do the driving. He was knackered. But Her Madge was probably right: this kind of thing was Lane's area of expertise.

'So what's the plan, Boyd?' asked Jacobs, breaking the silence.

'We'll get you to the station first and then get a recorded statement of everything you told me yesterday,' Boyd said.

'Then witness protection?' Jacobs leant forward between the seats. 'You know there's a killer out there, right? A fucking hitman?'

'I know. Which is why we *will* get you into witness protection as soon as we've finished with our interviews.'

'That had better not mean custody,' Jacobs said. 'I'm not doing that again.'

'No, it doesn't mean custody,' Boyd assured him. 'We're going to keep you safe until you can return home.'

'And when will that be?' Jacobs asked.

'I don't know,' Boyd replied. 'It won't be until we've interviewed and charged all the names on that list at the very least.'

Jacobs laughed. 'You'll be fucking lucky. Half of them are in government, the other half run the bloody media.'

He had a point. And, while they couldn't possibly 'do away with' the number of people who would know their little secret, there was no knowing how far these people were prepared to go to protect their own. Blanket denial? Superinjunctions? They could probably have the case re-assigned to another, more compliant force if they wanted to.

And then what waited down the line for Darren Jacobs? Slipping in his shower and sustaining a fatal head injury few weeks later? Or perhaps he'd be run over by some unidentified hit-and-run driver just like poor Chris Lewis.

'I honestly don't know how long, Jacobs. It could be a few weeks or several months,' Boyd said wearily.

'Shit,' Jacobs said. 'It's all fucking shit.'

Lane twisted in his seat to look at him. 'So what's this *list*?' he asked.

'It's a list of members of the Lambda Club,' Jacobs replied. 'Sutton gave it to me.'

'Let's save this for the interview room, eh?' said Boyd.

Lane turned back to face the front. 'He's right, Jacobs. Try to relax. We'll get you there in one piece.'

'Have either of you got any fags?' Jacobs asked hopefully.

'I don't smoke,' said Boyd. 'Plus, you're not stinking up *my* car.'

'And I'm out,' said Lane. 'Sorry, mate.'

'Shit,' Jacobs grumbled. 'I really need one. And I need a piss, by the way.'

'It's an hour and a half back. Think you can hold out?' asked Boyd.

'On neither front,' Jacobs said. 'Sorry... but you didn't give me much chance to go at the hotel.'

'There's a garage after the turn-off for the A21,' said Lane. 'I spotted it on the way up. We could let him take a leak there?'

Boyd shook his head. He really didn't want to stop at all.

'I'll take him,' said Lane apologetically. 'I could do with one too, actually.'

'Bloody hell,' Boyd said, exasperated. 'If there's a Maccy D's there, do you kids want a Happy Meal each too?'

Lane chuckled while Jacobs just scratched at his itchy feet. Boyd realised he'd have to hoover the floor in the back once he'd delivered Jacobs to safety. The thought of an early snowfall of dried flaky skin made his stomach turn.

'All right,' he said finally. 'Pee break in about fifteen minutes. Do you both think you can hang on that long?'

Lane nodded, trying to supress a grin. Jacobs continued to scratch away at his foot with one hand and his beard with the other.

For fuck's sake – what did I do to deserve this?

MINTER LEANT FORWARD, his nose practically touching the monitor. 'Bloody hell, I think you're right. It *is* Lane.' He looked up at Okeke. 'He's gone out with the boss. I've got no idea where...'

'Shit. Boyd's taken Lane up with him to collect our informant,' Okeke said.

'What informant?' asked O'Neal.

They all stared at her. Minter looked really pissed off. 'Informant?' he said. 'And how come you know about this and I don't?'

She explained about getting the lead yesterday afternoon and Boyd insisting that it stayed between the two of them until they knew what they were dealing with.

'Thanks for not trusting us,' grumbled O'Neal.

Minter glared at her. 'Call him,' he said. 'Now!'

66

Boyd swung the car into one of the parking spaces beside the garage. His tank was half full and on any other day he'd have taken the opportunity to fill her up.

'Right, quick as you can,' he said, resigned.

Jacobs climbed out of the back as Lane unbuckled himself. 'Do you want anything?'

'Just for you to be quick,' Boyd replied tersely.

Boyd watched them hurry across the forecourt, Lane walking briskly looking in all directions at once as though he was escorting the prime minister himself, Jacobs hobbling beside him in his sandals and flapping floral shirt. From behind they could have been a budget version of Tom Cruise and Dustin Hoffman in *Rain Man*.

LANE LED Jacobs to the toilet. 'I'll go and buy us some smokes. You got a favourite?'

'B&H... if you're paying,' Jacobs replied with a cheeky grin.

Lane eye-rolled and left him queuing behind a mum and a wriggling baby. He stepped into the petrol station's shop and pulled his phone out. He checked to make sure he wasn't in Boyd's line of sight, then hit the last number he'd dialled.

A voice answered after the first ring. 'Yes?'

'I'm in possession of your little weasel. What do you want me to do with him?'

'Get rid of him, of course. But, for the love of God, he mustn't be found. I've had a devil of the time trying to get Sutton's investigation hobbled.'

'Sir, no names.'

'Right... yes, of course.' A pause. 'That was clumsy.'

'Just be careful.'

'Chief you-know-what down south... has apparently been a difficult bitch and is pushing back against her superior. So I'm not even sure we *can* close this down. Let's just make sure they've got no more evidence.'

'There's a complication,' said Lane.

'What's that?'

'I'm with the senior investigating officer on the team.'

'*What?*'

'We had to collect the weasel together. He's to be formally interviewed later today.'

The man on the other end of the line let out a volley of expletives. In the background Lane could hear the muffled sound of men laughing and the clink of glasses. It wasn't rocket science to work out that the speaker was in the members' club privacy room: a small windowless, wood-panelled room with one desk, a few leather armchairs and an absolute cast-iron guarantee it was bug and camera-free. Not even the corridors of Westminster could offer that comforting assurance.

'Well, then you'll have to deal with him too.'

Lane didn't answer.

'Is that a problem?'

Was it a problem? In so far as he'd actually grown to like Boyd, yes, actually, it was a bit of a problem.

'I'm not sure adding yet another scalp to the pile is going to help, sir,' he said.

'The weasel *must not be interviewed*! Do you have any idea how much is at stake here? This is not up for discussion. Understood?'

Lane turned and noticed the lady with her toddler emerging from the corner of the shop. Jacobs would be out soon. He needed to get off the phone.

'Do it. And do it now,' the man said. And hung up.

BOYD PULLED OUT HIS IPHONE. He'd felt it vibrate and suspected, no, *hoped*, it was Charlotte. They hadn't spoken since Monday morning. He wondered how she was feeling.

There was no message.

He fumbled in his trouser pocket for his work phone. He was certain one of them had vibrated while he was driving. He lifted his bum off the seat, pulled his phone out and tapped the screen.

He saw Okeke's name beneath the green speech bubble. He'd not thought to text her to say he was going up to collect Jacobs, which must have stung when she realised he'd gone. He was about to swipe the screen to unlock his phone when the rear door was wrenched opened.

Jacobs clambered into the back, mid conversation with Lane. '... the bloody rush? I told you! I'm gasping for a puff, mate.'

The passenger door opened and Lane got in. 'Let's go,' he said.

'Did you get his fags?' asked Boyd.

'The queue at the till was too long.'

'What?' Jacobs blurted from behind. 'There was no bloody queue. And, anyway, why did you wander off? Aren't you meant to be protecting me?'

Lane twisted in his seat. 'You'll get your fucking cigarettes when we get to Hastings!' He turned back to Boyd. 'We should get a move on.'

Lane's manner had completely changed. 'You okay?' asked Boyd. 'Did something happen?'

'I'm fine,' came the reply. 'Sorry. I just want to get this job done.'

'Okay.' Boyd nodded. 'Okay. Me too.' He dropped his work phone into his lap, turned on the ignition and pulled out of the car park onto the sliproad that led back to the A21. He recalled from Dave Mullen, the child-porn-peddling van driver, that from here to Hastings there were no other pit-stops or petrol stations. They should have a clear run back.

He eased onto the A21. The traffic was still relatively light. 'All right. It's forty-five minutes to Hastings, Darren, then we'll get you a coffee from the canteen and you can have a fag before we go into interview. Sound good?'

'Fine,' Jacobs muttered grumpily.

Lane took his phone out of his pocket and swiped at the screen. Boyd caught a glimpse of a young boy on the lock screen before it vanished.

'Is that your lad?' he asked.

Lane nodded, busy thumbing his phone, looking for something.

The first creeping sense of doubt began to percolate into Boyd's bloodstream. The boy he'd glimpsed looked a lot older than *four*. Nine or ten, even.

'You said your son was four?' he said.

'No. He's older, mate.' Lane's face flickered with a smile. 'You must have misheard me.'

Shit. No, he definitely said 'four'. Why's that suddenly changed?

His phone vibrated again on his lap, ringing this time. The screen was *facing down* – thank God. He was certain it would be Okeke again.

'We'll need to come off the A21,' said Lane, studying his own screen.

'Why's that?' Boyd asked.

'There's been an accident,' Lane replied. 'Both lanes blocked on the A21 and backing up.'

Okay, Bill... you might be in trouble here, Julia's voice cautioned.

'It's okay,' said Boyd. 'It'll clear.'

'No,' said Lane more forcefully. 'The turn-off ahead is quicker; it's a much more efficient route.'

Boyd looked at him. 'It isn't, though... is it? That's bullshit.'

Lane, realising the ruse was over with, reached under his jacket discreetly – for Boyd's eyes only – and wrapped his hand around the grip of his gun.

'Just take the next left, Boyd.'

67

Minter dialled the phone number for Police Control in Lewes. It was answered almost immediately. 'Contact officer Ellie Bryant speaking.'

'This is DS Minter down at Hastings,' he said. 'I need an urgent track request for one of our officers.'

'Are they in trouble?' Ellie asked.

'They're in danger. It's quite urgent.'

'All right. What's his force-issue phone number?'

Minter read it out from his contacts page.

'One moment, sergeant...'

Minter turned round to face the others. Okeke was busy texting Boyd again. Warren and O'Neal were already on the ANPR module of LEDS, trying to pick up a match on the number plate of Boyd's Renault Captur.

'DS Minter?' Ellie was back on the line.

'I'm here.'

'Yes. We've got a real-time signal on his phone. It's actually in motion. Let me see... It's just south of Sevenoaks, heading along the A21 towards Tonbridge. Do you want me to put out a broad alert?'

Minter's brain was whirling. He really wasn't sure what to do. Would an all-channels scramble to Boyd's location put the boss in further danger? Would it be better to discreetly monitor and track his progress? Probably for the first time since he'd joined the team, Minter really wished that clumsy twit Sutherland was here.

'Sergeant?' Ellie prompted.

Minter took a deep breath. 'Yes, a broad alert,' he replied. 'We've got a senior officer in an extremely hazardous situation.'

～

'WHAT'S GOING ON?' asked Jacobs. 'Why the detour?'

Boyd answered. 'Are you going to explain, Lane?'

Lane twisted in his seat and produced his gun for Jacobs to see. 'You're both going to do as I say from this point onwards,' he said firmly.

'Shit!' Jacobs recoiled at the sight of his gun and struck the back seat with his fist. 'Fuck!'

'Just stay calm!' Boyd said, doing his best to *sound* calm too.

'Like he said,' added Lane. '*Calm* will get us all through this without incident.' Lane glanced at the winding country lane ahead. 'Stop up there,' he said, pointing at a widening of the country lane. It looked like a tractor entrance into a gated field.

Boyd did as he said.

'Right.' Lane unbuckled his seatbelt, opened the door and reversed out of the car. He pointed the gun at Jacobs. 'You... in the front seat. *Now!*'

'Lane,' said Boyd, 'we're keeping this calm, right? Keeping this –'

'Shut up, Boyd!' Lane swung the gun towards him. 'I want silence. Come on, Jacobs. Front seat. Now!'

Jacobs climbed out of the rear door on Boyd's side.

'Don't even think about running or I'll put a bullet in your spine. Then I'll walk right over and put another in that stupid little head of yours.'

Jacobs held his hands up high as he rounded the rear of the car. 'You... you're with them?'

'Shut up!'

Jacobs nodded.

Lane stepped back and gestured with the gun in the direction of the front passenger seat. After Jacobs had got in, he slammed the door shut and climbed into the rear seat.

'Now, toss your phones out of the window,' he ordered.

Jacobs complied quickly. Boyd spread his thighs to let his *work* phone slide down into the gap between them. He reached into his jacket and pulled out his personal phone. 'Lane, come on...' he tried, in a bid to distract him.

'I said, throw it out. Now!'

Boyd opened his window and tossed it out. 'There.'

'And the other one,' said Lane. 'DO IT!'

Boyd flung his work phone out of the window too.

'Now... drive. I'll give you directions.'

They headed on down the winding country lane, past high grassy verges topped with brambles and low-hanging trees that obscured the endless hectares of farmland.

'Lane,' Boyd said as coolly as he could manage, 'I had a text from Okeke while you were taking a piss.'

'Be quiet, Boyd.'

'They know you've abducted us,' he continued conversationally.

'I said, be quiet.'

'They'll have radioed a broad shout by now.'

'FOR FUCK'S SAKE, BOYD, SHUT UP!' Lane shoved the barrel of the gun into the side of Boyd's neck. 'The less you say, mate, the easier this is going to be!'

Boyd glanced sideways at him. The end of the barrel was

digging into flesh beneath his ear. 'This is just another job... right?' rasped Boyd. 'Is it worth it? Really?'

'Left,' Lane snapped. 'Take the left ahead.'

There was a small white sign pointing to Bitchet Green and beneath that a brown National Trust sign indicating Ightham Mote was a point of interest nearby.

Boyd drove on in silence, trying to work out how this was likely to pan out and what he could do about it. It wasn't looking good for either him or Jacobs, whichever way he looked at it. Lane had to be a *freelancer*. 'Hitman' was a word for Hollywood scriptwriters, but essentially that was what he had to be. Whether Lane was also a close protection officer for the Met – *Christ, did no one think to check?* – was pretty much immaterial now.

But he *was* human... with very human vulnerabilities.

'Okay, mate...' Boyd tried again. 'I'm driving. The phones are ditched. No one's zeroing in on us yet. How about we dial this down a notch?'

Lane shook his head. 'Quiet!' he said, audibly grinding his teeth. 'Or I'll put a fucking bullet right in the back of his head!'

'Shit! No!' screamed Jacobs, cowering down in the front seat. 'Please!'

'Lane...' said Boyd. 'This doesn't have to end messily.'

Lane looked at him. 'It's going to be fine if you just shut up and do as I say.'

It's not, though, is it?

The only conceivable objective for this detour was to find somewhere quiet to shoot Darren Jacobs and, as necessary collateral, shoot Boyd too. That meant somewhere remote enough for Lane to properly dispose of their bodies. Sometime soon he was going to say 'Pull over' then 'Get out', then walk them into some dense woodland and without any warning or ceremony – *pap, pap*. Job done.

Bill? Julia's voice. *You need to do something. And very fucking soon.*

68

Okeke had given up texting. There were four unanswered messages stacked one above the other in the chat history. If Boyd wasn't replying, it meant he *couldn't* reply. Her frantic mind kept cycling round to the worst possible explanation and then she'd mentally scold herself for doing so.

They were responding to a *potential* situation and doing everything possible. O'Neal had brought Hatcher scrambling into the Incident Room, and Hatcher and Minter were both on their phones, receiving a running commentary on the police units that were currently blue-ing and two-ing, from various directions, to the current location of Boyd's phone.

Warren pulled up a live screen-share, sent by Control, which had a red pin on a map for Boyd and half a dozen blue pins indicating units on their way.

'Come on, come on,' Okeke whispered under her breath.

Chief Superintendent Hatcher had somehow managed to sidle up beside her unnoticed. 'I can't believe it,' she uttered.

Okeke glanced at her and could see the colour had drained from her face. Whatever Boyd suspected about her motives during the Nix case, it was clear to Okeke that right now she was determined to get her detective back home in one piece.

Hatcher noticed Okeke looking at her. 'I can't believe it. I simply can't believe it.'

She was referring to the CCTV footage O'Neal had just played back for her, showing Lane in the tobacconists. Then her voice changed. 'Yes, I'm still here,' she said into her phone. 'What? You're sure?'

Okeke could see the blue pins edging closer to the red one, painfully slowly across the map. Out there in the Kent countryside, those patrol cars would be tear-arsing their way round blind corners and across traffic-light junctions, sirens blaring. On the screen, the pins shuffled silently.

Hatcher ended her call and turned to Okeke. 'They have no record of a DI Douglas Lane working as a CPO.' She shook her head.

'Didn't *anyone* do any checks, ma'am?' asked Okeke incredulously. She tried as hard as she could to keep it from sounding like a straight-out accusation.

Hatcher shook her head again. 'The call about Lane came in from the very top. I presumed...'

Okeke bit her lip, very tempted to remind her that that particular word prefaced far too many a police screw-up.

On the screen, the blue pins were converging. They were right on top of Boyd's location now. Okeke realised she was holding her breath, her mind repeatedly doubling back to that worst possible scenario again. And this time she broke through her own mental police tape and pictured Boyd's body sprawled in a ditch, leaking blood from a hole in the back of his head.

Minter lowered his phone. 'Echo Mike Nineteen's at the location, everyone!' He put the phone back to his ear. 'Come on! Report for Christ's sake. *What do you see?*'

The Incident Room fell silent as everyone turned to look at

Minter, focusing on the expression across his face, hoping to get the earliest hint of the incoming news.

Minter lowered his phone and let out a deep rasping breath. The relief was plain on his face. 'It's only his phone. No bodies.'

~

DARREN JACOBS HAD his very own survival strategy. He was pleading with Lane for his life.

'I don't know any names! I don't know what went on! Please! You can just let us go! PLEASE!'

In the rear-view mirror, Boyd could see Lane's hand on his gun, index finger flexing round the trigger, repeatedly curling round it, then off, round it and off.

'If this is about money? Jesus... Fuck knows who's paying you, but it's not worth this!' Jacobs whined. 'Come on! It's not w–'

'Another fucking word and I'll shoot you right here in the fucking car!' Lane snapped. He had the barrel of the gun resting on the top of the seat. Jacobs stared boggle-eyed at it.

He's losing it. Lane's gentle Scottish burr, his professional and calm demeanour, had been completely dispensed with along with his cover story.

'C'mon, man!' pleaded Jacobs. 'You can turn on them. Be a witness. You can –'

In a blur of movement, Lane aimed over the headrest and shot Jacobs point blank in the head.

Boyd watched it happen in slow motion – then the windscreen instantly fogged with a fine spray of red and tatters of skull and brain matter. 'FUCK!' he screamed.

Just like Lane, his hands made the executive decision to do *something* – because no other part of him was doing anything useful to save his arse. Unable to see ahead, he gripped the steering wheel tightly in both fists and jerked it hard to the right.

The Renault Captur slew across the country lane, the front bumper caught the raised grass verge on the far side, flipping it over into a frantic barrel roll.

Blue sky and grey tarmac traded over and over, as everything loose inside the vehicle clattered from the floor to the roof to the floor and back again. Boyd caught sight of Jacobs next to him, his arms, legs and bloody head flailing lifelessly like a lurid piped-air sales mascot outside a showroom.

Eventually they came to a stop with a jarring impact that shattered every window into a blizzard of glass crystals.

There was a prolonged stillness as Boyd hung upside down from his seatbelt. A silence filled with nothing but the ticking sound of the engine cooling down and the tweeting of the birds outside in the trees. Boyd twisted to look behind him and saw that Lane was conscious, intact and slowly regathering his own wits. He searched around to see if the gun was loose and within reach, but he couldn't locate it.

Gun or no gun, he didn't doubt for one moment that Lane could kill him with only his bare hands.

Don't be an arse, Bill... For God's sake, JUST RUN!

He reached for his belt buckle, clicked it and instantly collapsed down onto the roof of the car, his thighs smacking on the steering wheel as his weight was released.

'Ahh! Shit!'

As he began to pull himself out through the empty frame of his side window, he felt a hand grasp his ankle.

'Fuck off!' he shouted as he kicked back with his spare foot and caught Lane. He heard the man grunt with pain and felt him let go. Boyd pulled himself out onto hard-packed earth.

Behind him, he could hear Lane, unclicking his own belt and tumbling down to the roof with the same *booff* of breath and yelp of pain. Boyd turned round to see if he could spot the missing gun lying on the roof, or perhaps flung out onto the road. If he could get his hands on that before Lane, the immediate crisis would be over.

'Are you all right?'

It was a woman's voice. His head spun to see an elderly woman with walking poles standing on the grass verge on the other side of the lane. 'I'm on the phone to the ambulance,' she said. 'It won't be long.'

'Police!' Boyd gasped. 'POLICE!' Then: 'Get the fuck back!'

Lane had managed to get out and had found the gun. He was wobbling, holding it awkwardly and trying to keep his aim on Boyd. Blood was trickling down the left side of his face and into his eye.

'Boyd...' he wheezed. 'I'm really sorry, mate.' He pulled the trigger.

69

Okeke felt like a fifth wheel, like a useless gawping civilian. She and the rest of the team could do little more than watch Warren's monitor and Minter's facial expressions in an attempt to gauge the current situation on the ground.

A blue pin remained overlapping the red pin of Boyd's phone, the others were now diverging, shuffling along various faint grey hairlines on the map that indicated a network of country lanes.

'They're spreading out,' said Minter, stating the obvious.

The Incident Room was beginning to fill up with other CID and uniformed officers drawn by news of the unfolding drama, technically breaching all manner of department and team confidentiality tape-lines.

Even though he'd only been with them for six months, Okeke felt she'd become close to Boyd. Outside work she'd like to say he was fast becoming a friend. She'd never admit this to him – but, more than her senior officer, he almost felt like a big brother. And here she was, doing absolutely fuck all to help him. All she could do was watch as his fate unfolded as pixels on a monitor.

For fuck's sake, please... please be alive, you stupid bastard.

'A 999 just came in!' said Hatcher, relaying the news from Control. She had the whole room's full attention as she listened to the voice on the other end of the line. 'It's an overturned car and gun shots.'

Okeke realised a tear was threatening to spill down her cheek. Quickly checking no one was looking her way, she swiped it away.

BOYD WAS CRUMPLED down on the grass verge next to the old woman. She was bleeding out from a wound in her lower torso... and Boyd had had no choice, none whatsoever, but to drop down beside her and compress the bloody wound.

Lane hobbled across until he was standing over them, his shirt wet with blood from the gash on his temple. 'This could have gone better.'

'Lane, for fuck's sake,' Boyd snarled.

'At least you won't run now,' he said, indicating his own ankle.

Boyd could see that Lane's left foot was wrongly askew.

'You know it's over, Lane. The APUs are coming.'

'Yeah, I know,' said Lane.

'So fucking well put the gun down and help me!'

'I can't let you go, Boyd. You know who's on that list.'

'No, I don't.' Boyd lied. 'I glimpsed his bloody notebook. But I didn't get to –'

'Yes, you did,' Lane said, sounding tired. 'In or out of prison, I'm a dead man if I let you walk.'

'Witness protection is still an option for you. You know enough to bring down some big people.'

Lane smiled. 'Which is exactly why there *won't* be options for me. These big people have *reach*.'

'Not with me, they don't'

Lane smiled ruefully. 'You're a good man, Boyd.'

Lane's aim was wavering. Boyd nodded at Lane's left foot. 'That ankle broken? You know you won't be able to run.' Boyd nodded at the old woman's Nokia, lying where she'd dropped it. 'She made the call, mate. They'll be here any second. Put the bloody gun down and give me a hand with her. Make the right decision.'

They could both hear the sound of several police sirens warbling in the distance.

'The gun?' Boyd said. 'Put the bloody thing down, eh?'

'I'll do time –'

'If you don't get immunity, you'll do *easy* time, Lane. Well away from the general prison population. You'll be protected. We'll nail the lot of them. I don't care how many cabinet ministers are on that list –'

'You're so naive, Boyd, if you think any of those names are going to see the inside of a fucking prison,' Lane spat.

'There's more of a chance if we're *both* alive, though, right?'

The warbling sirens were getting rapidly louder.

'Put the gun down, mate. Don't let them see you pointing it at me.'

Lane lowered himself to the ground and set the gun down on the road beside him.

'You better kick it away,' said Boyd. 'Don't give the APOs an excuse.'

Lane nodded, kicked it with his good leg, and it skittered away across the tarmac.

The next moment the first patrol car arrived on the scene, slewing to a halt as it came round the bend, kicking up a rooster tail of burnt rubber behind it.

Boyd raised a hand as the coppers climbed out. 'DCI BOYD!

WE HAVE ONE GUNSHOT WOUND TO A CIVILIAN OVER HERE!' An ambulance would be on its way already, but at least the paramedics would know what they were dealing with on arrival.

'Lie flat, belly down, hands where they can see,' hissed Boyd in Lane's direction.

Lane nodded, lay down on the road and laced his hands over the back of his head...

70

Seeing Lane spread out on the ground and waiting to be arrested was the last clear, lucid recollection Boyd had. The aftermath – the other vehicles arriving, the APOs walking Lane through the stages of de-escalation, the paramedics working on the old woman, Jacobs pronounced dead at the scene – was all a blur.

He'd been examined by the paramedics and had got away with nothing more than whiplash to his neck and seatbelt abrasions across his chest that, the medic warned him, would hurt like a second-degree burn for the next few days once the analgesics wore off.

Boyd had then been blue-lighted to the hospital for a more thorough check, and eventually released. Okeke had taken him home, and had been the one to explain to a frantic and furious Emma that her dad had somehow managed to get himself involved in a life-threatening situation yet again.

He'd felt distanced from it all – like it was a boxed set of some TV drama playing out before him.

The whole muddled post-adrenaline-rush experience,

along with the tranquilisers they'd pumped into him, had left Boyd feeling exhausted and numb. He went to bed knowing that when he woke up the next day every part of him was going to hurt like a bastard.

71

'I'm sure you can understand, Tim, that we did the very best we could. But I'm afraid we've not managed to put it to bed.'

George had chosen another remote country pub. This time he wasn't sitting inside with a gin and tonic, but in his Jaguar in the gravel car park. There was no offer of a drink and no reassuring smile.

'What happened, George?' Tim asked nervously.

'The less you know, the better. Suffice to say it didn't work out the way we wanted it to.'

Tim Portman, erstwhile Secretary of State for Work and Pensions, felt his stomach roll queasily. 'George, tell me this isn't... this isn't going to actually break the surface, is it?'

George shook his head at the stupidity of the man. 'Of course it will. A version of it will, anyway.'

'Oh, God. Please, no!'

George shook his head. 'We'll probably manage to hide away the worst of it behind a clutch of expensive superinjunctions. And this is not for your benefit, Tim, you understand? You're done.'

Tim could feel his guts churning. 'What's... what's the p-plan, George?'

'You and your stupid *Spartans*... ' George sighed. 'Ridiculous bloody name.'

'But that was so long ago, George. We can –'

'Shut up, Tim.'

Tim Portman's mouth snapped shut.

'It only takes one idiotic twat who believes he can do what he wants, that he's above the law, to soil the drinking water for the rest of us,' said George, anger reddening his jowls.

'She drowned in her own vomit, George. She took too much of the stuff that night and –'

George raised his hand to silence him. 'I don't want to hear.'

'Listen to me... She got drunk. She wasn't used to... Look, it wasn't my fault!' Tim whined.

'No, you listen to me, you piece of shit! I already know what happened. I know you drugged her and then raped her.'

Tim felt his cheeks burning. 'It wasn't *just* me. There were others...'

'Fuck you, Tim. *You* are the one linked to our party, to this cabinet and to this prime minister.'

'What's going to happen to me?' Tim could feel tears brimming.

'You're going to be expelled, Tim. And then very shortly afterwards the nation is going to find out precisely why. We'll find child pornography on a government computer. The worst kind of pornography. The prime minster will announce that he's horrified and disgusted, that he thought he knew you, and that there's no room for a paedophile in the party.'

'Oh no... not that. Please!' Tim, white as a sheet, began to shake.

'You'll be arrested, you'll definitely do time, and you'll be on a register for the rest of your life.' George pressed the central-lock control on his dash and the doors clicked. As far as he was concerned, their meeting was over.

'And if you say one thing. One. Little. Thing – to *anyone* – you'll be found hanging in your cell.' George glared at him.

Timothy Portman began to sob into his hands.

'Get out of my bloody car,' snarled George.

72

Boyd had been quite right. The following morning, he'd been unable to get out of bed. Moreover, his body was mottled with livid purple bruises. And, yes, the nice young paramedic had been correct: the diagonal abrasion caused by the seatbelt across his chest and belly stung like the worst case of sunburn he'd ever experienced.

He was signed off work for the rest of the month, with a medical and psych evaluation, PTSD screening and counselling scheduled for the end of the month. He suspected the bruises, aches and scrapes would be long gone before Sussex Police would let him get back to anything vaguely resembling an operational role.

A bit of time off work sounded just fine to Boyd. Time to wind down, to finish redecorating the house and turn the garden into something presentable. And of course, with Emma starting her new job at the hotel, he'd be at home to mind Ozzie. Unlike the cliché of the battered, bruised and stoic TV detective, he wasn't particularly desperate to get back to policing the 'mean streets of Hastings'.

He spent the morning alone at home with Ozzie, nursing a

neck that spasmed every time he made the mistake of absently turning his head. He'd resorted to wearing the neck collar that had been given to him, which Ozzie stared at with great interest, and would have laughed, if he could, at the bizarre picture they made, sitting together with their cones of shame.

He purveyed the headlines on his iPad over toast and marmalade. The newspapers hadn't got hold of the story yet. In fact, they were salivating this morning over the news that a married Premier League footballer had been caught sending dick pics on Instagram. Of less interest to them was the story about the PM's cabinet reshuffle, which had been postponed while unspecified 'scandalous' allegations regarding a recently appointed minister were examined.

Boyd suspected he'd be combing the papers every morning for the next few weeks to see what exactly *was* going to break the surface. He was relying on an unofficial daily update from Okeke and at the very top of his list of questions would be what was happening with Douglas Lane.

He'd texted her private phone earlier.

Is there any chance of an update on the case sometime today?

She'd replied:

Tomorrow lunchtime maybe? Her Madge holding a team briefing on the Sutton case tomorrow AM. Minter acting SIO, but rumour that maybe Met stepping in. Need anything dropping in meantime, guv?

He had several packs of paracetamol and some weird healthy lentil gunk that Emma had left him for lunch.

Maybe you could drop by tomorrow? Beers? Update me then? Pls bring real food.

She replied almost immediately.

Deal

AT ONE O'CLOCK, with the painkillers finally kicking in, Boyd felt mobile enough to attempt a walk with Ozzie down to the beach. If they both took it slow and steady, with no sudden jarring neck swivels, he figured they'd be okay. At this time of day, mid-week, the beach wouldn't be too crowded despite the hot weather. With the recent sunshine, the old town, particularly the east end, was a no-go zone at the weekends.

He'd picked this time, poo bags in hand, hoping to catch sight of Charlotte. He'd sent her several texts this morning. None of them had triggered a reply from her so far.

He'd also had a go at calling. But it had rung through to the voice-message thing and he'd bailed out rather than say anything. She would have known it was him. His name would have come up.

Even a dimwit would conclude from the available evidence that she wasn't interested in hearing from him. He'd puzzled over what had weighed the scales in that direction. She'd seemed so pleased to see him at the barbecue, turning up with the Pavlova and that *pleased to meet you all* smile. He was pretty sure he'd been well behaved in spite of things, although recollections of the afternoon varied depending on who in his team he asked.

As he hit the shingle and let out Ozzie's extendable lead, he looked left towards Rock-A-Nore, then right towards the pier. It looked as though he had the beach all to himself. But then some movement – a figure silhouetted at the base of one of the pier's legs – caught his eye.

There was a small dog splashing into the surf and a person idly walking along the sand, just shy of the water's reach. The figure was too far away for him to be sure it was Charlotte and he was damned if he was going to go charging down, calling out her name like this was an episode of *Poldark*.

He pulled out his phone and texted her once more.

Is that you by the pier?

A moment later, the figure stopped walking. It could have been coincidence, but he was pretty sure the dog walker was now looking down at something in their hand. And then his phone pinged.

Is that you too?

He smiled as he tapped out a reply.

Fancy some chips?

THE END

DCI BOYD RETURNS IN

THE LAST TRAIN available to pre-order
here

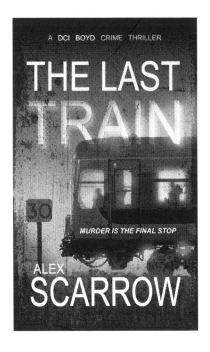

ACKNOWLEDGMENTS

It's time, once again to send out some thank yous to the other less visible members of the team behind DCI Boyd. First and foremost, a big thank you to my wife Debbie who has to digest the hideously rough first drafts that I write and make them digestible enough for others to read. Without her this series would simply not exist.

Also, a shoutout to Wendy Shakespeare, my copyeditor. We worked together on another series ten years ago, and as she was then, she is now, the safest pair of hands in the business.

For this book I want to thank two people from the Facebook group UK Crime Book Club. Firstly Kon Frankowski for some detailed and grisly information on forensics and burned bodies. Secondly, to Paula Najair for crucial information about the Hastings Fire Service. You were both very prompt and more importantly... very right. Any mistakes in the book are mine and mine alone...

This amazing group has also introduced Ozzie and myself to a whole host of invaluable ARC readers. They are an incredible group who read at short notice and are quick to give feedback. A special mention goes to Maureen Webb, Lynda Checkley and Lesley Lloyd for your error spotting... It's a heartfelt thank you from me and a big sloppy kiss from Ozzie!

Following on from this, I'd also like to thank the UKCBC as a whole, members and admins, for being so supportive of this series. It is much appreciated.

My heartfelt thanks as always go to Spaniel Aid UK, for allowing us to adopt our adorable boy Ozzie in 2017. He's as much our dog as he is DCI Boyd's. If you would like to know more about Spaniel Aid and the work they do, please visit their website: www.spanielaid.co.uk

Finally, to my partner in crime - or grime to be more accurate - Ozzie himself. When writing Boyd I have to reach inside, with Ozzie, I only have to reach down. He's always right there... aren't you boy?

Gruff!!

ALSO BY ALEX SCARROW

<Other books by Alex Scarrow>

Thrillers by Alex Scarrow

LAST LIGHT

AFTERLIGHT

OCTOBER SKIES

THE CANDLEMAN

A THOUSAND SUNS

The TimeRiders series (in reading order)

TIMERIDERS

TIMERIDERS: DAY OF THE PREDATOR

TIMERIDERS: THE DOOMSDAY CODE

TIMERIDERS: THE ETERNAL WAR

TIMERIDERS: THE CITY OF SHADOWS

TIMERIDERS: THE PIRATE KINGS

TIMERIDERS: THE MAYAN PROPHECY

TIMERIDERS: THE INFINITY CAGE

The Plague Land series

PLAGUE LAND

PLAGUE NATION

PLAGUE WORLD

The Ellie Quin series

THE LEGEND OF ELLIE QUIN

THE WORLD ACCORDING TO ELLIE QUIN

ELLIE QUIN BENEATH A NEON SKY

ELLIE QUIN THROUGH THE GATEWAY

ELLIE QUIN: A GIRL REBORN

ABOUT THE AUTHOR

About the Author

Over the last sixteen years, award-winning author Alex Scarrow has published seventeen novels with Penguin Random House, Orion and Pan Macmillan. A number of these have been optioned for film/TV development, including his best-selling *Last Light*.

When he is not busy writing and painting, Alex spends most of his time trying to keep Ozzie away from the food bin. He lives in the wilds of East Anglia with his wife Deborah and four, permanently muddy, dogs.

Ozzie came to live with him in January 2017. He was adopted from Spaniel Aid UK and was believed to be seven at the time. Ozzie loves food, his mum, food, his ball, food, walks and more food...

He dreams of unrestricted access to the food bin.

For up-to-date information on the DCI BOYD series, visit: www.alexscarrow.com